EVIL WOMAN
. . .Takes Revenge

Also by Carol M. Creasey:

Biography:
  My Life is Worth Living!

Fiction:
  Fatal Obsession
  Not Just an Affair
  Evil Woman

EVIL WOMAN
...TAKES REVENGE

SEQUEL TO Evil Woman

Carol M. Creasey

UNITED WRITERS
Cornwall

UNITED WRITERS PUBLICATIONS LTD
Ailsa, Castle Gate, Penzance, Cornwall.
www.unitedwriters.co.uk

British Library Cataloguing in Publication Data:
A catalogue record for this book is
available from the British Library.

ISBN 9781852001742

Printed and bound in Great Britain by
United Writers Publications Ltd.,
Cornwall.

I dedicate this to my lovely
daughter Andrea, who has always
shown great compassion to people who
need understanding and support.

Chapter One

"So Sadie Morton Brown is being let loose again!"

Michael Bull ignored the tone of voice that Elizabeth Fowler had used. She always thought she knew everything, but she didn't know Sadie like he did. Like all women she saw her as a threat. He felt he was more able to make a judgement about Sadie. He had spent the last three years studying her and working towards her rehabilitation; a beautiful young woman such as Sadie still had her whole life ahead of her, and it was his duty to help her recovery.

"It's such a shame the way people judged her, even though she was never convicted of anything. She was declared insane when, in fact, most of her mental problems were caused by severe post natal depression, made worse by being separated from her baby."

Why did he feel the need to justify himself to Elizabeth? Women were strange creatures, in his experience, always ready to bitch about each other. He wished Elizabeth would adopt a more professional attitude towards Sadie; the young woman needed all the support she could get to rebuild her life.

"That is true, there was an open verdict about Danny's death. He was all washed up, wasn't he? Not wanted in the team, and Sadie was about to tell his wife they had a love child, if, in fact, it was his child."

"That's right, her main problem was that she was a pathological liar, she couldn't tell the difference between fact and fiction."

Elizabeth nodded her agreement: "Well that is what set people against her, you know, the lies: she boasted that she killed her brother and then admitted it was all a joke, a very sick one if you ask me."

Michael could feel the psychologist in him vying to get out, so he let it.

"Well, subconsciously she felt guilty because he had drowned when she was not that far away, so inside her mind was the feeling she might have caused it. One can feel guilty even if you haven't lifted a finger to control the situation."

Elizabeth wasn't quite ready to accede defeat.

"Well boasting about it didn't do her any favours. It made her appear heartless, and raised doubts in people's minds."

Michael could see she was coming round to the idea, even if it was unwillingly.

"Yes, I have spent three years getting to know the person she is, helping her to deal with her issues. She's had pills, and every bit of new treatment that there is, but underneath that tough exterior is a very hurt and vulnerable young woman. She certainly is not evil, and if she stays on her medication we shouldn't see those uncontrollable rages any more."

Elizabeth paused, her fingers hovered over the keyboard of her laptop.

"Her lifestyle now is so different, I must admit. She keeps herself to herself, reads a lot, does everything she is asked, and has become very religious."

"Precisely! So we had a meeting, and the whole panel decided she was no threat to society, probably never was actually. The medication controls the hallucinations; she now knows she hasn't done anything. The whole situation has been badly handled. She was kept in prison for a year whilst they tried to find evidence to convict her; no wonder she appeared to be insane, can you imagine her frustration at being locked up for so long and not really knowing why?"

Elizabeth pushed her doubts aside. There was something about Sadie, she could sense it, but nothing that could be proved against her; and her job as Michael's colleague was to support his decision, because it would not have been taken lightly.

"OK, I agree, she should be allowed to go free, but she will need family support at first. Is that very likely?"

"Don't remind me," sighed Michael. "Yet another very sticky

situation to try and iron out, but for Sadie's sake we will do our best."

Elizabeth excused herself and left the room, trying to ignore the sense of unease so deep inside her. She had known Michael for ten years; he was happily married with a young family, and he was also very good at his job. He successfully managed to separate his working life from his family life, and he kept his relationships with his patients on a strictly professional basis. But Elizabeth could see that Sadie was beautiful, sexy, and very alluring. She mustn't allow her envy of that to cloud her judgement. As for Michael, he was a very shrewd judge of character, he had trained in that field for years, so it was unlikely that Sadie had fooled him with her looks, he was surely a much smarter man than that.

Denise McKane was looking forward to visiting Sadie today. As a prison warder, she was used to working amongst all kinds of women. Most of them were hard nuts from underprivileged backgrounds; thieves or prostitutes, they were so desperate they would do anything to keep their heads above water. Many of them were alcoholics or on drugs, and it was her job to watch over them and make sure they didn't harm one another, because they frequently fell out. Once inside prison, they were given help to conquer their demons. Suddenly drugs and alcohol were no longer available and, as withdrawal symptoms manifested themselves, they needed medical help to cope with that.

Denise was a tough Scottish woman, her blonde hair was cut short in a bob and her build was stocky and strong. There was nothing feminine about her job as a prison warder, and in everyday life Denise was not feminine. She had no time for men, having been abused by an uncle at only seven years old, this had put her off the male sex for life.

Sadie had been so different from the other prisoners, she was neither an alcoholic, nor a drug taker. She came from a very middle class background, and after all the tales she had heard about Sadie's evil doings, the reality was not what she expected.

She had been arrested mainly because of her involvement with Danny Foster. He was just the sort of man that Denise despised, a womaniser and a coward, but Sadie had loved him, and had his child. Her tough exterior melted when she saw the frail girl with the huge haunting eyes. She had lost all her fight; the man she loved was dead, and she had been parted from her new born daughter with no idea when she would see her again.

Denise found herself taking on quite a challenge with Sadie. She had gone on hunger strike; it seemed she wanted to die. Denise found herself defending the girl when it appeared her only crime had been post natal depression, and no wonder after the way she had been treated.

The public had turned against Sadie. Hysterical female fans of Danny blamed her for his death, which resulted in her being kept in prison for a year before it was decided she couldn't stand trial. It was felt she wasn't mentally fit, and also there was no real evidence.

Denise believed that Sadie's 'insanity' had been caused by being in prison, and the jeers and bullying from other inmates hadn't helped. Sadie had rages which were frightening to witness, but after a while she seemed to lose her spirit and give up. Denise was assigned the duty of suicide watch and, against her will, she found herself getting involved.

She encouraged her to eat, and rejoiced inwardly when Sadie's gaunt frame filled out and her face regained its former healthy look. Sadie confided her innermost thoughts to her. Her life had been full of men who had taken advantage of her. She had been pregnant at thirteen after being raped, and her mother had forced her to have an abortion. Denise had an empathy with her, having also suffered in the same way herself, although she had thankfully not got pregnant.

Danny had been the only man she had felt warm feelings for, and although he was married, he had told her it was a sham, they were only happily married for the newspapers, and he had planned to leave his wife and start a new life with Sadie. Who could possibly imagine that she could have killed him, whatever would her motive be?

Sadie kept herself away from the other prisoners, and then she found God. She told Denise he was the one person who knew she was innocent. Denise now firmly believed this was true too, and although she didn't want to be parted from Sadie, she was relieved that Sadie was to be taken from prison and moved to a rehabilitation unit. Here she could receive treatment and get better, and then pick her life up again. No longer were mental patients locked away from society, they were put through all sorts of programmes, given medication, and encouraged to rebuild their lives.

Denise was devastated when Sadie did leave the prison, and she realised at that time she was in love with her. She had experienced only a couple of relationships with women in the past, neither had been serious, but this time it hit her like a sledge hammer, not only had Sadie needed her, she also needed Sadie. They hadn't even slept together, but they were so close, they could tell each other anything.

She had confessed her feelings to Sadie, who had admitted that she was bisexual. This gave her hope for the future, so every time she had a day off, she spent most of it with Sadie. The unit encouraged patients to have visitors from the outside world, and if they did find it strange that Denise spent so much time with her, it was never remarked upon.

Then they started to make plans for the future. When Sadie was allowed back into society, Denise pointed out she would always be there for her. They could move away and make a new start. Living round this area would never give Sadie a chance to rebuild her life. She had suggested Australia. They could maybe get a house built; Denise had savings, and if Sadie became united with her daughter Danielle, maybe they could bring her up together. What a perfect life that would be.

As soon as she entered the room, she could tell by the animation on Sadie's face that she had good news.

"I am going to be free. I'm cured. In four weeks' time I leave this place!"

Denise hugged her, suddenly her life of happiness seemed to be in sight.

"Are you sure? Oh my goodness, I need to go ahead and find us somewhere to live, somewhere suitable to raise Danielle."

"That's a good idea. I have to spend some time bonding with her again, and then I'll be right out to join you."

"Shall I book you a ticket, say a month after?"

Sadie's eyes sparkled with animation. "I have a better idea. If you can leave me some cash, as you know I leave here with nothing, I will buy the ticket as soon as I can. It might even be less than a month after you; and when I join you, we can work out a plan where we both work and share the child care so I won't be living off you." Oh how easy it was to say all the right things!

"As if I care about that!" said Denise, although she did respect the fact that Sadie wanted to retain her independence. There was a spring in her step when she went back to her poky little flat. She would leave all this behind her and start a new life with Sadie, and she couldn't wait.

Sadie went quietly to her room after Denise had gone. She had so much to think about. During the last four years that she had spent virtually in isolation, she had changed, and this change had caused her a lot of mental confusion. In the beginning, because the normally free spirit inside her was cooped up in one place, she found it very stressful. She grieved for the loss of her daughter; they had so suddenly been parted, and Danielle was so much a part of her brief union with Danny, she couldn't bear to be without her.

These powerful feelings of love were so strange to Sadie, who had only felt hatred for everyone in her life, and until then she had got pleasure from using and abusing everyone around her. Ever since she could remember, she had wanted to hurt people as much as her own mother had hurt her. She still remembered those angry words her mother had flung at her all those years ago. That terrible secret that she could never share with her father, the man she had always looked up to ever since she was a little girl. It would have caused him so much pain, and Daddy had always been her rock, that was until Jeremy was born.

But the hatred inside her grew bigger and bigger until it had totally consumed her. Sadie was hurting so badly. All she had was her looks, and she soon found that these gave her a power over men and women. Knowing she was desired assuaged a little the grief that was ravaging around inside her. But none of her sexual encounters had truly satisfied her, only briefly did they feed her vanity, until she met Danny.

She had felt a warmth inside when she was with Danny. She hadn't meant it to happen, he was far from perfect, she knew that, but being with him had made her view her life in a different way. When Danielle was born, she had loved that baby in a way that totally consumed her, and her first feelings of guilt for Ricky, the baby she had sold, started to manifest themselves. When Danny had rejected her and Danielle she hadn't believed him.

She knew that if he had lived she would not have been able to accept his decision; she would have tried with all of her being to change his mind, but she had been robbed of that by his untimely death. Her pride would not allow her to tell anyone that, so she pretended, as she had all her life, that her future would have been secure.

Sadie knew that Alice had made a fool of her, and even wanted Sadie to take the blame for Danny's death. Alice was a mad woman, she had killed Danny, Sadie knew it, but she couldn't prove it, and before she could do anything, she herself was being held culpable for it. She had tried to tell them that Alice was mad, but they wouldn't listen, they were all as mad as Alice, they must be, and it seemed to Sadie that she was the only sane person.

Once again, Sadie felt that hatred sweeping over her. She had wanted to break free from this prison and get her revenge on Alice, and her mother, the person Sadie felt had shattered her life in such a way that she had never managed to rise above it, nor share it with anyone. That story was more horrific than any of the other ones she had told, but that one was true, yet so disgusting that she had no doubt that she wouldn't be believed, and it remained locked up causing devastation deep inside her.

Sadie had been plunged into a deep depression. Alice had killed the man she loved, wormed her way into her parent's house and taken over her daughter, and Sadie was in here, locked up, and unable to do anything about it. She felt she had nothing to live for, so she went on hunger strike; death would release her from this pain and torment raging away inside her. So she lay on her bed and waited for death, but her torment wasn't over yet. She was to receive a visit from Ricky. They were now divorced, but he wanted to trace his son, and when she saw him her guilt was tremendous. The only way she could cope with the situation was to use her perceived madness to deny that she knew him, and it worked. For the first time ever, Sadie experienced guilt, his bleak face was to haunt her for a very long time.

But her spirit was not totally defeated. She could see that Denise had an empathy with her, so she planned to use her to gain her escape. She was hated by the other women prisoners, they bullied and spat at her, so she was put in solitary confinement.

She took up reading, and decided to pretend she had found God. Lots of prisoners did that, in the hopes their sentence would be shortened.

Denise continued to watch over her like a mother hen, and she was taken for endless tests until she was finally pronounced unfit to stand trial; and then her luck changed.

Sadie was moved to a secure unit and her rehabilitation programme began. In the beginning she flushed her pills down the toilet; she didn't think she needed them, but after being caught out, they made sure she did take them. After a while her depression seemed to lift, and she felt more able to cope with her situation and the loss of Danielle.

The visits from Denise gave her hope. She planned to use Denise and her money to give her a start when she was finally set free. She was absolutely determined to be reunited with her daughter, and her hatred for Alice had not diminished; she would get her revenge, but all in good time. As for her mother, Sadie could not forgive her for what she had said and done, it may have been some years ago, but it had stuck in her mind, it haunted her, and she felt it had affected her life. If only she had the courage to speak about it, and why oh why hadn't she told Daddy? But she knew the answer to that so well, the pain it would cause him, and herself, and the knowledge that it was so preposterous she doubted anyone would believe it. Her mother, for sure, would deny it to protect herself, as she had done for the last thirty years, and it would be thought of as just another of Sadie's outrageous stories. But sometimes she felt if she could let it out, it might help the turmoil that had plagued her for all of her life.

Chapter Two

Isabel had mixed feelings when she heard the news that Sadie was going to be released back into society. Her daughter had mental problems, and she lived in a fantasy world. Isabel had tried to love her daughter, but she had always been a difficult child, and had grown up to be a completely selfish and uncaring young woman.

She had always been closer to her father. Isabel had felt jealous of their closeness, and when Sadie became a teenager Sadie had found out something that could shatter Isabel's own life as well as Sadie's, so she'd had to act quickly, she just had to sweep it all under the carpet. Then very shortly after that, her darling son Jeremy had been taken from her, and even Sadie's ordeal seemed to pale into insignificance.

Isabel had worked hard to make her own life, as the wife of a very wealthy and distinguished man, completely normal. She had blocked out her heartbreaking past and moved on. But then that same heartbreak had happened to Sadie; such an unbelievable coincidence, and she knew that the one person who must never find out was Philip.

Philip never had, not even from Sadie.

As Sadie grew older, she had continued to reject her mother and moved even closer to Philip, which was what had inflamed Isabel's jealousy to the point that she had not had any problem in telling Sadie the truth, and then there was no way back for their relationship. Philip hadn't known why they were both so cruel to one another, they both hid their grief, but he saved the day by providing Sadie with her own apartment.

Isabel felt like she had spent her whole life living a lie through no fault of her own. Although her family were not as wealthy as Philip's, they were still very middle class, and Isabel went to good schools and had nice clothes. She was the apple of her father's eye, and for three years the only child, and then along came Victoria.

Victoria was always craving attention, she was no blushing violet, and the two sisters clashed frequently. Another three years later, Joey came along. He wasn't like either of them; he didn't argue with his sisters, he played alone, he was a quiet boy who loved playing with model cars. Her parents were delighted to have a son, and everyone said that Joey was so quiet because, with his two feisty sisters, he couldn't get a word in at all. He was very bright at school, especially with maths and sciences, but he didn't have many friends. Self-centred Victoria found him boring, but Isabel felt he was lonely and vulnerable, and all her protective instincts towards her little brother were aroused.

He grew into a handsome but lonely young man, and because she bothered about him, he relied on Isabel. He never showed much affection to anyone, but continued to be a loner, although many girls noticed his dark and captivating looks. He was not interested in clothes or fashion in any way, but his passion for model cars had spurred him on to have cars in his life, always fast sports cars, and when he got one of his own, Isabel was as worried as her parents that he might crash it.

He went to Oxford University after getting the right grades quite effortlessly, and during the term he was away, Isabel met Philip. She was now twenty-four, she had also got a degree in Physics, and was currently working as a research assistant at a London hospital. It wasn't many months before they decided they were in love, and wanted to get married, and the only thorn in her flesh was Joey; how would he take it?

Joey had met Philip briefly in the Christmas holidays. He had only been with his family for Christmas Day, and that was after much persuasion, as he had been happy to stay alone at the place the students rented. Isabel knew her parents worried about Joey's strange attitude, and the fact that he was happy to spend most of his time alone, but they consoled themselves by telling people how bright he was; getting to Oxford spoke for itself.

Isabel had been shocked when he left the room after being

introduced to Philip, and then got in his car to drive away. He was upset and angry that he might lose her, and although she tried to explain having Philip for a boyfriend would not interfere with their brother/sister relationship, Joey didn't seem convinced, and took himself out for a long fast ride in the car to soothe himself. She had laughed it off with Philip at the time, her kid brother showing off, and as their relationship got closer and closer, they both knew they wanted to spend their life together, and a wedding was planned for the next summer.

Joey had not been home since Easter, and in March all the preparations were being made for the wedding, so she guessed he was staying away because he wasn't happy about it. Her heart ached for him, he wasn't good at showing his emotions, but clearly they were there for him to be so jealous.

Isabel took the coward's way out by posting an invitation to the place he stayed with the other students. She didn't expect to get a reply, and realised with a heavy heart, Joey might not even attend her wedding. But it made no difference; she was madly in love with Philip, and the sooner they could get married the better.

Even after over thirty years it hurt her so much to recall that night, a few days before her wedding, the night Joey had turned up at home. Her parents were out and she was alone and ready for bed, planning to have an early night, as she had a very busy day ahead of her. His rage was terrible to see; she just didn't recognise this side of her brother, and even now she wretched and her mouth filled with bile when she remembered what he had done to her. Her own brother had raped her, and when a few weeks later she had found herself pregnant, as much as she wanted this child to be Philip's, in her heart she knew it wasn't.

But that hadn't been the end of the horrors of that night. Joey had driven his car at top speed into a wall. He had been killed instantly. Everyone had believed that it was an accident, and tests had shown he had been drinking, so it seemed like Joey had been another young person who had thought he was invincible, and had died through his own carelessness.

But Isabel knew differently. Her brother had in some twisted way wanted her, and the fact she was his sister made no difference to him, so realising what he had done and that he couldn't have her, he had taken his own life. The truth was so shocking to her, she had hidden it away inside her. It was her shame, so she just went along with what her grieving family believed; it was easier that way.

So she married Philip, who never suspected a thing. He was there to comfort her over the loss of her brother, and when he found out she was pregnant he was over the moon. He took great care of her through her pregnancy. She knew how much she needed this calm and dependable man. Each day the horror of that night grew a bit further away, and she concentrated on keeping herself fit and feeling so grateful that she would never have to face her brother again.

Remembering the day that Sadie was born, the feelings of unrest she felt when she saw her came back to haunt her. Her baby wouldn't stop crying when she held her, she only wanted Philip and those dark eyes bored into hers, reminding her so much of Joey; and she felt almost as though Sadie was the curse he had sent to torment her for the rest of her life.

But Isabel had one more shock in store, because not long after Sadie was born, Laura, who it appeared had been Joey's on and off girlfriend, turned up at her parents home with a one year old son, which she claimed Joey had fathered.

Her parents had no choice really but to be supportive. Laura was as poor as most students are, and when Matt was born, the facial resemblance to Joey with his dark eyes and black hair was unmistakable. Isabel had seen the baby only once, and she shuddered with emotion when she saw how similar to Sadie he was. But then she had been spared further involvement, when after a generous payoff from her parents, Laura had taken Matt and gone to live in Scotland. By all accounts she had got on with her life, and eventually met a man who had married her and brought up Matt as his own son.

She had thought that was the end of it, as Laura rarely contacted her parents. They were getting older now, and if they wanted to keep contact with their grandson they never said, and Isabel didn't feel any bond with him.

The day she found that photo on Sadie's mobile she had initially assumed he was a pop singer, or someone a thirteen year old would revere, but when she had looked closely at him her heart lurched with fear, and she felt that overwhelming panic come over her. This fourteen year old boy had an uncanny

18

resemblance to her dead brother; but surely it couldn't be, his son was living in Scotland?

She plucked up the courage to confront Sadie. She had to, she didn't like the idea that this lookalike might be hanging around her daughter, it would only dredge up old painful memories. She should have knocked before she entered the room, but the door was slightly ajar and Sadie was facing the other way, so she didn't see her. Isabel, even after sixteen years, could still remember her shock when Sadie turned towards her with a pregnancy testing kit on the bed, and the word PREGNANT, defiantly flashing on the results stick.

She hadn't been able to control her anger, or her fear, and the knowledge of what had happened to her thirteen year old daughter consumed her with panic. Normally Sadie would be bolshie and unco-operative with her mother, but right now she needed some support. She told her mother about Matt, who had moved from Scotland with his parents. She had met him whilst she was out with Sunita during their holidays from boarding school. And when Isabel had become hysterical, she had added that she had only wanted him as a friend, but he had raped her.

Isabel had no way of knowing if Sadie was for once telling the truth, but one thing was for sure, she was pregnant by her half brother. So she told her who her real father was, and that Matt was her half brother, and she also told her in no uncertain terms that she couldn't keep the baby. Not only was she much too young, it was incest, and the child could well be born with physical and mental defects.

"You don't want a reminder of the person who raped you, abortion is the only way out," she said harshly. Sadie had gone very quiet. Isabel knew she had shocked and hurt her; the man she had loved as her father for thirteen years was not. She had been given no choice, she had to tell her.

So Sadie had her abortion, and Isabel had visited Laura and told her she must move away right now, or else Isabel personally would report Matt to the police for rape, and her bluff worked. Laura, her husband John, who knew nothing about any of it, and Matt, vanished into the mist and never came near the family again.

Isabel's relationship with Sadie went from bad to worse after that. Then she had lost Jeremy, and her life had felt like it had stopped. Thank God Philip had been there to support her; they were even more united in their grief, and she was so wrapped up in that, she couldn't imagine anything worse than to lose her child.

Sadie appeared to recover and move on from her abortion, and her infatuation with Matt, but now she knew that Philip was not her biological father, instead of being angry and rejecting him, Isabel was shocked to discover that Sadie seemed to be viewing him in a sexual way, which was even more disturbing.

Isabel only knew peace of mind when Sadie was away at boarding school, away from Philip, and when she spoke about her fears to him he laughed it off, saying he could handle his precocious daughter. She trusted him implicitly, and she knew that Sadie would never tell him he was not her blood father, she loved him too much to hurt him. The only time Sadie appeared to show any emotion was when she spoke about Philip or was with him. With everyone else she seemed to enjoy hurting them.

But Isabel had blamed herself for Sadie's vindictiveness towards others. If Laura had stayed put in Scotland, the past would have remained buried and no one would have been hurt. She knew Sadie had been hurt and she had taken that anger out on anyone and everyone who became a part of her life. Isabel didn't believe her daughter had murdered anyone, but she realised Sadie's twisted attitude towards people, and her desire to cause trouble, stemmed from Sadie's own feelings of insecurity because she had suffered.

It was amazing that Philip was blissfully unaware of any of this; only two people knew who Sadie's true father was, and neither of them would ever reveal it. Isabel so wanted her daughter's torment to be over, and with her usual optimistic nature, which had kept her sane over the last thirty years, she wondered if Sadie came home and bonded with Danielle, would that mother/daughter relationship help to erase the pain from the past so that Sadie and Isabel could both also move on.

But there was another feeling inside her of uneasiness. Life had calmed down since Sadie had been sectioned; Danielle had grown into a bright and happy little girl without any apparent issues, she was the complete opposite of her mother, being a warm, demonstrative and loving girl. She had been a joy to have around for almost five years now, and although Isabel didn't like

20

to admit it, it was probably due to Alice, who had cared for her as if she was her own child.

Isabel's reverie was interrupted when the door opened to admit the tall and sturdy frame of Nathan. He brushed back a lock of dark hair that persisted in falling across his forehead, and his face lit up with a smile that reached up to his dark grey eyes which always sparkled with animation. He was so far removed from the gaunt unshaven man with haunting eyes and hollow cheeks that Philip had brought home from the flat over ten years ago now.

"Isabel, I am off to Canterbury, is there anything you need?" he enquired. Then he noticed that she seemed uneasy. She handed him the letter that had stirred up all the memories again, saying simply:

"Sadie will be free soon."

After glancing over the letter, Nathan gave a low whistle as he folded it back up and handed it back to her. He had known it would happen one day. Sadie had not been charged with anything, she had been ill and received treatment, but she had always been too much for her mother to handle. Her most precious possession was in this house, Danielle, so she would obviously want to come back to claim her.

"How do you feel about it?" he enquired gently. So many unspoken thoughts were tumbling around inside his head. His memories of Sadie were hazy, he had known her at probably the lowest and darkest time of his life. But if he hadn't known her he might still be a useless bum, an alcoholic and drug addict. Maybe Sadie wasn't the best thing that had ever happened to him, but certainly Isabel and Philip were.

"I'm not sure. I would love to see her bond with Danielle again, but you don't need me to tell you she's not an easy person to get on with. Philip understands her better than I do."

"Well I wasn't easy to get on with when we were together. She may have grown up now," said Nathan defensively. Why on earth was he defending her? Both himself and Philip knew, even if Isabel didn't, that Sadie had done her best to bump him off; all that petrol scattered around the bedroom. Philip initially had funded him to make sure he didn't go to the police and report it, a sort of pay back, but it had been the making of him. Nathan now had two people in his life who actually felt responsible for him. After a mother who had neglected him so badly, and then a succession of children's homes, where he learnt to be tough and survive any way he could, more often on the wrong side of the law, life had suddenly got much better.

Nathan had reformed, he had a steady job, and he would never forget what this family had done for him. He had now made his own money and he lived in London in a penthouse, but his ties with Philip and Isabel were for life, they had lifted him out of the gutter, given him a chance, and he had taken it. But none of this would have happened if he had not known Sadie, it must have been fate.

"She's not going to get on with Alice," Isabel reminded him.

Danielle had a strong bond with Alice, but they had certainly needed Alice to help them when Danielle was a baby. At first Danielle had been difficult, crying a lot, but no doubt the sudden separation from her mother had affected her, too. The nights had been very disturbed, so it seemed only natural that Alice should move in with them. Even when they decided to leave Richmond, and they bought their splendid Victorian house overlooking the downs at Herne Bay, Alice had still come with them, it seemed she didn't mind leaving the London life behind her.

Nathan wasn't keen on Alice, she was too intense for him and too possessive about Danielle. To him she seemed to think Danielle was her own child, and whenever he came to visit at the weekend, instead of using her free time to go out, she always seemed to be hovering around, listening to what was going on, and not allowing Danielle out of her sight.

"Well I can understand that, Isabel. Alice herself won't give up Danielle easily. Maybe you and Philip should insist she takes a holiday, a couple of weeks off when Sadie arrives, just to give Sadie a chance to get to know Danielle."

Isabel looked gratefully at him. "Oh yes, I hadn't thought of that. I don't need anything by the way. She's due back from ballet with Danielle pretty shortly, it's supposed to be her day off, but she can't seem to let go of her, she had taken her to ballet before Philip and I had even noticed."

"Yes, I know what you mean. Where is Philip, by the way?"

"Outside with our new gardener, planning some landscaping. We want to get the benefit of the wonderful sea views, so that is his latest project."

"Brilliant," said Nathan with genuine enthusiasm. Philip and

Isabel had certainly not moved here to take early retirement. Philip had enough money not to get his hands dirty, and he was already a member of the local golf club; they had both joined a group of bridge players, and been shown such friendliness by the people of this seaside town that it had been easy to settle.

He left the room, anxious to avoid Alice when she returned. Her presence here was the only downside of visiting, but on this very pleasant spring morning, with the birds chirping merrily and the blossoms on the trees shining in the sunlight, it was easier to put her out of his mind.

Alice was the bane of his life. He was aware of her fixation with him, and she was also a powerful influence on this family because of her links with Danielle. It's true she had taken care of her since she was a few months old, and no doubt in her mind she almost imagined she was her own daughter, but she was possessive and stifling, and Isabel and Philip knew this. If Sadie was coming home, apparently to try and bond with her daughter, it would not sit well with Alice.

He saw her enter the drive as he pulled out, giving her a friendly wave and blowing a kiss to Danielle, who was sitting in her car seat with her nose flattened against the window pane in an effort to catch his attention. Then he felt guilty. It wasn't Danielle's fault that Alice freaked him out, so he jumped out of his car, and ran up the drive. Alice stopped immediately, as he guessed she would, and he gave her a watery smile as she wound down the window.

"Hello Princess, how was ballet?"

"Good!" murmured Danielle, giving him a smile that could melt any heart. She was dressed in a little pale pink leotard, and her very dark thick hair was swept back into a pony tail. She had the dark mysterious eyes of her mother, and those eyes sparkled with animation and happiness. There was nothing complicated about Danielle; she was a sunny child, she had no hang ups, everyone loved her, and she had brought much peace to this family after the storm had erupted over four years ago.

Alice had hoped, just for once, that he had stopped because of her, but he barely gave her a glance. Nathan was a good catch for any woman, not only had he already made himself enough money to live comfortably for the rest of his life, at the age of thirty-two, he was a very handsome man. He was tall and lean with a fit body, his taste in clothes was good, and today he was wearing a petrol blue check shirt with cream trousers, which looked great on him. Those grey eyes of his that looked so serious one minute and then sparkled with humour the next, had captivated her, Alice was in love again, and when she loved it was with all her heart and soul, it completely dominated her senses.

She was aware that Nathan had no interest in her, but that only made the flame in her heart burn even more fiercely. Nathan was now a big part of this family, and so was Alice, her involvement with Danielle meant she had made herself indispensable. Philip and Isabel needed her, so in her mind it would make perfect sense for herself and Nathan to become a couple. Who knows, one day they might become the nearest to being parents to Danielle that anyone could be. Their own little family unit. All she needed to do was make Nathan realise he couldn't live without her.

Her looks had not gone unnoticed by Nathan. Her long auburn hair with its reddish brown highlights, and those vivid green eyes, were impossible to ignore, but he could sense an intensity and a possessiveness about her which he didn't like. Nathan was a free agent and he wanted to stay that way. She was the sort of woman he couldn't have a fling with, she wouldn't let it rest there, and seeing as she was almost part of the family, there was no way he would upset the present family situation.

Sadie, on the other hand, frequently filled his thoughts. When they had been together he had been a poor excuse for a human being. When he looked back he felt ashamed, always drunk and tanked up with drugs. He had no doubt that she had used him to get herself away for a new life, but he now wondered why she had left such a caring family. He remembered her as a very beautiful and striking young woman. He also remembered her nature had been a little unpredictable; she had been a typical spoilt little rich girl, so why would she leave it all behind? He knew that the person he was then could not have offered her a future, but how would they get on now that he had self respect? He was certainly curious to find out.

It was ten years since he had known her, by all accounts she had got herself into a lot of trouble with her imaginative stories, even been sectioned at one time, but there was something very exciting about her that continued to attract him and the challenge she presented appealed to his senses. But would the person he had

24

become be of any interest to her, and what of her parents. Would they approve of them picking up where they had left off?

He had frequently thought about going to visit her, but there was always the fear she would turn him away without even seeing him. Her own parents had only visited occasionally, Philip more than Isabel. He knew Sadie and her mother had often clashed in the past, but they were hoping now that their mutual love for Danielle would bring the family back together.

The one person that could ruin this possibility was Alice. She may well have been Sadie's friend in the past, but the little he did know was there was no love lost between them now. Philip had confided in him after visiting Sadie just how upset she was that it was Alice, and not herself, that was helping to care for Danielle.

He was spared any more conversation with Alice when Philip appeared from around the side of the house where he had been planning some changes with the gardener.

"Nathan, just the man I wanted. Can we chat?"

Philip's dark hair tinged with grey made him look distinguished. Although now in his late fifties, he was still a very handsome man. His placid nature was in complete contrast to his wife's, and was no doubt the reason their marriage was so strong and had survived all the traumas of the past years. Isabel needed his calmness, and he admired her strong character and feistiness. Together they made a strong couple, and it was plain to see, after over thirty years, just how much Philip was in love with his wife.

Philip drew him inside the Victorian conservatory with its splendid views of the downs. It was a large and comfortable room with sofas and a fluffy rug, and they stood in there, away from Alices's curious gaze.

"Did Isabel tell you that Sadie is being released very shortly?"

"Yes." Nathan waited for him to finish.

"I mentioned it to Alice, and she was anything but welcoming about it. I thought they were friends."

"They used to be." He wondered if he should speak his mind, and decided it was the only way, it was best to be honest. "Philip, I think Alice almost believes that Danielle is her own child, so she won't like Sadie coming back now."

"Yes, that is what I thought. Maybe we won't need Alice any more, but her nature is such that it won't be that easy to let her go. But Sadie comes first, she is our daughter, she's been through a

25

lot, and maybe when she sees Danielle she can start again, we can all start again as a family."

Nathan looked at Philip. Sadie was still so important to him, and he saw renewed hope in his eyes. His desire to give his daughter some support was clear to see.

"Yes, I know what you mean. There is an intensity about Alice which makes me feel uncomfortable. Would you like me to go and see Sadie, and find out exactly what happened in their past?"

There, he had said it, he had admitted he didn't like Alice, and Philip hadn't batted an eyelid.

"Oh, would you?" Philip was so grateful for his strength and support. "As long as you feel OK with her after what she did to you."

Nathan smiled. "She had good reason, you know, I was a bum! Don't worry Philip, it's water under the bridge now."

Philip smiled gratefully back. Nathan was almost the son he had lost. Both he and Isabel felt as if he was a part their family now, and his strength and common sense made anything seem possible.

"Good luck with her. She can be difficult, and you need broad shoulders. Her tongue can be very acid!"

"Don't worry, I will tread carefully, and then we will have to see how we can let Alice down gently."

They exchanged rueful smiles, both knowing that nothing would be that easy, but in this family nothing ever was. Nathan made up his mind at that moment, if he could help the situation in any way, he would. It was the least he could do after what Philip and Isabel had done for him.

Chapter Three

Sadie was waiting for Nathan's visit with distinct unease. After Alice and her mother, Nathan was probably the person she most hated, and it gave her a great deal of satisfaction to contemplate how she could get even with him.

He had escaped death after living off her allowance from Daddy for quite a few months, and then to cap it all, her parents had taken him in, straightened him out, and used him as a replacement for Jeremy; how pathetic was that? On Alice's last visit, the time when she told her that she was Sarah's twin, she had also exalted in telling Sadie that Nathan was so 'in' with the family now, he was mentioned in their will to inherit everything when they died.

Sadie had realised just how Alice had duped her and why. She was making sure that Sadie took the rap for her own murderous act. Alice had killed Danny and put the blame on Sadie because her own twin, the ill fated nanny, Sarah, had to take the blame for Jeremy's death.

Sadie realised now what a fool she had been to tell Alice that she had killed Jeremy, her own brother. But it had worked out OK in the end. Sadie was famed for making up stories, it was part of her medical condition, so denying it had been easy and believable. At this time people thinking she was mad was a distinct advantage.

But Nathan had some power over her. They both knew she had scattered that petrol around the bedroom whilst he was sleeping, to rid herself of him. Being found by Philip had not only saved his life, but also given him a new one. Sadie didn't believe for one minute that the drunken slob had reformed; he'd just taken advantage of a situation where he needed to be kept quiet with money, just like she would have done. She had every intention, when she got out of here, to find some way of discrediting him to her parents. She would have to pretend to get on with her mother, and that would be hard, but Danielle was there, the daughter she could not forget. There was a pain in her heart for the four years of her daughter's life that she had missed and soon she would rectify this. Once she got home, Alice and Nathan had to go, they were both too well in with her family for Sadie's liking. The only reason she had agreed to see Nathan was pure curiosity. What did he look like after ten years, and more importantly, why was he coming to see her when he had never bothered before?

It had been a good excuse to tell Denise not to come today. She had come to the end of her usefulness, although Sadie would get at least the cost of a plane ticket to Australia. As if she had any intention of following after her, what a laugh! But the silly cow was in love and would believe anything. She had to endure one more visit. Denise's plane was flying out at the end of the week, and Sadie would be richer by about £1,000, which wouldn't last long, but it was better than nothing.

Denise had been useful when she was at her lowest. She had encouraged her to pick up her life again and start eating, but she had no need of her now. She was back to full health and soon to be free. Denise was one of many people that Sadie had used during her life for her own benefit. Once cast aside she would soon be forgotten, just like the others before her.

The room they ushered him into was pleasant. Now that she was no longer locked up and almost ready for release, Sadie was allowed to receive her guests in a small room not much bigger than a study, with comfortable armchairs and a coffee table. The staff were never far away, but Sadie had no intention of behaving in any way that might prolong her stay here. As soon as she tired of someone she just invented a headache and the staff would usher them out. Oh no, she wasn't daft, but they all were, and she also made sure everyone saw her saying her prayers so they knew that Sadie Morton Brown was a reformed woman.

When she saw him, Sadie was completely taken by surprise. The last ten years had been kind to Nathan, he had kicked out all

28

his demons, learned how to dress smartly, and she wasn't prepared for the handsome young man in the grey suit and blue tie, who held out his hand to shake hers, and looked her straight in the eye.

All her memories were of an unshaven, often unwashed person, whose main interest in life was doing drugs and sleeping it all off. The only reason she had got involved with him was because he did have connections and had managed to get her a fake passport. On the few occasions he had been sober, and washed, there had been a sex life, but it was few and far between, and in the end she had decided that this drunken bum deserved to perish with the flat, he was of no use to anyone.

But seeing him today she felt confusion. This man was not only well turned out, he oozed confidence, and as much as she hated him, his charisma was not lost on her and she could see why her parents believed he had reformed.

"Hi Sadie, you are looking great, how are you?"

He took her hand lightly, and she felt a very powerful emotion sweep through her at his touch. Oh how she hated him, the opportunist! She pulled it away.

"I am very well, thank you, and today must be my lucky day, you've actually taken a shower."

"I have, it's something I do quite often now. If I showed up at work the way you used to see me I wouldn't last long."

"Quite the city gent," she said sneeringly. "All thanks to Daddy, no doubt."

Nathan brushed off her attitude as though it were a very inconspicuous crumb.

"Your parents played a huge part in helping me turn my life around Sadie, and I will always be grateful to them."

"So I heard. You are quite the favourite son now, can't put a foot wrong."

Nathan could see she hadn't changed at all, so why should he care whether Alice's presence in the house would upset her or not? But he did care. He cared about the tramp he had been when she knew him before, and for some reason that he didn't understand himself, he cared about her. The last ten years had only enhanced her beauty. Those eyes to die for; black mysterious pools. That unbelievably soft hair; long, dark and lustrous. How he longed to run his fingers through it, to hold her close and tell her not to be jealous, she could rebuild her family ties, but he could see the anger and uncertainty in her eyes. He somehow had to charm his way into her good books.

"I don't live with your parents. I have a good job and a nice pad in London, but it was because they believed in me, and encouraged me, that I was able to rebuild my life. They are the parents I never had."

Sadie had heard this sob story before. Poor little neglected boy, does his round of children's homes, ends up in the gutter, and then bingo, he makes good. What did he want, a medal? Trouble is, as much as she was trying to fight it, this new Nathan had her admiration, and he was fit and so easy on the eye. She decided to mention the one thing that hung between them and get it out of the way.

"I was stupid that day to scatter the petrol. I didn't want to do you any harm. I knew Daddy was coming round."

Nathan laughed. " 'Course you did. But do you know, I wouldn't blame you if you did want to bump me off. When I look back now I am not surprised, I was a drunken drug taking slob. You did me the biggest favour ever, and what a wake-up call it was!"

Sadie was relieved. She had been getting ready to defend her actions but she didn't need to. She couldn't help admiring the way he owned up to his faults. Most men wouldn't, and she certainly never thought of herself as anything less than perfect.

"Why have you come to see me?"

She looked him directly in the eyes, so he came straight to the point.

"Obviously your parents are delighted to have you home, and it will be wonderful for you to bond with Danielle again, but there is Alice. Most of the care of Danielle has been done by her, and I know you used to be close friends. . ."

"Close friends; never!" Sadie declared passionately. "Alice did her best to frame me for Danny's murder. She did it, and used the fact that I was sick to make up stories to get me arrested. Her twin sister was Jeremy's nanny, the one that neglected him when he drowned, the guilt got too much for her so she committed suicide. But Alice blamed me, and we can't live under the same roof. She is mad and dangerous, and quite honestly I have always worried she might harm Danielle. Trouble is, they thought I was the mad one, and no one would listen."

30

"Well, I am listening!"

Nathan knew she was famed for not knowing the truth from fiction, but his instincts told him she was telling the truth. He had always been uneasy around Alice; he could believe she was capable of anything, and Sadie had been the victim. A girl who had issues of her own had been used in such a way that no one would believe anything Sadie said. It was sickening.

"Do your parents know about Alice being Sarah's twin?"

"Not from me, I have never said."

"Well it's time they knew now. Their granddaughter might be in danger. We all believed she was just a friend you met in Spain."

"Trouble is my life inside has been a bit of a blur, with all those pills and medication, and the day she came to gloat that she had care of Danielle I lost it and tried to attack her, then I spent some time in solitary confinement. It took me ages to get them to trust me again. Being in there you lose a sense of reality. All I wish is that I could have recorded her words. She admitted what she had done, and why she did it, for revenge. No one in our house is safe from her. She needs to go!"

This was far more serious than Nathan had ever imagined. They had a murderer living in the house and taking care of Danielle. Now he had to go back and break the news to Philip and Isabel. The police would not be interested, it would just be Sadie's word against Alice's, and so far her word had not proved to be reliable.

Getting rid of Alice would be the hardest thing of all. Because of her obsession with Danielle, she would not go quietly. Oh dear, this poor family surely had more than their fair share of stress to deal with.

After he went, Sadie made plans. Her hatred for Nathan would have to wait. Right now she needed him as an ally to get rid of Alice. Her version of the events was what Nathan believed. The only way to see Alice was gone from her life would be to kill her, but she knew Nathan would not be up for that. Maybe she would have to arrange an accident, surely that would be the answer? With the sort of things that had gone on before, maybe that wasn't such a good idea though. Someone around her dying from an accident, especially Alice when they had such history, would be very suspicious. Sadie realised that in the future she would have to tread very carefully.

31

Nathan drove back wondering how he was going to tell Isabel and Philip about Alice. They knew she had faults, and they both tended to turn a blind eye to them because of Danielle. No one could fault the way Alice had taken care of Danielle ever since she was a baby. She was close to the age of her real mother and she had virtually taken on that role. Because they were older and more set in their ways, Philip and Isabel had been happy to take a back seat as grandparents often do, and spend time with her when it was convenient for them. But because she had been brought up in their home, there was still a close bond. In spite of all this though, if Alice had murdered Danny and then put the blame on Sadie, there was no question about it, she would have to go.

When he got out of the car, he saw Philip and Isabel sitting out on the balcony, enjoying the afternoon sun. To his relief there was no sign of Alice which meant he could speak freely. He took the stairs two at a time; he was not looking forward to this conversation, but he knew it had to be done.

Isabel greeted him with a smile.

"How did it go? Is Sadie looking forward to seeing Danielle again?"

She mentioned Danielle, because she was only too aware that Sadie wouldn't be coming home to see her. If only they could get on, but Sadie knew too much about her and she felt like she had been judged by her; that bad smell was always hanging over their relationship.

Nathan sat down in the chair next to her. So engrossed was he in what he had to say, that even the sun sparkling over the sea was lost on him.

"Is Alice around?" he cautiously enquired.

Philip had his shorts on and he stretched his legs lazily. Nathan knew he was about to destroy this very peaceful little scene.

"She's at a birthday party collecting Danielle, so we thought we would make the most of this lovely afternoon. When she gets back, Isabel and I will insist she takes the rest of the weekend off and we'll take over. She needs to have her own life outside of Danielle. She's our granddaughter, and we want to spend time with her without Alice always in the background."

Nathan seized his opportunity and went on to explain Alice's full involvement with Sadie, watching their faces change. There was fear in their eyes, and horror that once again not only would they suffer, but innocent little Danielle would as well.

"Maybe this is one of Sadie's stories," suggested Isabel. "There have been so many over the years!"

"It's possible, but in the meantime I am going to check out Alice Lorenzo. I have to agree with you Philip, she is too possessive towards Danielle."

"We need to get rid of her amicably, with a good payoff, otherwise she could turn nasty," suggested Philip. In his world where money was no object, he felt it could cure all ills. Nathan wasn't so sure. Alice wouldn't go that easily, he was sure. Thank goodness Isabel and Philip had realised how dangerous the situation was for Danielle; and in all this, that little girl was really the person that mattered most of all.

When he was back in London on Monday, Nathan made some enquiries that confirmed his suspicions. Lorenzo was a married name, Alice had been born a twin with the surname of Townsend, and her sister Sarah, the nanny, had committed suicide. Her parents still lived in Richmond, and in her attempts to keep her former life away from her present employers, she had lost touch with them, so they had no idea about her new life. All this information was provided by a woman named Lisa who knew Alice for most of her life because they had been at school together. Alice had told her things about Sadie too, but Nathan was not interested. His suspicions had been confirmed, Sadie had told the truth, and now her parents knew they would have to act very quickly.

Chapter Four

Elizabeth drove up the hill noting the downs that wound their way down to the beach. She passed the building known as The Kings Hall and she could see sailing boats on the promenade. People were walking their dogs, enjoying the warm spring weather. It was too nice a day to work, she thought ruefully, and then she spotted the house.

It was a Victorian building set back from the road, with a path winding from the front door to the gate which opened directly onto the sea front. The wrought iron gates opened obediently for her after she had pressed the buzzer to announce her arrival. As she proceeded up the drive, admiring the mature shrubs and clumps of daffodils, she could see how well cared for the garden was. She swept across the gravelled parking area, which was generous, two other cars were parked there and there was plenty of room for hers, and more if needed.

She admired the impressiveness of this building. There was a balcony facing out to sea, a Victorian conservatory built on the side, and a big front door, so she knew before she entered that the interior would be resplendent and in keeping with the period in which the house had been built.

Elizabeth's role today was to make an assessment as to whether it would be in the best interests of Sadie and Danielle for her to return to her family. As a family liaison officer, her role was to be the mediator or peacemaker when there had been troubles in the past, and to decide whether there was enough of a family bond for Sadie to return there, or whether it might affect her mental health in the future. That was a situation that had to be avoided at all cost. During counselling sessions Sadie had been adamant that she wanted to bond with her daughter again, it was just whether it would work amongst her own family, or whether she would need support to make a new life for them both elsewhere. Obviously Danielle would have strong ties with her grandparents which must not be broken, and then there was the hope that Sadie would be a fit mother. So many loose ends to tie up.

Isabel opened the door to her, noting her businesslike appearance, her smart grey suit and blue blouse, and her hair dressed neatly on top of her head, and guessing her age to be about early forties. This visit, coming so soon after Nathan's revelations about Alice, was difficult. They had to act as a united family, and that included Alice. It was all one big play act, because as soon as Elizabeth had gone, Alice would be going too. There was no way they wanted her anywhere near their very precious Danielle.

"Good morning, what a lovely day it is again, do come in."

Elizabeth shook her hand, and then Philip was there too, introducing himself, and explaining that Alice, their nanny, was collecting Danielle from preschool as she only attended until 12pm, although next term she would be starting school full-time.

Whilst Elizabeth sat in the conservatory chatting to them both and sipping coffee, she formed her own opinion of them. As a couple she could see how close they were. Philip's eyes showed his adoration of his wife, which was touching, but quite unusual after so many years together. This was a strong marriage, she could see. Isabel was the more dominant partner, the most opinionated and a feisty woman, but wasn't it just as well she was, setting up a group to help others after losing her own son took strength of character. Philip seemed a very easy going man, the perfect partner for her, and he spoke caringly about Sadie. His concern was obvious, whereas Isabel seemed a bit more uncomfortable.

"Of course we want her home. Bonding with Danielle is everything, the loss of her baby caused a lot of her mental problems!" said Philip defensively.

Isabel was determined to be as honest as she dared to be. She wasn't sure if Sadie had let it be known that they didn't get on in the past.

"Sadie and I clashed in the past. I never found it easy to cope with her, and we both agreed that we had spoiled her. . ." she looked over at Philip for support, and he nodded his head slightly, and touched at her hand showing his support. " . . .But that was when she was a teenager. We all love Danielle as she does, and I am sure we can make this work. We both want to see our daughter settled and happy. Later she may want her own home, but right now she can get to know Danielle again in a warm family atmosphere.

Elizabeth studied them both and saw sincerity in their eyes. So far so good.

"How much does Danielle know about this?"

Isabel explained. "We never pretended her mummy was dead, we said she wasn't well and the doctors were taking care of her, but of course she doesn't remember her. She knows she is coming to visit her. She will be five years old in a couple of months, and right now she is excited about her mummy sharing her birthday with her.

"I see, do you intend to keep her nanny on?"

This was the part that Isabel had been dreading, but over the years she had learned to mask her emotions, just to survive. Her voice became firm.

"Alice has been a good nanny, especially when Danielle was a young baby, but I think Sadie will want to take care of her own daughter."

"We are going to take care of her financially. A small reward for all she has done," Philip added quickly, with slightly less composure than Isabel, which Elizabeth noticed, but she decided that they felt a slight guilt about dispensing with her now. After five years, it was only natural.

At that moment Isabel heard Alice's car sweep up the drive.

"Danielle's home. You can meet her, she's a delightful little girl," she said proudly. She could have easily added that she was far less complicated to bring up than her mother had been, but in the present circumstances that wouldn't help the situation at all. The reason Danielle didn't have issues was because she didn't remember her mother, and they had all, including Nathan, who was a sort of surrogate uncle, showered her with love and made her feel wanted. Sadie had been a disturbed child because of the way she was conceived. She had inherited her father's looks as well as his unusual character, and when Isabel had to tell her the one thing she didn't want to, who her true father was, for her own good, any sort of mother/daughter relationship that they had was gone forever. Deep down Isabel wished she had been there for Sadie when she had her abortion, but the shock of knowing that Sadie's own half brother had come into their lives and made her pregnant had been such a trauma to deal with, and by the time she had started to accept it, her own darling son had drowned and that huge loss had changed her life ever since.

Still, it was no good having regrets, many years had passed, and it was the present that counted. Nathan seemed sure that Sadie had told the absolute truth, but after years of being fooled, Isabel realised it might not be the whole truth. Just because Sarah had been Alice's twin, it didn't prove that Alice had murdered Danny. It had been an open verdict; either an accident or suicide. Alice might well have a grudge because of her sister's suicide. Maybe this was why she was trying to pretend that Danielle was her own child. Who knows, Alice may have blamed herself and Philip for it all, so winning over Danielle would be a sort of satisfaction for her.

She made up her mind to discuss this possibility later when Elizabeth had gone, but in the meantime, they must satisfy her that it was in everyone's interests for Sadie to return.

Suddenly Danielle burst into the room in typical five-year-old fashion, bouncing over to give her grandmother a spontaneous hug.

"Grandma, I've done a drawing of our house," she said, holding it out in front of her. Isabel admired it, then passed it to Philip.

"Danielle, say hello, this is Mrs Fowler," said Isabel, anxious to make a good impression.

"Hello, are you Grandma's friend?" asked Danielle curiously.

"Yes, sort of."

Elizabeth noticed how confident she was, with a captivating smile. She felt drawn to this happy little girl.

Alice came in saying, "Danielle, you shouldn't just run in like that. Grandma and Grandad were having a private conversation."

Elizabeth turned to see the nanny. She looked to be in her early thirties, a good looking young woman, with reddish brown hair, and very startling green eyes, which right now flashed with annoyance.

"Mrs Fowler, meet Alice, our nanny," said Philip quickly, sensing Alice's feeling of being left out of things. He put his arm around Danielle, who snuggled into him, seemingly unaware of Alice's displeasure. Philip knew she was right to teach Danielle how to behave, but he suspected her icy attitude was mainly because she knew why Elizabeth was here.

"How do you do?" said Elizabeth, shaking hands with her, and noticing how she barely took her eyes off Danielle at any time. Elizabeth made no reference as to why she was there, that was up to the Morton Browns to tell her if she didn't already know. But judging by her body language, Alice did know, and she didn't like it. Well that was something that both of them and Sadie had to resolve.

She stayed for another half an hour chatting to them and making notes. After a short but polite conversation with her, Alice took Danielle with her to give her some lunch. Everything that Elizabeth had seen today had convinced her that this was the best place for Sadie to bond with her daughter.

She had a loving family who were concerned about her welfare, a daughter who seemed to be uncomplicated, just a normal happy little girl, and although a little stern, her nanny was obviously working to make sure she understood manners. Elizabeth knew she was going to recommend that Sadie returned here, then it was up to Sadie to prove, with the help and support of her family, that she could be a responsible mother.

After Alice had given Danielle her lunch, she sat with her for a few minutes of what she called 'Quiet time'. It lasted for about an hour, whilst Danielle was allowed to watch CBeebies. She no longer took a daytime nap, but this hour recharged her batteries to get her through the rest of the day. Danielle snuggled up to her on the sofa, clutching her favourite cuddly bear, and although she was watching story time, Alice's mind was elsewhere.

She was so angry. She couldn't help it, but she must keep it from Danielle. Her baby was not to blame. It was all locked up in her mind, longing to escape, but not when her little one was around. Alice had never thought of herself as a bad person, only a wronged one, and when that happens it causes you to act in a way that is best for you. As far as she was concerned, Sadie was the cause of everything going wrong in her life, and for this Sadie had to pay.

Sadie, by her own admission had killed her own brother, and then caused her beloved twin Sarah to take her own life. So Alice had to put that right, and as it was too late now to bring Sarah back, Sadie had to pay. So she had taken matters into her own hands by killing Danny, the man they were both in love with, and then framed Sadie for it. Alice's love for Danny had turned to hate after he rejected her, so what a good idea it was for her to kill him and then let mad Sadie take the blame.

It was even better with Sadie locked up. She had become Danielle's nanny. In the beginning it was to spite Sadie, and also her parents, but she had grown to love this little girl, she was her last link with Danny, and now she felt like her own daughter.

If only Nathan had returned her affection, together they could have brought Danielle up. Because her grandparents were not going to be around for ever, and because Alice had done most of the caring, and getting up at night with her when she was very young, she really felt that Danielle could not survive without her.

But it had all gone wrong. Evil Sadie was coming home to cause even more trouble and Nathan didn't want her, in fact no one wanted her, she had regretfully lost contact with her own parents since she came to work for the Morton Browns, and now they were going to discard her like a dirty sock after all she had done.

They hadn't said so, they had only mentioned that Danielle's mummy was coming home, but it was like a knife in her heart. She had made herself a comfortable life here in the last five years, and that bitch had got away with her crimes and was coming home to her family as though nothing had happened. But worst of all, she was going to lose Danielle, she knew it, and that little girl was her whole life. She was fun to be with, loving and affectionate. Alice had given up her own family ties to care for Danielle, and she had never regretted it because she couldn't let the Morton Browns find out she was Sarah's twin. Danielle had been everything to her, and even as she was thinking all this, Danielle leaned closely up to her and put her arms round her neck.

"I love you Mama Alice."

"I love you too!"

It was their little secret that Danielle called her Mama, only when they were alone. It meant everything to Alice to hear those words, but for how much longer?

39

Later when she was in bed, she allowed the emotion to sweep over her; she sobbed, and her tears flowed. Her future without Danielle stretched out in front of her, empty and meaningless. How would she ever cope?

But after the tears came the determination. Sadie was not going to ruin her life again, she would stand up and fight for Danielle. She had made a fool of Sadie before, and she would do it again. All Alice had to do was make sure that Sadie's sins were known about. Just because she was coming home, it didn't mean she had turned into Mother Teresa. She would carry on with her evil work, but just as before, and Alice would be one step ahead of her. All these thoughts tumbled around in her brain, until eventually weariness overtook her and she went to sleep.

Chapter Five

"Danielle, when you come back, Grandad and I are taking you to the beach. The tide will be out, and we're going to have some fun."

"Cool," said Danielle. The word sounded good, she had heard some older girls saying it when she was out the other day.

"Alice, you can take the afternoon off," said Isabel firmly, ignoring the look on Alice's face. This young woman did not own Danielle, and Isabel was determined that she would sever the reins that were bound much too tightly between Alice and Danielle.

"Take this, and go and buy yourself some new clothes for your holiday," said Philip warmly, handing her a generous wad of notes.

Alice allowed herself to take the money. They hadn't got rid of her yet. She was clinging on to her job by a thread, and she didn't want to go on holiday, but it was booked and paid for, so she really had no choice. She knew that whilst she was away, Sadie would get her foot back through the door. Alice just had to grin and bear it, but whilst she was doing that, she intended to think of a way to get rid of Sadie, out of their lives, once again.

"Thank you." She gave Philip a watery smile and left the room. Danielle skipped after her; Alice was taking her to the dentist. Danielle liked the dentist, he was a kind man with twinkling eyes, and he always let her spin the chair round, it was fun. And he told her she was cleaning her teeth well, so she was quite happy to go there.

41

Danielle was looking forward to her fifth birthday. She would be really grown up, and go to school all day. Grandma had bought her some school uniform, a grey skirt with a white blouse, and a royal blue cardigan. She liked wearing it; all her friends wore it too, and almost everyone in her class had been with her at play group, so going to school had not been a difficult experience.

Ever since she could remember, Danielle's life had been full of happiness. Grandma and Grandad were there, as was Alice, and they all made her feel loved and secure.

Grandma and Grandad might be very old, but they still knew how to have fun. Last time they went to the beach, Grandad had helped her to make a sandcastle and a boat, he had put flags on the boat, and then he had buried her in the sand so only her head was sticking out, then Grandma had laughed, taken a photo, and had told him to get her out now in case she got sand in her eyes.

When Alice had been ill one day, Grandma had asked Grandad to take Danielle and her friend Hannah out to eat, because Alice had a bug, and Grandma was getting the cleaning lady to make sure all the kitchen was free from germs. Grandad had taken them to McDonald's at Whitstable, so they had a happy meal and ice cream. Afterwards Danielle's tummy was so full, but she didn't care, McDonald's was her favourite place to eat, and the fish fingers were brill!

Danielle felt like Alice had always been in her life, and she did love her. Alice was very beautiful, and she too could be fun, but sometimes she made her feel a bit like they were bound together, and she mustn't do anything without her. And sometimes she knew that Alice and Grandma were a bit funny with each other, and she felt like a little doll they both wanted.

She had seen photos of her mummy. She was even more beautiful than Alice, and Danielle knew that with her own glossy black hair and very dark eyes, she looked like her mummy, and she felt very proud of that. Grandad had shown her lots of pictures of her mummy and told her about when her mummy was her age. Alice never spoke about her mummy, and she could sense that only Grandad was the one to talk to about her. Grandma had said she was in hospital getting well and children were not allowed to visit. But now her mummy was well and coming home to spend her birthday with her. That made Danielle very happy. All her friends at school had mummies, and she wanted to be the same. Her secret with Alice to call her Mama Alice was because Grandma might not like it, and although she did it, Danielle still wanted to see her real mummy and call her Mummy without it having to be a secret.

She had asked Grandad who her daddy was, and he had looked very sad and said he had died. So she would never see him. She was glad that her mummy was well now and she hadn't died; all she knew about dying is that people went to heaven, and you never saw them again. There must be something special about heaven if no one ever came back, but Danielle didn't think anything could be nicer than living in Herne Bay, having nice friends, and playing on the beach. The only person she knew who wasn't so nice was Sammy. He had tried to get her Crunchie off her and he was bossy, but Danielle wasn't scared of him, she had grabbed it back. Then he had told Miss Morris that she had bad manners, but Danielle wasn't having that. She might not be five yet, but boys were rough, well Sammy was, and she told Miss Morris that it was her Crunchie bar, and Miss Morris had smiled and said, "Go Girl!"

Boys it seemed, were stronger and bossier than girls, so now that she knew, she wasn't going to let any of them get the better of her. Since she had stood up to him Sammy hadn't bothered her again, so that was good, and being of a naturally happy and generous nature, the next time she had a Crunchie bar with her, she had given him half, then they had made friends, and it seemed that Sammy liked her again.

"Right, open your mouth and let me help you with your teeth, they have to be extra clean for the dentist."

Danielle obediently opened her mouth. Normally she would have skipped past Alice, daring her to catch her, giggling and would have said, "I can clean my own teeth." But she knew it was hard to reach the back, and she did want the dentist to praise her, so she allowed Alice to guide her electric toothbrush right round behind her teeth.

When Alice was satisfied her teeth were clean enough, they got in the car and drove down to the town where her dentist had his surgery. Herne Bay town had a high street with shops, a supermarket, library and bus garage. Then there was the cobbled pedestrian area; with more shops and cafés the pedestrian area ran parallel to the sea front, and it was pleasant to walk down with a sea view to the left.

There were only a couple of ladies-wear shops in this area and Alice decided there would not be enough choice for her. So after lunch, seeing as she had been given the time off, she would go to Canterbury, where there was a vast selection of shops, departmental stores, and fashion outlets. Her resentment started to fade, she was going to make the most of this holiday. She reckoned Danielle might miss her, and when she came back she would have worked out a plan to rid them all of evil Sadie. Then life could carry on the same as it had been. If she couldn't attract Nathan, what the hell, there were plenty more men out there, and she had her youth and her looks, she might even meet someone in California. That would give them all a shock, if she found 'the one' on holiday and never came back. But she knew that would never happen, she was too firmly attached to Danielle to do that.

Whilst Danielle was at the dentist, Isabel and Philip had an early lunch. It was very pleasant sitting in the conservatory eating the smoked salmon salad that had been prepared by their housekeeper, Ann. Isabel was quite happy to give her the afternoon off too, she would come back later from the beach with Philip, and order a pizza takeaway. It was a treat for Danielle, most of the time they enjoyed good healthy food, organically sourced, but today they wanted time to talk to Danielle about her mother coming to visit without Alice around. Spending quality time with her this afternoon was the best way to do it.

Danielle had been the reason they had managed to keep their lives on track these past few years, in spite of all the heartbreak they had suffered. This little granddaughter, of whom they were so very proud, had given them a reason to carry on. The one good thing Sadie had done in her life was to give birth to Danielle. She wasn't perfect, and they wouldn't have wanted her to be, she was just a happy little girl with an uncomplicated nature, who could be a pickle at times, even a bit disobedient, but she was warm and loving, unlike her mother, who appeared to lack emotion. But then Isabel had to question herself on that. Was the lack of emotion inherited from her own father, and because of the way she was conceived, not in love, but with violence by a man who was so sick himself? And had the abortion she had to suffer at thirteen affected her? Isabel couldn't help blaming herself when she thought about that. She had been in such shock when she found out that of all the boys Sadie could have met up with, it was

44

Sadie's own half brother that had made her pregnant, that she had not been there for Sadie to support her. She had just arranged for a very quick private abortion, never to be spoken about again, and then bang, within days, her own dear son Jeremy had drowned, and her grief was so all consuming that Sadie's abortion, and how she might be feeling about it, was pushed right out of her mind.

"Shall we take her along to Tankerton and go on the street of stones, she loves that?" enquired Philip, interrupting her thoughts.

"Why not, the cream tea shop will be open as the weather is so good. We can pop in there after. She'll enjoy an ice cream, and there's plenty of room for her to run around on the grass outside."

"That sounds nice." Philip stretched his long legs in front of him, putting his empty plate from his lap onto the table.

"I am going upstairs to change into my shorts, it may not exactly be the South of France, but it's still only early May, and the weather is so mild."

Isabel left the room and Philip wondered if he would have time for a quick nap; women were noted for taking a while to get ready. But then Isabel's voice floated back to him and he grimaced with good humour. How well she knew him!

"Philip, can you put the deck chairs and other bits in the car. You know what Danielle is like, as soon as she puts a foot through the door she will want to go out again."

Philip acceded defeat. He was surrounded by women in this house; feisty opinionated women. He was outnumbered, and when Sadie came home, there would be one more. He needed Nathan to balance it up a bit, but Nathan had his own life, although he did still visit some weekends. He was so proud of how that young man had turned out, everyone had good in them if you looked for it.

Even Sadie had good in her. Philip had seen it. It was a shame that Isabel hadn't, but now would be the chance to remedy that.

He so wanted this homecoming of Sadie's to work. It wasn't just about Sadie and Danielle bonding, although that would be a good start. His dearest wish would be to see Sadie and Isabel bond at last, and if there was one reason for that to happen, it would be Danielle. Even Sadie would realise that they had to be a united family for her relationship with her little girl to work.

Like all fathers, Philip wanted to think the best of his daughter,

45

and they had every reason to believe her depression had been treated and any mental problems had been resolved by the experts, otherwise Sadie would not have been allowed to come home. The reports he had seen suggested that Sadie had reformed and turned towards religion to guide her. She had been a good prisoner, this is why she had been moved from the secure unit to one allowing more independence and freedom.

She was not popular with the female inmates, but that was because they believed she had killed her own brother, and those sort of crimes did not sit well with others inside. Sadie's amazing stories had not helped her, so she had become a loner, but since she had been treated, not only had her temper lessened, he had been told that she no longer lived in a fantasy world.

He was longing to see her and hold her, his heart ached when he thought about what she had been through. His greatest pleasure would be to see the three women he loved most in the world all bonding together. Today they would tell Danielle that her mother was coming for an afternoon visit tomorrow, just after Alice had flown out to California. If that went well, then she would move back in a couple of weeks, and then their family would once again be complete.

Chapter Six

Sadie sat in the car next to Elizabeth, glancing out of the window whilst they were travelling. She had dressed casually, in jeans and a pink tee shirt, which was in stark contrast to Elizabeth, who looked immaculate with her hair dressed in a top knot, and a striped navy blouse which went well with her grey suit.

"How are you feeling?" Elizabeth enquired sympathetically. She could imagine how very nervous Sadie must be today, after not seeing her daughter since she was a baby.

"Oh, I am OK," Sadie sounded unconcerned. In the past that would have been true. Sadie had never cared what anyone thought of her and had gone her own way in life doing whatever she wanted to, even when her son Ricky had been born. Why should she love Ricky when she had only married his father to get her hands on his money? Why should she love any child when her first love had resulted in a baby that she had no say in, and it had been cruelly ripped from her body? Losing that baby so suddenly, with her mother not trying to understand just what she was going through, had filled her head with thoughts she had no control over, thoughts that if her baby could be taken from her without anyone caring, then her mother should suffer the same fate.

It was easy to store up all that hatred and bitterness, to allow it to dominate her life and her behaviour, until it all changed. Even when she fell in love with Danny, she wanted to be a better person for him, but she would still stop at nothing to get what she desired, and that included removing Petra from his life, his very attractive maid, whose presence in the house made Sadie feel threatened.

But Danny had died, and when her grief subsided it was replaced by an even deeper grief: the sudden parting from her newborn daughter. Sadie had never experienced pain like it. From the moment that little girl was born she had felt a love she didn't even know she was capable of, a deep all consuming love for that child who had been conceived with a man she actually had feelings for.

After four years she had accepted that Danny was lost to her. In her mind she had imagined they would have made a life together, the idea of any resistance from Danny had been put firmly out of her mind and forgotten. But Alice had spoiled that, she had murdered him because she didn't want Sadie to have him.

Danielle was all she had left to remind her of Danny, and she too had been taken from her so suddenly that Sadie had been plunged into a deep despair, that is until Denise had come along and helped her.

This had made Sadie evaluate her life. She knew that once she had been diagnosed with mental illness, and had left prison, she had a chance of getting her daughter back one day. Her love for Danielle was so strong; she vowed to be a model prisoner, show she had reformed, and really try to be a better person. She still had those bad thoughts inside her, they would never go away, but she wanted Danielle to love and respect her, so she would have to try and be a good mother. That also included treating her own mother with respect, something she had never done.

She sneered at herself for going soft in the head. Hating people had always been very satisfying for her, but being a mother had changed her, and her biggest fear was that her daughter would reject her, and if she did then Sadie would have nothing left to care about, so she might as well be dead! She knew how she would do it too, a handful of pills would do the trick, but only if she had to, because that was one rejection she would not be able to take on the chin.

At one time she would have sneered at the idea of her parents leaving Richmond; such a classy area, and near enough to London to enjoy all it had to offer. If they wanted to bury themselves on the Kent coast she really didn't mind. If she didn't like it here, once she had bonded with Danielle they could move to wherever they wanted, Daddy would more than likely fund it.

But even Sadie could find no fault as the car drove up the hill towards the house; the sun shone brightly, and the air was fresh with the scent of blossoms of pink and white. Gazing towards Reculver Towers, which were clearly visible at the top of the hill, pointing towards the skies, she could see the rugged cliffs, and below the sea was gently lapping the shingle, creating such a serene atmosphere it soothed her anxiety a little. The gates were open for them, and as the car swept up the drive and into the gravelled area, she noticed how grand the Victorian house was. Daddy loved period houses and they were always decorated in keeping with the time they were built. Maybe living here wouldn't be so bad. Plenty of fresh air, and Canterbury nearby, which was almost like a mini London, with plenty of good restaurants and night life. But then she reminded herself, if she was being a mother to Danielle, night life wouldn't matter any more, and to her own surprise, she found it didn't really seem to matter.

Elizabeth glanced at her as they got out of the car. Her face was impassive, whatever was going on behind that tough exterior it was hard to tell. Here was a woman who was able to hide her emotions, if she had any. She had heard it suggested more than once that Sadie was devoid of all emotion.

Isabel was at the door with Philip. Sadie dutifully kissed both her parents, and Elizabeth noticed that Philip seemed the most comfortable with her, Isabel had seemed a little awkward. But then it was a long time since they had been together, and so much had happened.

Sadie had kissed her mother for the first time since she had been a young child, and then even as a child, it had only been because Daddy had insisted. The body language between the two of them had been awkward. Isabel had been taken by surprise, she had always been used to anger and insults from Sadie. She scarcely dared to hope that Sadie really had changed for the better.

Sadie's dark eyes darted around her, and Philip guessed exactly what she was thinking.

"Danielle is in the play room, she is very excited about meeting you, but also very shy. Come through."

Danielle's excitement had turned to fear and shyness, and when they opened the door, she was nowhere to be seen.

"Are you hiding, Danielle?" tried Isabel, and Sadie's heart

49

turned over. Her own daughter didn't want to meet her. What had that bitch Alice said to her? It would be her fault, she was sure.

Philip spotted her first, at the far end of the room. She had drawn the curtains, but in typical five year old fashion, had forgotten to hide her feet, which were poking out the bottom. He crossed the room in a flash, pulled back the curtains and said "Boo!"

Danielle loved hide and seek, and she collapsed laughing into his arms. Philip was going to make sure this reunion would not be an ordeal. He scooped her up like a wriggly puppy and carried her over to Sadie, unceremoniously setting her down next to her mother.

"Danielle, meet your mummy. Sadie, you know who this is."

There was a pregnant pause whilst they surveyed each other. Sadie's only memories were of a baby who slept, fed, and cried, she had not seen any photos of her daughter's progress, but she liked what she saw, a mirror image of herself. A beautiful little girl, her dark hair was her shining glory, and her very dark eyes sparkled with fun and good humour. She was of slender build, and her flawless peach-like skin looked soft.

Sadie opened her arms and held them wide. For the first time in her life she was scared that someone might not like her, and this time it truly mattered.

Danielle met the eyes of her mother; she was just like her photo, with her dark hair and eyes, and suddenly Danielle felt complete. She was no different to any of her friends, she had a mother. All shyness now forgotten, she ran into her mother's arms. She felt the warmth of her body as they hugged and she liked the feeling.

"Mummy, I am glad you are well."

That sounded polite to her. Alice and Grandma had both told her she must always be polite, so she backed away in confusion when suddenly Sadie's body started to tremor, and was then racked with sobs. She looked up at her mother, the tears were rolling down her face whilst Sadie made desperate attempts to wipe them with a tissue. Danielle wondered why she had upset her.

Philip and Isabel stood aghast: Sadie in tears, she really must love this child.

"Don't take any notice of me. I am being silly, but it's been a long time, you were a baby last time I saw you."

50

Sadie was composed now; she smiled at Danielle. This little girl was even more special than she remembered. She didn't want to do anything to scare her. She cursed herself for getting emotional, whatever had happened to her?

Elizabeth had been watching the scene very carefully. All those who said Sadie was devoid of all emotion were wrong, or else she was a very good actor, but Elizabeth felt it was genuine, and in spite of herself, she felt empathy for Sadie. Since she had been given the task of ensuring that it would be in everyone's interests for Sadie to return home, she had changed her opinion of her. She had love for her daughter, that was very clear, and living without her for the past four years must have been heart wrenching.

"Shall we go into the conservatory, Ann has made us some afternoon tea," said Isabel hospitably. She still felt bewildered by the change in her daughter, but she welcomed it. There was hope for this family yet.

"Thank you," said Elizabeth. It was certainly no hardship to sit in their beautiful sun lounge, gazing across the downs and out to sea, which looked particularly blue today and calm, as blue as the sky was.

They all went into the conservatory, where Isabel poured the tea and handed round a plate of scones and cakes. Sadie had remembered to bring a tube of Smarties, which made Danielle warm to her even more. They all sat drinking their tea and commenting how nice the weather was, and Danielle got excited when she saw a seagull hovering nearby.

Danielle used the new word which she really liked.

"Mummy, do you know the street of stones?"

"No, whatever is that?" asked Sadie, loving the sound of that word Mummy.

"It's magic, you have the sea around you, but you don't get wet."

Sadie was even more mystified until Philip explained that it was a narrow strip of land that jutted out to the sea, it was comprised of stones, and when the tide came in, for some reason it remained dry with water around it, so you could walk along it like a pier.

"That sounds nice," Sadie said smiling, but wondering what was happening to her. Normally the only beaches she liked were in exotic locations and sandy, and stupid stones jutting out to sea

51

held no thrill for her. But because of Danielle she would like them, and visit them. If anyone had asked her in the past if she would be like this she would have thought they were going mad, even she didn't recognise the person she was any more.

So they sat there as a family, discussing all the places they would like to visit, and Elizabeth was suitably impressed. Later, on the way back, she noticed Sadie had withdrawn into herself a little. No doubt the poor girl was wishing that she could have stayed there today where she belonged, with her family.

"You did well today," she said encouragingly, and Sadie smiled politely and thanked her for the ride. Normally Sadie didn't do polite, but she had her reasons now.

Later when she was in bed, so many thoughts invaded Sadie's mind, making sleep impossible.

Oh how muddled and confused she was! All her life she had been a sword in the side of her family, and now to gain her daughter's love and trust she had to assume what she felt was a goody two-shoes exterior. All the satisfaction she had got from hating people and causing them the sort of pain she had put up with, was no longer there. If she wanted her daughter to love and respect her she had to behave like everyone else. But that was a tall order for Sadie, the person she was trying to be now was not her real self, and she realised that not even for Danielle could she totally change.

Her best plan was to gain her daughter's trust, and then make their own life away from her family except for occasional visits. All she had to do was keep anything that she did that was from her own agenda away from Danielle, she would never know. People might say it was wrong, but Sadie had her own ideas.

Denise was on her way to Australia, she had given Sadie one thousand pounds to buy a supposed ticket to join her. That was never going to happen. Denise had given her back her life, and she didn't need her any more. Sadie felt no pity for her. Let her wait forever, she wasn't going to join her, and this thought gave her huge satisfaction. Denise was buying land and having a house built, but no way did Sadie want to spend the rest of her life with boring Denise. No matter how nice the house was.

Being nice to everyone was going to be hard, it would be the best play acting she had ever done, especially towards her mother. How could she forgive her mother for having sex with her own brother and getting herself pregnant? Poor Daddy, her mother had betrayed his trust, and knowing where she came from made Sadie feel her own life was messed up. Her mother had said he raped her, but hadn't Sadie said those self same words when her brief encounter with Matt had resulted in pregnancy? Anything to save yourself grief, and her own mother was no different. It was hard to respect her mother after that, and it made Sadie herself feel dirty.

But now she had a chance to lead a clean life with her daughter, away from her mother. Since she had lost Danny, she had lost her libido. Being shut away with only women around her had not made her promiscuous; sex had not happened with anyone, there was too much pain and grief inside her to work through. She knew that she could have easily seduced Denise, she had even planned to if she had to. But luckily for her, she had been moved out of prison, and then her only thought was not to put a foot wrong so she could come out and claim her daughter back again.

Lying in bed like this, trying to psychoanalyse herself, made Sadie realise she was still the same person inside. Danielle would only ever see her good side, but that other side, the one she had tried to subdue, might well still come out depending on the circumstances and how she was treated. And anyone who tried to upset her daughter would have Sadie to reckon with. She would go to any lengths to protect her daughter, and if anyone got hurt along the way, well tough, Sadie reckoned whatever she did to stop them would be justified.

Chapter Seven

Alice yawned and stretched as the plane started to do its descent into San Diego Airport. Philip had booked her a first class ticket and she had enjoyed travelling that way. The food was served on proper plates and was far nicer than the normal airline food that was given to the masses. Philip may have thought that money would win her over, but in this instance he was wrong. She planned to enjoy the holiday and spend the money, because he had been very generous with it, but when she returned, if Sadie was back, Alice had plans to get rid of her and take up her own rightful position as Danielle's Mama. It was all so clear in her mind, Danny's daughter had been given to her to bring up, and she was now her child.

Later, in her hotel room, which was equally impressive and had its own sitting room as well as a huge TV, she laid on the bed, which was big, just like everything in America was, and contemplated what she would do this evening.

The flight had been ten hours and she felt very weary, so after a short nap, she took a shower and got changed into a light summer dress. May in San Diego was very pleasant, a little too early for the sizzling temperatures it would have in summer, but still warm enough not to need a cardigan, unless of course the air conditioning was up high; so just to make sure, she took it with her down into the lounge to enjoy a pre-dinner drink.

There were mostly couples downstairs, and a feeling of loneliness swept over her. She had not had a boyfriend since Danny. She had given the last five years of her life up to Danielle.

Not that she regretted it, but now she was away from her she didn't feel complete. She decided not to sit in there, as nice as it was, with soothing music playing softly in the background, she would take a walk outside.

Maybe she would skip dinner anyway, she had eaten plenty on the plane, and sitting still for so long she still felt full, so stretching her legs was a good idea. The warmth hit her as she exited the hotel, so she tied her cardigan round her waist. The air felt humid, no wonder everywhere inside had the air conditioning going full blast. It was so different to England in May. After sleepy Herne Bay, with its carpets of daffodils covering the downs, and pink and white blossoms on the trees, these wide roads with so many lanes and traffic everywhere were like another world; there were palm trees, and people were walking about on this very pleasant evening.

San Diego was a little overwhelming. Alice searched for a side street to slip down, and then she found, tucked away, a small bar where she could have a quiet glass of wine.

Already she was missing the little village pubs in England where everyone knew her and she would be greeted with a smile when she came in. The exterior of the bar was very bland but inside it looked a little better. There were wooden tables with leather-look padded chairs, behind the bar was a man looking rather bored. The rest of the room was empty except for one man who sat over the far side busily working what looked like an iPhone.

Behind the bar, Rory brightened when he saw the young woman enter. Her red brownish hair flowed around her shoulders, and how cute she looked in that green mini dress, with such great legs. His evening was already getting a whole lot better.

"Good evening, ma'am, what can I get you?" his eyes appraised her, it was unusual for a woman to come into a bar alone.

Alice felt out of her depth. This man was devouring her with his eyes. Back home in the local pub this just wouldn't happen, they were friendly, but not lecherous.

"Allow me to buy you a drink, it's not often we get a lady like yourself in here."

Alice turned in surprise, it was the man on the iPhone, he had left it on the table and his warm brown eyes held hers, and she could see friendliness in them, and not lust.

"Thank you, a white wine would be good."

"There you go, ma'am."

Rory felt disappointed. Cliff had got in first, with his tanned skin and looks like Leonardo DiCaprio what chance did an ordinary guy like him stand? He handed Alice her glass of wine, smiling widely, revealing the gap in the front where he had lost a tooth.

Alice stifled a shudder, did this man really think she would look at him? In his dreams, maybe!

"I am Cliff by the way, how do you do?" said the man with the iPhone.

"I am Alice."

She looked at him and liked what she saw. A young man with a broad face and friendly brown eyes. He had a look of Leonardo DiCaprio about him, an actor she had always enjoyed watching. His jeans were well cut, and his open necked shirt looked cool and casual. She was drawn to him immediately, and suddenly she felt this holiday would not be lonely. It seemed perfectly natural to her to follow him over to the corner where his iPhone was; he carried her drink, and they then sat at the table together.

When she looked back on it afterwards, the only way she could excuse her behaviour was that she felt like he had cast a spell over her. His eyes were hypnotic, charisma positively oozed out of him, and it was ages since Danny, some six years or more, and there had been no one else. Suddenly, like an answer to a prayer, she had met this man in a bar, maybe not the best place, but at a time when she was feeling very lonely, he was there.

They spent an enjoyable evening together, Alice lost count of the number of glasses of wine she had drunk, and she didn't really care. Suddenly the freedom that she had was more intoxicating to her than any wine, and she was enjoying the easy attitude of her companion. Time stood still for her now, all thoughts of getting back to her hotel were gone. He was funny and witty, a man who didn't take life that seriously it seemed.

In the past Alice had met men on her travels, but always her main focus had been Danny. She wasn't naïve, and she knew that meeting a man in a bar was not the best way to start a relationship, those sort of men were not looking for anything more than a fling. But this man drew her to him like a magnet. She couldn't help herself, what harm could it do to have some fun with him?

So they sat at the table flirting and laughing together until the bar started filling up.

"Let's go somewhere a bit quieter."

Alice couldn't stop giggling, everything was spinning around her, but she didn't care.

"I could always smuggle you into my hotel room."

He was back on his iPhone again, and she wondered fleetingly why she felt so dizzy. Surely she hadn't had that much wine?

Cliff stood up and tugged at her arm. Alice hung onto his arm, in spite of her dizziness she was absolutely determined, with a little bit of help from Cliff, she would walk right out of this bar and remain upright. It all seemed so funny, she could not stop laughing.

Cliff had been having such fun; this little lady was up for a good time. Fancy her coming into this bar when he was there and feeling bored. He'd even spiced up her drink a little, so no wonder she felt a bit dizzy, but he had better get her out of here soon, it wouldn't look good if she passed out on him.

As he rose to go he saw the door open, and in came the all too familiar sight of an FBI man with a gun in a holster around his waist. Suddenly this broad was a hindrance to him. He let go of her, and in slow motion she slid down the table and onto the floor. At any other time he would have found this funny, but not now, although it did have the desired effect of causing a diversion. A couple of people ran over to help, closely followed by the FBI man, but in the meantime Cliff had used this opportunity to slip out of the side door and then to keep going until he had left that chaotic scene behind him.

When he reached the block of flats where he lived, he took the elevator to the top floor, and breathed a sigh of relief when he was inside his home.

Ricky Scott was pleased that the girls had gone to Easter camp this week. For the past eight years he had to juggle home life and working life. It wasn't easy, and he wasn't always as available as the other guys to take assignments that took him away from Greenview.

His mother helped when she could, but he didn't like to ask her too often, and since Marina, alias Sadie, had plunged his whole family into complete devastation, when she married and then left very shortly afterwards, for a while life had become much harder for them all. But that was over seven years ago, and when he looked back at it now, it just seemed like an unpleasant nightmare that was best put right out of his mind.

She had taken them all in, but what hurt him the most was that she had used the girls to get him, and then when he was safely ensnared, she had left them without a backward glance. Never mind that she had hurt him, it was the pain she had caused his three princesses. Oh, how he wished he could have taken it away, coming so soon after the death of their mother, it was heartbreaking to see.

But his girls were strong; that grief had bound them even closer to each other, and they had worked through it now. They were all doing well at school, had plenty of friends, and were surprisingly independent already. Brenda was now sixteen, but was very protective of her two sisters; he felt proud of her.

Two years ago Ricky had met Kirsty at a parents' evening. She was a single mother with three children of similar age to his, and they became friends. Since then their friendship had blossomed to a very contented relationship. They didn't live together, but they spent as much time together as they could, and the two families all got on very well. He had no plans to even think about marriage again whilst the children were so young, but Kirsty had given him back his faith in women and this had helped him to put the past behind him.

Except for one thing, his son. Even working for the FBI, Ricky had still failed to track him down. Little Ricky would now be seven years old, and his heart grieved that he had never seen him. For this reason only, Ricky had kept up with Sadie's exploits, had even been to see her, but she had refused to recognise him. How heartless she was, or was it mental illness? Her character was far too complex for him to analyse.

He really didn't know whether his son was alive or dead, and he realised, with a pang of pain, he might never know. Luckily his working life had always been busy, so he'd grafted hard, and his girls were his reward. His hope was that, if little Ricky was alive and well, one day his son might seek him out and he could then explain why he had been absent from his life.

Maybe he should have hated Sadie for the havoc she had caused in all their lives, but Ricky had long since realised that her behaviour had not been normal, so maybe she was to be pitied rather than hated.

She had been released from prison, had received treatment at a special unit, and it now appeared after four years, she was going to be released as she was not considered a danger to anyone. He had used his FBI secret contacts to keep track of her. Maybe he should have let it go by now, but all he did know was he had an obsessive desire to know about his son, whatever the news, good or bad, and Sadie alone was the person who knew the answer.

He hadn't yet worked out how he would do it, but he planned to track her down in England. She had refused to tell him last time, but he would find out, he was determined. In his job he was paid to be suspicious, and her reaction when he had seen her in prison had been, oh, so suspicious. He had spent the last five years mulling it over in his mind and now he wanted answers. If he had to use his annual leave to take a vacation in England he would do it. Kirsty understood his need to find out the truth, that was what was so good about Kirsty, she supported him in everything he did. If he went to England, she had already told him she would take care of the girls and keep them happy until he returned.

But right now he had to focus on the assignment they had given him. They had tracked down the guy who was the main part of a drugs ring that they had been trying to bust for years. He was living it up in sunny California, and Ricky's mission was to act on the tip-off they had been given, get over there and track him down. If he could successfully make this arrest it would be a job well done.

His hotel was not far from the airport, and he had continuous contact via his phone with the office. He wasn't even allowed to take a shower before instructions were issued for him to go to Rory's little bar, tucked away round the back. He was to burst in and surprise Cliff Johnson. This time they had him, peddling drugs in a local bar, and he didn't even know they were onto him.

He had been given clear directions as to the location of the bar, so it was easy to find. He could scarcely believe that after ten years of trying to pin something on him, in a few minutes he could well be arresting wily old fox Johnson. He could call back up if necessary, but on his own he would be more able to reach the man before he realised just what was going on.

His hand felt for the holster that held his gun, only to be used if he had to, and he gently pushed at the door. There were quite a few people in there, a babble of voices greeted him, and he recognised Johnson right away, he had studied that photo so many times.

Johnson was holding a young woman by the arm, and it was clear to see she was very intoxicated, whether it was with drink, or drugs, or both, he had yet to find out. But even as he sprang across the space between them, Johnson acted quickly, releasing the woman who, unable to remain upright, slid to the floor. A couple of people rushed to help her, and blocked his path, so in spite of his efforts to get through, Ricky could only watch helplessly as his suspect slipped out of a side door and was gone.

He swore under his breath that he had been outwitted; the old fox had done it again! But the girl would talk, he would arrest her and take her to the local jail. She would know where Johnson had gone; well that is after a night in the cells sobering up. He would have her tested to see if she was on any drugs. He hadn't lost out yet, all he had to do was call for backup. He picked up his phone.

"I am arresting a white female, heavily intoxicated, and I need backup."

He slipped his phone back in his pocket and then went to her aid, poor chick was just like a rag doll, what had the swine done to her?

Philip and Isabel took the opportunity, whilst Alice was away, to move Sadie in with them. She had been given the largest bedroom, with its own en suite facilities, which happened to be next to Danielle. In the past it had been Alice's room, but they had moved her along the corridor when it had recently been decorated, and she was now settled in the other room. Nathan came to stay for a few days when she arrived; he wanted to make the most of Alice being away, and he also wanted to see Sadie, she still held such a fascination to him.

Sadie came with very few belongings; every time she had moved on, most of her personal things had to be left behind. When she was detained in prison, and the secure centre, she needed even less, so she arrived home in the jeans and pink T-shirt she had worn on her visit.

It didn't take Philip long to remedy that. What better idea than to send Isabel and Sadie on a shopping trip together; maybe not Danielle if they were trying to choose clothes and shoes. He had plans to take Danielle down to Herne Bay seafront. The recent mild weather, which happened to coincide with the Easter holidays, meant that not only had the crazy golf and ice cream parlour opened, but also the bouncy castle and trampolines on the beach. He could sit having a cup of coffee at the open air café and watch her enjoying herself. Then after that he would take her to McDonald's, it would be busy of course, everyone was on holiday, but Philip didn't mind. He was proud of his little granddaughter, and very much enjoyed spending time with her.

Sadie would have refused to go shopping with her mother at one time, but she knew, for Danielle's sake, she must make an effort. She was trying to convince herself that she was becoming a better person. Maybe her mother did bring out the worst in her, but she had learned over the years to be a good actress.

So they spent a whole day choosing a complete new wardrobe of clothes and shoes for Sadie. All day she kept her composure, listening and agreeing with what her mother said; even she marvelled at her self control, but it was for a reason, she kept reminding herself.

Isabel was bewildered, she had never been given any respect by Sadie before. She kept expecting scornful remarks, anger and bitterness, but there was none. For the first time ever she spent an agreeable day with Sadie shopping and having lunch, and by the time they came home, because like any parent she wanted to think the best of her daughter, she was confident that Sadie had finally reformed.

Sadie congratulated herself on managing to fool her mother that she was a changed person. It had been a strain, at times, not to retaliate in an angry and bitter way when her mother made suggestions. In Sadie's opinion her mother didn't have a clue about anything, she was out of touch with modern life, and her worst fault, along with her father, who was just as guilty, was allowing Alice to care for Danielle. Mad dangerous Alice, who she knew had killed Danny, and was therefore capable of anything. Nathan had warned them just how dangerous Alice was, he did believe her, but instead of getting rid of her immediately, all they had done was send her on holiday.

The anger she felt that Alice was being rewarded for her evil deeds was all consuming, and later that evening, after her parents had retired to their room, she vented it on Nathan; she no longer cared what he thought of her, he was just a hanger-on who had charmed his way into her family.

"Why is she still here? How can they let a killer take care of my daughter?"

Nathan looked at her. The passion in her voice and those dark enigmatic eyes that flashed with anger excited him. When he had first met her it had been one of his lucid moments, and her strong character and enticing looks had reeled him in, but then he had spoiled it by using her and behaving like a bum, and in return she had used him back and got a fake passport. In his stupid state he had believed her when she said they could go away together. Well she had gone away all right, but her plans had not included him, he had been left in the flat to burn.

And yet he couldn't blame her. Somehow he felt he was to blame for her desperate act; he had pushed her to the limit. She was still reeling him in now, no matter how rude she was to him, or how damning her attitude, she stirred an excitement inside him that no other woman had. The need to see her was more addictive than any drug he had ever taken, and being reviled by her was better than being ignored.

"I did speak to them about Alice, but they seem to think Danny wasn't murdered, they believe it was an accident."

"They're mad! She did kill him, then tried to blame me! How many times do I have to say it?"

Oh, how he loved the fire in her when she was angry, what an exciting woman she was. He side-stepped her bitter criticism, no way was he going to argue with her.

"I believe you Sadie, and when she returns, they just won't need her any more. Danielle has taken to you already, she loves having her real mother around. I think they are going to gradually phase Alice out of her life so it's not too much of a wrench for her, she's still very young."

His words did soothe Sadie a little, but she knew what his game was, he was trying to get into her good books, and she wasn't going to let him succeed.

"Oh that's fine words coming from you. I haven't forgotten you spawned kids all over the place."

Her face was twisted with spite. She wanted to hurt him, and she was even more angry to see how unruffled he was by her words.

Nathan smiled. "Not quite, you know one woman tried to tell me I was the father of her son, and he was a cute little kid that I would have gladly supported, but the DNA test proved otherwise, and then the bloke she had used me to make jealous, turned up out of the blue; it was his son, and it brought them back together."

Sadie had no answer to this, so Nathan continued.

"Sadie, I know you have a lot of anger and bitterness inside you, I get that, but until you stop acting like a spoiled child, we are just going to go round in circles. For your own sake you must put the past behind you. Alice will go in time. I know you haven't got much patience, but if you don't want to blow your relationship with Danielle, you need to develop some."

Sadie was shocked. She was usually the one who did the talking and everyone did what she wanted, but not Nathan, he didn't fear her wrath, and he spoke his mind. Even though she wouldn't admit it, she liked his strong attitude, there was nothing wishy-washy about him. He was so far removed from the useless bum she had known in the past. And even though she didn't like what he had said, she knew he was right. She went to bed knowing on this occasion she was defeated.

Chapter Eight

"I keep telling you, I never met him before yesterday in that bar. I was just having a glass of wine and a bit of a laugh with him, he seemed very nice!"

"Nice?" echoed Ricky. "He's a known drug dealer, and the results of your blood test prove that he slipped a little something into your drink."

"Oh, that was why I felt so giddy then. I knew I hadn't drunk that much, and he seemed fine."

"They always do! If you had left that bar and gone anywhere with him, you would probably have been the victim of date rape," said Ricky grimly. He believed her story; she wasn't Johnson's moll, just an English woman on holiday and lonely. She wouldn't be able to help them track him down. Disappointment flooded through him at the failure of his mission. This woman was not a suspect, just a very reckless tourist who was nearly taken in by Johnson. His voice became stern.

"So how would the family you work for react if they found out you were in jail for being drunk and disorderly, and under the influence of drugs."

Suddenly it all became too much for Alice. She had a kingsize headache, her mouth felt dry and nausea kept sweeping over her. She was being cross-examined by this man whilst his companion sat making notes and saying nothing.

She sobbed, running her fingers through her hair with an involuntary gesture.

"Please don't contact them, I will lose my job, and I can't leave Danielle, she's like my own daughter!"

Then it all came tumbling out: her connection with Sadie, and how she had become a nanny to her child and helped to raise her. Ricky was totally amazed that here in front of him was the one person who could lead him to Sadie again. What an unbelievable coincidence that she had been in that bar last night and had crossed his path. Surely this was meant to be.

"Did Sadie ever speak about the son she had by her husband?"

"Maybe." Alice wasn't sure just what she could say to this man.

Ricky's tone became cajoling.

"If you give me a very important piece of information I will release you without charges today, but if you ever come before me again for behaving in that way I won't be so kind!"

"If I can," said Alice, her hopes raised, wondering what he wanted from her.

Ricky was not going to unburden himself to her and admit Sadie had been his wife. He knew his companion, who was writing notes about the interview, could be trusted, so he continued.

"Sadie Morton Brown is known to us. Seven years ago she had a son who simply disappeared into thin air. We have to track him down."

Suddenly Alice could see a way that she could rid herself of Sadie, and legally too. How amazing. She could get the FBI onto her and, with a bit of luck, she'd be back inside where she belonged, and no one would ever guess that Alice had anything to do with it.

"Well, as long as no one in England ever knows that you arrested me."

"You have my word." Ricky looked her right in the eye. If only she knew just how much his heart was thumping and that he was silently praying she would tell him what he needed to know.

"She changed his name to Billy. Well, she didn't, his new parents did. She sold him to a childless couple. Apparently they paid her a fortune to get him they were that desperate."

Ricky kept his face impassive, but inside him there was anger, disbelief and pain, in equal measure, all vying for supremacy. He could scarcely believe that any woman, even Sadie, after giving

65

birth, could sell their own child, but his face masked his emotions.

"What was their name? Can you remember?"

Alice screwed up her face trying to remember. How she was enjoying this, once again dumping Sadie in it. Well it was only right, her evil actions deserved to be punished. So far she had got off scot free.

"Sadie called the woman Jill Hopkins. Not sure what her husband's name was." She felt quite proud that she had remembered the woman's name. "I'm not sure about that, and anyway, they moved when they adopted him, and Sadie came to Las Vegas with the money, and that is where we met up. They had to move, she told me they had sold the house to raise the money for her, and they were going somewhere to buy a small apartment, that was all they could afford."

Ricky struggled to keep his expression wooden. How sick was all this; the more she said, the worse it was! Well they didn't have much to go on, a child named Billy with a mother called Jill Hopkins; and America was a huge country.

"OK. Well if I release you, then no more chatting to strangers in bars. San Diego may be a beautiful part of California, but sadly it has its share of low-life like any other city."

Alice agreed readily, and very shortly she was released into the warmth of the outside. She made up her mind that the rest of her holiday would be spent mainly round the hotel swimming pool or clothes shopping, and over here men were off limits. She was not going to make the same mistake twice; she felt a bit like a naughty teenager. She had given the FBI man the address where he could contact Sadie. Selling a baby was a criminal offence, so it wouldn't be long before Sadie was behind bars again and Alice could resume her rightful place back with the Morton Brown family and Danielle.

After she had gone, Ricky's companion spoke for the first time.

"I know what you're thinking; that news must be devastating to you. But if you want her arrested, you need to butt out of the case. You're too close for comfort; it's your ex-wife, for God's sake, man!"

Ricky sighed. "I know, but first I want to try and find the Hopkins and see my son, after that I can hand the arrest of Sadie over to you. Do you understand what I mean?"

"I certainly do. So you want me to look the other way whilst you go and find your son. I guess if I was in your position I would do the same. Look buddy, we never had this conversation, I know nothing."

Ricky felt relieved. He had known Dave since their induction training. They were close friends, and being divorced himself, with an unreasonable ex-wife who didn't allow him much access to his children, he would fully understand Ricky's torment.

Sadie was enjoying very much being a mother to Danielle. The little girl accepted her back into her life easily, such was the friendliness of her nature. Sadie had been expecting a bit of mistrust because she had been missing for so long, and also that Danielle might pine for Alice. She felt angry when she realised Alice had that covered; she made a point of Skyping Danielle at about four o'clock every afternoon, which was eight in the morning in San Diego, just before she went to get her breakfast.

So after putting up with it for a week with a smile firmly fixed to her face, whilst uttering every oath she could think of under her breath to make herself feel better, Sadie started arranging different trips out. Danielle, like any young child, was quite oblivious of time; the first time she missed her Skype call with Alice she was sorry, but after that she was having such a good time she forgot all about it. Sadie was smiling to herself with satisfaction that it had been that easy to divert her daughter's attention. That was one in the eye for Alice!

Even when Alice rang up and complained to Isabel that Danielle was never there when she tried to Skype her, Isabel didn't care. In this instance she agreed that Alice was away on holiday and she would see Danielle soon enough without the continual need for Skyping.

Danielle shared her mother's love of nice clothes. Even at this tender age she knew exactly what she wanted to wear, and her greatest pleasure was to be invited to Sadie's bedroom to watch her mother trying on new clothes and shoes. Now that Danielle knew her mother, she felt complete, just like her friends. No one could tease her for being 'different'. She had learned already that not everyone in life was nice; other children sometimes said things she didn't like, but her buoyant nature made it impossible for her to dwell on it for long. She found life amusing and exciting, and most of her friends were fun to be around.

Another thing Danielle liked about her mother was her voice. She had a good singing voice and she knew all the latest songs. So instead of nursery rhymes and baby songs, Sadie and Danielle performed on her karaoke machine. It was such fun dancing round holding the microphone, pretending to be cool like the older girls she had seen on Saturday morning TV.

Sadie had remembered how entertaining Ricky's daughters had found the karaoke sessions, so it seemed a good idea to try it on Danielle, and it had worked. She didn't really know much about young children, but music seemed to be something they all enjoyed.

Looking at Danielle she felt so much pride that she and Danny had made this beautiful child. If there was ever a reason to be a better person, it was standing right next to her. Warm cheeky Danielle, who could melt any heart with her spontaneous hugs, and in Sadie's case she certainly had.

But life was never that easy for Sadie. No matter how much she wanted to change and be a better person for Danielle, there were people like Alice who wanted to spoil it. And her mother, who made Sadie feel dirty because of the way she had been conceived. That voice in her head told her she must rid the world of these bad people, and it was so difficult to ignore it.

"Danielle honey, it's time for your bath," she said, deliberately trying to block out all the negative thoughts which always seemed to bubble up inside her and threaten her happiness.

"OK Mummy, can we just sing that song once more?"

Sadie smiled, the little madam was using delaying tactics, but she couldn't blame her for trying, it was normal for children to fight going to bed. She must be firm, she mustn't spoil her.

"You have your bath and get your PJs on, then we might."

She was rewarded by a spontaneous hug before Danielle skipped out of the room to get herself undressed for the bath. My god, how good was the feeling of being a mother to such a loving child!

But then something passed through her mind that she would rather forget: her other child, the son she had given away. Her conscience stirred. She tried to put that thought to the back of her mind, excuses sprang into her head. He was Ricky's child, and

68

she had parted from Ricky. But there was that voice inside her head again, reminding her that Ricky wanted his child but she had sold him to someone else. She didn't like that voice, she wished it would go away. Danielle was her child and she must concentrate on that and put everything in the past out of her mind. But that voice was determined to punish her. It reminded her she could have had two children, and her son would be seven years old now. With a supreme effort Sadie brought her mind back to Danielle, who was standing naked in front of her.

"Mummy, can you come and wash me?"

Sadie felt a thrill go through her at the sound of her name.

"Come on then, let's see if the water is high enough, and your hair needs washing, too."

She followed after Danielle into the bathroom. The bathtub was empty.

"Come on, let's get some water in here then."

She soon had enough water in the bathtub, then found a warm and soft towel from the airing cupboard, and Danielle got in the water. Sadie busied herself bathing her daughter, but still those thoughts were floating through her mind, and that voice saying maybe she wasn't a very nice person, and how would Danielle feel if she knew she had a half brother that her mother had given away?

Well she would have to make sure that Danielle never knew, she wanted her to think her mother was a good person; and she would be in the future, she would change just for Danielle and make her proud of her. With this lasting thought in her mind she felt more at peace with herself.

Later, when Danielle was fast asleep, she touched her soft cheek; there was such a look of innocence on her young face. Sadie wished she could go back to that innocent age herself and start her life again. Whatever happened, she would make sure she always put her daughter's happiness first. My, how she had changed, and she knew it, and all because of Danielle.

Chapter Nine

Philip and Isabel took advantage of the Whitsun half term by arranging a short break for Sadie and Danielle in Portugal. Alice was due home from California after a six week holiday, and this seemed a good time to tell her that she was no longer needed. Isabel would have loved to go with them to Portugal, but she knew she could not just disappear and leave Philip to break the news to Alice, that was definitely a coward's way out of a difficult situation.

Sadie was secretly chortling with glee that firstly, she didn't have to spend a week being nice to her mother, and secondly, when she came home, Alice would be gone. She hadn't realised it would be that easy, and she knew that if she had actually seen Alice, face to face, it would have been very difficult to act a part, there was so much hatred between them, she wasn't even sure she could have kept her hands off her.

Her parents now realised just how much Sadie blamed Alice for her arrest. What they were not sure about was whether Sadie was justified in thinking Alice had lied about her to the police, or was her imagination taking over as it had in the past? But one thing was for sure, it seemed best to keep these two women apart if peace was to continue to reign over their family.

Isabel wasn't sure just how affected Danielle would be when Alice was no longer around; five years of her being there was the whole of Danielle's life. But keeping the ties was not a good idea, there was too much history between Sadie and Alice. Isabel was grateful for those years Alice had taken care of their precious granddaughter, but now that relationship had to end or else these family ties could never be bonded back together again, and for Isabel and Philip that was the most important thing of all.

Philip had decided that a nice financial reward might soften the blow. He would go so far at to give Alice enough money to set up in her own flat somewhere; but preferably away from Herne Bay, he was hoping her new life would take her elsewhere.

Neither of them were looking forward to letting her go. Alice was not particularly a person who inspired affection, but she had always shown herself to be an excellent nanny, so they would miss her care of Danielle, although not her rather obsessive need to monopolise her young charge. Isabel wondered if Alice were to meet someone special and get married, then have her own children, it might make all the difference and help her to forget Danielle, because although it was quite customary for nannies to keep in touch after they left a family when the bond between them and the child was so close, in this instance it would not work.

Ricky looked out of the taxi window as it passed slowly through the traffic in Canterbury. So many old buildings; they just didn't have anything like this in America. Dave was looking forward to exploring some of the cobbled side streets, and of course Canterbury Cathedral, they might be here for work, but they couldn't go back home without experiencing some of the culture and atmosphere that was unique to Canterbury.

As the taxi passed through the Westgate Towers, Dave admired the medieval architecture,

"Hey buddy, look how narrow it is, yet all the traffic passes through the middle."

"Yup, we'll get some pictures tomorrow, after we've done what we came for," agreed Ricky. He was trying to inject some enthusiasm because he knew it was Dave's first time in England, but there was only one thought on his mind; to find out about his son.

Glancing to his left he saw the gardens full of flowers, lovingly planted in patterns of colour, and behind them flowed the river Stour, with families of ducks lazily gliding past and seemingly oblivious of the people who walked through those gardens to get to the shops.

71

A group of students from the local university made use of the benches and the grass, they looked to be busily writing, and what a delightful place to further their studies.

"I am looking forward to fish and chips and a pint of ale in an English pub," remarked Dave.

The taxi swept into quite a narrow passageway that led to their hotel. Their week long stay was to be at a building with a wealth of character dating back as far as the sixteenth century. It boasted of oak beams and hops, and other period features.

After being used to such space in their own country, the winding narrow stairs and low beams were of great fascination to them. Their bedroom was quite small, with just a narrow space between their beds, although it did contain an en suite shower room. Even Ricky's interest was captured by the different culture and surroundings.

Later, when they returned from the pub, they discussed their plans for the following day. A hire car was going to be delivered to the hotel in the morning complete with satellite navigation, and then they were off to Herne Bay, some six miles away. Ricky spoke animatedly about it.

"Well Dave man, we are here, what happens next?"

Although his boss didn't know it, Ricky was using this trip to kill two birds with one stone. And it was all thanks to Rory. Poor Rory the barman, he had to lean a bit heavily on him after losing Johnson that night, and threaten to close down his bar because he had 'allowed' someone to hand out drugs there. He guessed Rory didn't really have a clue, but it had worked, he couldn't afford to lose his livelihood, so he'd spilled the beans on where Johnson was hiding out. Ricky and Dave had gone round there and surprised him, even arrested him, but now they needed a statement from Alice, who had spent that evening with him. Her evidence, added to more that they had from people he had sold drugs to, would put that lousy excuse of a man in jail for a good few years.

Dave had spent the last few weeks chasing up every Jill Hopkins that he could possibly locate, but America was a big country, and he had drawn a blank. Ricky hoped this visit would further his search.

"Ricky, I know what you're going through, but there is no 'WE', it's 'ME' only!"

Ricky's lips were set in a stubborn line, as Dave knew they would be, but on this occasion he was taking control. He couldn't let Ricky blow it, because in this instance his heart would definitely rule his head.

"The only reason we have this week over here is because the chief was so delighted that we finally got Johnson. He could have easily arranged for the British police to pay Alice a visit, but instead he has sent us, and given us a car, and all I have to do is collect a statement from Alice. She won't even have to leave the country, she can testify by video link. . ."

Ricky butted in impatiently.

". . .I know all that, but I promised that the family she works for wouldn't find out she had been arrested. If we went together, I could question Sadie, and her parents wouldn't know we had really come to interview Alice."

He tried to make himself believe this was a good idea, but he knew it wasn't. He was clutching at straws.

"Ricky, you can't go anywhere near your ex-wife. If she turns out to be guilty of anything, your presence will compromise the situation, as you well know!"

Ricky was silent, knowing this was true.

"This is my plan. I am going over there in the car with you, and the car must be parked at least a street away. I will be dressed real casual, and if Sadie or her parents open the door, I will pretend I met Alice on holiday. I will do my utmost to question her and Sadie. Buddy you must be patient!"

Ricky sighed, he knew Dave was right, if he made the wrong move he could lose his job. He had his girls to support and his mortgage to pay. Although finding out the truth about his son was important to him, taking care of his three princesses would always be paramount, and nothing must ever jeopardise that.

"Thanks buddy!" he said, touching Dave's arm lightly.

"That's OK. Now let's get our heads down."

"Yea, I'm pretty tired after that flight."

It didn't take either of them long to fall asleep; even Ricky with so much on his mind had to surrender to the weariness that enveloped his body. He would have to wait and see what tomorrow would bring. Dave was so glad he had come with him. He knew that normally Ricky was one of the best FBI agents, who always did his job conscientiously, but right now his head

73

d

was all over the place, and was it any wonder after all he had been through in the past few years? Dave wasn't his best friend for nothing, he was going to keep him in check right now, and eventually he could help him to get to the bottom of what exactly had happened to his son, but it would be done properly.

Sadie was enjoying her time with Danielle; just the two of them this week. Even with her daughter beside her, she still got admiring glances at the open air swimming pool. There were lots of fit men here this week, sporting their tanned bodies in tight swimming trunks which left nothing to the imagination. At one time Sadie would have just made herself available, but even though she had not had sex for a long time, none of them could replace Danielle. She realised that a fling for self-gratification was not lasting, but if she could earn her daughter's respect, the bond between them would be.

These men with their plastic smiles irritated her. She was quite happy to sit on the balcony with a glass of wine after Danielle had gone to sleep, and she couldn't stop the feeling of regret sweeping through her; if only Danny had been there to share his daughter with her.

She had frequently questioned herself as to why she had fallen so deeply for Danny. He didn't have much of a personality, could have even benefited from elocution lessons, he must have left school too early, but he had roused feelings inside her she didn't know she had, and it was those feelings that had created Danielle. No wonder she was so special.

But she told herself she was over those feelings now. Danny was not around to share that love with her any more. At this time in her life she found men and women a nuisance. She had no desire to go and find a partner, which surprised even her. Danielle was the focus in her life.

The only man to make any impression on her was Nathan, and he got right under her skin. She hated him with an intensity. He was just using her parents for his own advantage and no one outside the family was allowed to do that.

She really didn't want to waste time thinking about him, he was bossy and outspoken, so unlike the druggy that she remembered from the past. Sadie had to admit he had the power

74

to make her obey him, and deep inside her was a grudging respect of his strong character; not that she wanted to get involved with him, it was much safer to go on hating him.

The only blight during her holiday was when Danielle mentioned Alice. She was missing her. The six weeks away from her had finally caught up. Sadie didn't mind her saying she had missed Grandma and Grandad, but when Alice's name was mentioned she felt an intense pang of jealousy sweep through her, realising that even being with her own mother wasn't enough for Danielle. She felt such hatred of Alice, but she had to hide it, so she just murmured:

"Don't worry, you will see Alice when you get home."

This seemed to satisfy Danielle, and Sadie comforted herself in the knowledge that Alice would not be there and she would then have the opportunity to slowly plant the idea in her daughter's head that Alice had deserted her. Any feelings of conscience she might have suffered over that were quickly dispelled when Danielle asked to Skype her from the laptop just before she went to bed.

"There's no Internet connection here," Sadie said quickly, then realised, even at five, Danielle would remember Sadie using it the day they arrived. So she added. "Well, today there isn't."

"Oh," said Danielle, visibly disappointed.

"If you get some sleep now, we can go in the pool tomorrow. We only have one day left. We can tell Grandma and Grandad you swam two strokes today."

"Oh brill!" Danielle's lively mind was now diverted and she settled down to sleep. Sadie breathed a sigh of relief, the sooner that bitch Alice was out of their lives the better.

She waited a couple of hours to make sure Danielle was asleep, then she texted her father's mobile to ask if Alice had gone yet. When the reply came back that she had gone, Sadie felt really jubilant. Tomorrow if Danielle asked to Skype, she would get her grandparents and she would be told Alice wasn't there. She had told Daddy to only say Alice was out, because there would be time enough for her to realise that Alice was gone and would not be coming back. Although that gave Sadie a feeling of satisfaction, the thought that Danielle might grieve for the loss of Alice did not sit well with her. Her feelings ran amok: jealousy of the love Danielle had for Alice, and regret for the pain her daughter would suffer for her loss. These conflicting emotions continued to torment her. She didn't know herself any more, she was no longer self centred, her feelings were all centred on Danielle.

Doubts and insecurities flooded into her mind; worries that she couldn't live up to the image that Alice represented to Danielle. Would her daughter ever love her as much? That feeling of rejection came back to haunt her, and the need to prove herself. All her life she had used her sexuality; but now she had to make her daughter proud of her. She loved her so much, and she needed Danielle to love her back to make her feel worthy. Oh curse Alice, how she hated her!

The next day was the last one of their holiday, and as promised, she took Danielle to the open air pool. Sadie went down the steps and into the shallow end with Danielle, who now felt confident enough to move around without her armbands. She moved a little way away from her, encouraging Danielle to swim to her; and to her delight, the little girl let go of the side, and doing her own dog paddle type stroke, showed how fearless she was and swam to her.

Sadie felt so proud. She looked too little to swim, but she was gutsy. She liked the courage that Danielle showed, and she wasn't the only one to notice it.

"Well done, she's a natural!" enthused Sam. He had spent the whole week trying to chat to Sadie, every time his wife Susan wasn't looking. Initially she had been annoyed; who the hell did he think he was? But as the days progressed, she started to enjoy his attention, and it pleased her to think that he obviously found her more attractive than his wife. She hadn't planned to do anything about it, even though it was a long time since she had an active sex life.

Maybe that was the trouble, and it was certainly the excuse she gave herself when it happened. Susan took Danielle with her daughter Lyn to get an ice cream; they had perhaps ten minutes alone. There was a female toilet nearby, and Sadie knew by the look in his eyes exactly what was going to happen when she went in there. It was empty, she locked the door and took her bikini off, so when he tapped on the door she was naked and ready for him.

There was not much room in the cubicle, but that did not stop them. Sadie felt desperate for sex, it had been so long, and the

76

sight of him day after day in very tight swimming trunks had kept her in a constant state of excitement; and he had known that, he had read her signals.

She sat on the closed toilet seat whilst he fondled her, and when she stripped of his trunks she couldn't wait to get her hands on him. It was so erotic, and totally wrong, which made it all the more enjoyable, and when he entered her they both gasped with pleasure.

Sadie wanted to shout. She felt liberated again and she was having so much fun, but then she heard someone come in the cubicle next door. Sam was pressed up close to her, and he released his lips from her nipple, but carried on thrusting deeply into her, saying, "Enjoy it quietly, sexy Sadie, we have company."

That excited her even more; oh how good it felt to be shagged again. But suddenly he withdrew. She was jerked back to reality, but Sam hadn't finished with her. He stroked her buttocks as he encouraged her to kneel on the toilet seat, and she opened her legs wide so he could enter her from behind. When she felt him thrust again she was transported into a world of pleasure, his free hand was stroking the very centre of her sexuality, and she whispered urgently, begging him to make her come.

Now they were both working up to a crescendo, his thrusts became faster and deeper and Sadie could no longer keep quiet. Her cries of pleasure matched his; nothing could stop them now, and their mutual orgasm was perfectly timed and left them both gasping, and then giggling when the person in the next cubicle banged on the door and told them they were disgusting and she was going to report them.

By now Sadie could not stop laughing, especially when Sam made a quick exit out of a rather small window. He was a bit worried now that he would be found out. Sadie was perfectly calm. She put her bikini back on, and by the time the offended woman had returned with the person she had complained to, Sadie had finished washing her hands and someone else was occupying the cubicle she had been in. She smiled to herself when she heard them rap loudly on the door, and left to the sound of angry voices.

When she walked round the corner to the pool, Susan appeared within about five minutes, both Danielle and Lyn were eating an ice cream cornet, and shortly Sam appeared from the men's

77

toilets. After the two girls had finished their ice creams, Sadie explained that they were leaving the next day, so they would have to go and get packed, and then Danielle would need to get some sleep because they had an early start.

"It's been great meeting you," said Susan enthusiastically.

"It has!" said Sam, and when Susan wasn't looking he gave her a broad wink.

"Yes, we've both had a lovely time," said Sadie with feeling, keeping a straight face.

Later in their hotel room, when Danielle was fast asleep, she relived the experience in her mind. She didn't think she had done anything wrong, they were both consenting adults with no strings attached, and Susan would never know. It was a relief to be able to have sex again without any emotional feelings to get in the way. She was well and truly over Danny now; a liberated woman who could lead an independent life with her daughter. What she had done would not affect Danielle in any way, or hurt her, so there was no reason to feel any guilt about it. She would never see Sam again, nor did she want to; let him stay with boring mousey Susan, who Sadie was sure could never give him the sort of thrills that Sadie had.

Chapter Ten

"Alice, you have done a fine job with Danielle, we could not have asked for a more devoted nanny, but she's now at school, and between us we can cope with her."

Isabel avoided mentioning Sadie's name as it would not help this very tense situation. Sadie and Danielle had been on holiday for three days now, and every day Alice wanted to Skype her. She would not let go. They had talked her out of it; she'd done it when she was in California and it was getting too much, now was the time to break the news to her.

"Danielle has been very fortunate to have had someone like you in her life and we want to recognise that, so we are prepared to make sure you are comfortable in life after you leave here. We will fund a new home for you. There are some new flats going up in Chelsea, I think you might like one."

Philip was hoping this might soften the blow, but all he saw on Alice's face was misery, and he felt a wave of pity for her. She had given up five years of her life and now she had quite an adjustment to make.

"And of course, any time you are passing, just pop in and see us."

Even as he said it, he knew it would never happen. They had a secure entry system; those iron gates only opened to people they wanted them to, so if she ever did come back it would be easy to say Danielle was not there. He did feel guilty, but family always came first.

Isabel added another softener.

"We will, of course, give you the very highest reference that we can, you will have no trouble in getting employment elsewhere."

They glanced at each other, her silence was a little unnerving. They wondered what exactly was going through her mind and if she would, in fact, speak to them, or had this news been too devastating?

It was almost a relief for Alice to hear those words; she had been expecting it ever since she had found out that Sadie was returning home. She had been so jealous when Sadie and Danielle went on holiday together, and then she wasn't allowed to Skype Danielle, so it didn't take a genius to work out what was going to happen next.

There were so many things she could say, angry and bitter remarks about being used for all these years. It was love of Danielle that had kept her here. She had respected Danielle's grandparents, but had no affection for them. Between them they had created a monster in Sadie, and Alice didn't think she was fit to care for her own daughter. If only they had kept her in prison like they should have done, then nothing would have changed.

Alice had always excused her own behaviour in all this and blamed it on Sadie. Sarah, her twin, had committed suicide because of Sadie's lies, and the sight of Danny and Sadie together had inflamed her jealousy, even though it had been her own idea, so she had no choice but to kill Danny, and then put the blame on Sadie. Sadie had been the bane of her life, who made her do bad things, but when she had become Danielle's nanny she had put all that behind her. Initially she wanted to spite Sadie, but Danielle inspired love, she was such a sunny-tempered child, and Alice believed that looking after her had made her a better person. Now a cruel twist of fate had allowed Sadie to come back into their lives, so all her plans of revenge had fizzled out to nothing, and she was left with a heart that was not only broken at the sudden parting from Danielle, but also full of bitterness and hate. However, for now her pride took over, she wasn't giving them the satisfaction of knowing just how hurt and angry she was!

"I did realise all this. Danielle is now at school, and her mother is home, too," she couldn't bear to utter that name. That evil uncaring bitch might be Danielle's mother, but there was absolutely nothing of her vile nature in her daughter. She didn't

80

have Danny's weakness of character either, she was like Isabel, even at five, strong and feisty, but also warm and loving. A wave of pain shot through her at being parted from the only good thing in her life.

Isabel and Philip had been expecting tears and recriminations, but there were none. Could she let go of Danielle that easily? Her reasonable attitude was obviously a huge relief to them both, but somehow it didn't fit in with the sort of person she was. How could she be obsessive one minute and then unconcerned the next? It just didn't make sense. They both sat there, saying very little, waiting for something more to be said.

Alice did not disappoint. She knew she would have to give the performance of her life, her reward would come later. So many thoughts tumbled through her mind, but she still managed to keep her voice calm and matter of fact.

"The offer of the flat in Chelsea is very generous of you, but I actually plan to go and live abroad. I can easily get work in Spain as a nanny. I have seen an agency that frequently advertises for English speaking nannies."

This was exactly the words that Isabel and Philip wanted to hear. Alice living abroad would be perfect, right out of Sadie's way and away from Danielle too. In those sort of circumstances Philip was prepared to be very generous.

"Well Alice, I have a better idea. If I settle a regular income on you until such time as you find employment, and then when you find yourself a home out there, if you contact my solicitor, it can all be done through him."

If Isabel thought he was being a bit over the top she didn't show it. To get Alice out of their lives without any animosity was well worth it. All they really wanted in their lives was peace and so far it had always evaded them.

Alice smiled grimly to herself, she had no qualms about taking his money, but if they thought she was just going to accept what they had done to her, and walk away from this house and move on, then they were deluding themselves. She had other plans, and very soon she would put them into action and the Morton Brown family would wish they had never treated her so badly. "Thank you so much, that sounds perfect," she murmured, allowing herself to smile. Saying she was going to Spain was just leading them up a blind alley. She could collect the allowance Philip was so generously providing her with for a while until it stopped, which it would when they found out what she had done. Her bank would never divulge her address to them no matter where she went, she would make sure of that, and once the money stopped she would close that account and set up another elsewhere. What she would do would be life changing for her, so she must get it right.

"You can leave tomorrow if that suits you," said Isabel. This was going far better than she had hoped. "We are out for the day playing golf."

"Absolutely fine," murmured Alice, but inside she was seething, they couldn't wait to be rid of her before their precious daughter came home. They would certainly pay for that!

Later that evening, after she had packed all her belongings, she sat in her room drinking a glass of wine. The realisation that she had no one in the world who cared about her, hurt. After having to cut her parents out of her life she had relied solely on the love that Danielle gave back to her, and without that she realised she had nothing, no boyfriend or lover even. Nathan had been her focus, but he had shown no interest whatsoever.

She tossed and turned in her bed that night. Her plan was an audacious one, and she realised the enormity of her actions. It was all she could think about. This was her last night at this house, and as much as she needed to sleep, it didn't happen. Eventually she dozed off when the dawn was breaking, and woke up suddenly when she heard their car pull out of the drive. It must be about 9 o'clock, and they had gone to golf.

She was relieved to breakfast alone. She hadn't wanted to say any goodbyes, she was too choked with emotion for that. Ann hovered nearby, ready to get her whatever she wanted, but she felt nauseous so she settled for orange juice and toast. Her cases were in the hall and Philip had very generously paid for a tank full of petrol to help her on her way.

She was finishing off her breakfast when she heard the entry phone go, and Ann went to answer it.

Ann hovered by the dining room door.

"There's a man with an American accent asking to speak to you, he said he met you in California."

It all came flooding back to Alice, how could she possibly have forgotten? The FBI agent was coming over to question Sadie about the sudden disappearance of her son. Selling a baby was illegal, Sadie's past would finally catch up with her. Hope flooded through her. If Sadie were arrested, Isabel and Philip would need her again, maybe she wouldn't have to go too far.

"OK Ann, can you show him into the library, I will speak to him in there."

The library was only a small room; the size of a study, it had shelves of books all around, and it overlooked the back of the house where Danielle's swing set was. During her free moments Alice had often watched her playing, out of the window. It was quiet and private, which was the reason Alice wanted to speak to the FBI man in there.

When she entered the library, she felt a wave of disappointment that it wasn't him, it was the man who had been sitting in on their interview, who had done all the writing. Obviously he had sent his friend to do the interviewing, and he had asked for her.

"Good morning, ma'am, Dave Kent, we met in California, and I have come to take a statement from you now that the suspect has been captured."

"You captured him, that's good. I can't tell you much other than I shared a couple of drinks and a few laughs with him."

"Yes, that is what you need to tell me about, as he drugged you that night."

Dave met her eyes and she flinched a little; his stare was intense. She didn't think Ann was listening, and she certainly didn't want any gossip about her passed onto the family, even after she had gone from here. She decided the best means of defence was attack.

"When the other man interviewed me he said he was coming over to ask Sadie about when she sold her son, where is he?"

"Don't worry, we have it all in hand. He will question Sadie, but we have been sent to get a statement from you right now, and you need to tell me where Sadie is."

"Sadie and her daughter Danielle are on holiday in Portugal for another four days, and her parents are spending the day on the golf course."

Dave wasn't an FBI man for nothing.

"And those suitcases in the hall belong to who?"

"They are mine, I am leaving today. Now that Sadie is home, and Danielle is at school, I am not needed any more.

83

Dave saw her lip tremble and knew she was not happy about that situation. An idea came to him.

"Well, if you are leaving today, how about you come with my friend and I to a nice quiet English pub, and we do the interview there?"

Alice considered his words. It was hard to let go, and deep inside she hoped that Sadie would be arrested, so instead of vanishing into the mist, she would stay at a local bed and breakfast. Philip and Isabel had her mobile number so they still had contact with her. If she did meet up with the other agent, that would give her a chance to drive the knife in even deeper and make them realise just how cruel Sadie had been, and make absolutely sure that they would arrest her.

"Yes OK," she said very casually, but her heart was beating at such an alarming rate it felt like her chest would burst. Now was her chance to expose Sadie's evil character.

Later, in the pub, Ricky dropped the bombshell; he was Sadie's ex-husband. It wouldn't take them long to tape her statement against Johnson, but then with her help he needed to know more about what Sadie had told her.

When Alice realised just who Ricky was, she couldn't get over the fact that she had actually met Sadie's ex-husband, and she racked her brains to give him more information.

"Jill Hopkins, that was definitely her name, her husband worked for CNN advertising. Oh yes, Sadie referred to him as simple Simon, that was his name, Simon, he didn't have a clue she was taking advantage of their desperate need for a baby to charge them a sum of money that could bankrupt them. She was so proud about how much money she had got out of them!"

Her words made Ricky feel sick inside. He realised that he could never have known the real Sadie, she was so callous, but then hadn't she proved that when after inspiring such love from the girls, she had left them with broken hearts, and then tried to bleed him dry!

Dave was right, he was too emotionally involved, but they had both agreed that Alice must know who he was to get the information out of her. It was obvious from the way she spoke about Sadie that she had a grudge against her, and so that was a huge advantage, because she would tell them anything they wanted to know.

"Well, that's a help. If Simon Hopkins still works for CNN, we can trace him maybe? Many thanks."

"Can you not arrest Sadie first?"

Alice looked disappointed, she really did hate Sadie, that was obvious. Dave explained.

"Although we believe you, it's just your word against Sadie's, and of course she will deny it, she will say they adopted her son because she couldn't care for him."

Ricky cut in excitedly.

"But if we can trace the Hopkins, and get them to admit they bought the baby, then we have the proof to arrest and charge her."

"Well yes, that is my job," Dave reminded him. "And it will happen, this is why all the information you have given us will be very useful."

It hadn't quite gone the way that Alice had hoped. They wouldn't be hanging about to arrest Sadie, and knowing that evil cow she might well get away with it. When she left the two FBI men, after promising not to share anything they had spoken about with anyone, she felt let down; once again Sadie had evaded trouble. They might never trace that family or the little boy. There was no point in her trying to convince Philip and Isabel their daughter was evil, they didn't want to believe that, and if she betrayed their confidence, these men could tell them about her arrest in California and she still would not be reunited with Danielle, and that was all she wanted.

Alice left the pub in a taxi. The two men had thanked her for her help, they no longer needed to question her, so now she turned her thoughts as to where she could live until she put her plan into action. If they had arrested Sadie she wouldn't have needed to take action, but now she felt desperate. She needed to be fairly near to the Morton Brown family to keep an eye on things, and when the time was right she would carry out her plan. They had left her no choice.

Ricky and Dave returned to their hotel discussing what had happened with Alice.

"Can we trust her, she's very bitter?" said Ricky anxiously, not wanting anything to affect the new information they had.

"Yes buddy, we can, she's got an axe to grind and she won't

want Sadie or her family to be pre-warned about us, nor will she want them to know you arrested her in California."

Ricky liked Dave's common sense, it was just what he needed right now. The whole situation was so traumatic for him, and he was now happy to step aside and let his best friend pursue this inquiry.

"Don't worry, I'll get her buddy, if it's the last thing I do!"

Dave's words were comforting, and Ricky had no doubt they came straight from his heart. They were almost brothers; such a close friendship, and that support made him feel that all hope was not lost. Sadie had not won, he was still fighting back.

Chapter Eleven

When Sadie and Danielle arrived home from Portugal, it was to find that Alice had moved out. In the beginning Danielle was upset and Isabel tried to explain that Alice had gone to a new family who had a young baby that needed her and, now that Danielle was at school and growing up fast, she didn't need her.

Sadie said very little about it. Inside she was gloating, but she knew she had to keep it from Danielle. It was that other side to her that she had no wish to control except when her daughter was around.

Life seemed to be very busy right now. With the half term over, Danielle returned to school for the other half of the summer term, and plans were already in place to give her a very lavish fifth birthday party, with everyone from her class invited.

Sadie planned to talk to her father, once the party was over, about living in Canterbury. She had already mentioned it to him in passing; she was hoping for a town house that he would fund. Now she had Danielle to care for, it was the perfect excuse not to work. Canterbury had a thriving community, with a lot of clubs and night life, and Sadie wanted to be a part of this.

She had realised just how limited her life would be now she was a mother, and that fling with Sam had made her realise she could not give up everything for her daughter, no matter how much she loved her. Canterbury was very close to Herne Bay, Danielle's school was there, and her doting grandparents would be more than willing to look after her when Sadie went out, she was sure, and they would enjoy having her to stay overnight too.

Sadie felt she had done a good job of being polite to her mother, but living with her indefinitely was asking a bit too much. She was sure Daddy would understand, he still had a soft spot for her. But she hadn't reckoned on Daddy discussing it with Nathan, nor the arrogant way Nathan spoke to her about it. He was really hard to take, and she didn't have to pretend to like him, her hatred for him was so strong she really wished she had done the job properly when she'd shaken that petrol can!

When Philip had spoken to him about Sadie's request, and asked his opinion, Nathan was horrified. He was sure Isabel wouldn't be too happy when she knew either. Danielle was growing up in a lovely house with fresh sea breezes around her, places to walk and a playground nearby. She had just lost her nanny and was learning to cope, but she needed to still be with her grandparents right now. Sadie needed to realise her timing was all wrong, she was being selfish.

The other reason, which he couldn't tell Philip, was that if she moved, he wouldn't see Sadie. Since Alice had left he had been coming to visit most weekends. He had told himself it was to help Danielle with the loss of Alice, but deep down he knew that when he drove down on a Friday evening the thought of seeing Sadie thrilled all his senses. Even though he could see how selfish, rude and uncaring she was towards him, it made not the slightest difference. He knew there was a softer side, she showed it towards her daughter, so where had all this bitterness and hate come from? He needed to find out because this enigmatic woman fascinated him in a way that no other girlfriend had even come close to. Even knowing she had wanted him dead only fuelled his desire to get inside her mind and discover what she was all about. Sadie was a challenge, and he wanted to rise to that challenge.

He had read Danielle her bedtime story whilst Sadie took a shower and got herself ready to go out. It had been the suggestion of Isabel and Philip that Sadie went out more. She was only twenty-nine, and they were perfectly happy to babysit, especially as they were having a bridge night and had friends coming over.

Sadie had told her parents she was going to a play at the Marlowe Theatre. She hated having to explain herself just like a teenager, but when she got her town house and her freedom that would all stop. In truth she was going to a night club with the intention of finding a man for the evening. The whole night would have been better, but until she led her own life that was impossible. There was no way she was going to creep guiltily into the house the next morning and face a cross examination.

When Nathan saw her in the vivid red minidress and killer heels, as she carefully negotiated the stairs, his heart flipped. Her jet black hair was flowing around her shoulders, her vivid red lips were shiny and tempting, oh how he longed to kiss them, and those dark mysterious eyes of hers were accentuated with deep green eyeshadow, she reminded him of a cat, with her graceful moves and air of mystique.

"Nathan, have you seen my handbag, Danielle was playing with it earlier?"

"Which one?" he enquired. Sadie had so many.

"The black patent one, it matches my shoes."

Nathan remembered he was angry with her. Never mind how gorgeous she looked, he was going to have words with her.

"I can't say I have, but it may be in the lounge. By the way Sadie, I need to say something to you."

Sadie didn't like his tone, he sounded bossy again.

"Well you had better make it quick, I am just about to call a taxi."

"Not here. I will give you a lift, and I can say it in the car."

Sadie bridled against his words. Who the hell did he think he was?

"Oh will you? Try asking me first."

She didn't really care if he gave her a lift to the Marlowe. As soon as he had gone she could make her way to the night club; it was very close, and it would save her the cab fare. But she didn't like his high handed attitude.

Nathan came to a quick decision. Maybe a tactful approach might work; instead of being angry he would discuss her options with her. He could sense Sadie's hostile attitude towards him, and he wanted to appeal to her better nature, he was sure she had one. He turned on the charm.

"Sadie, will you allow me to run you to Canterbury? It will give me the opportunity to have a private chat with you."

Sadie had found her bag by now and was ready to go out. She picked up only a light cardigan on such a warm evening, it was all she needed.

"Come on then."

When they were in the car, Nathan chose his words carefully.

"Philip says you want to move to Canterbury. He hasn't told your mother yet, only me, and I am worried about Danielle, how will she cope with parting from them so soon after losing Alice?"

Sadie stared into space, digesting his words. She was annoyed that he expected her to explain herself to him. It was her life, not his.

"Danielle is doing fine. It's mostly her birthday she talks about now, she accepts Alice has gone."

He glanced at her profile; she was avoiding his gaze, staring straight ahead, and he could see by the rigid way she sat with her arms folded, she would not change her mind.

"Sadie, I will miss her too. I have known her since she was a tiny baby."

As soon as he said it, he wished he hadn't. She didn't need any reminder of how much of Danielle's babyhood she had missed. What a bloody idiot he was!

"Well my heart bleeds for you!" her sarcasm hit him full in the face. "You've seen a damn sight more of her than I have." And now she wanted to shock him, to make him hate her as much as she hated him, so her words came tumbling out and she didn't care what she said.

"Nathan, I am twenty-nine, and I can't live with my parents any more. I want my own life with Danielle, in my own home. I don't want to say where I am going when I go out. Tonight I am not going to the Marlowe, I am going out to find a man or a woman because I need sex, and plenty of it, I need to have fun! And before you say anything else, they won't lose Danielle, she will stay with them when I go out, she is still my priority, but I am like any other woman, I have needs."

Nathan couldn't help being impressed by her honesty, but he felt jealous at the thought of her finding someone for sex. As well as jealousy, he felt desire rise inside him; what a night he could give her if she would only let him.

He had driven the car along the Hoath Road and into a country lane, so he now pulled over to the side of the road, and turned to her.

"What do you mean, man or woman?"

Sadie laughed; she had shocked him.

"Didn't you know, Nathan, I swing both ways? I can enjoy myself with men or women."

Nathan gulped. This sexy little woman was turning him on. He felt a hot flush go through his body and he couldn't stop himself from saying:

"If you spent one night with me, I promise you Sadie, there is nothing any woman can do any better than I can."

The passion in his voice was obvious; she was enjoying teasing him.

"Oh yes, I remember the last time we got together, you couldn't even keep it up."

She was mocking him. Of course, when he was on the drugs he had failed her, but he was clean and virile now, and oh, how he wanted her!

She turned provocatively towards him; her perfume was sweet and musky, and suddenly Nathan's self-control snapped. He pulled her into his arms. Her lips were close and he was drowning in her senses, it was as though his body was being taken over by an alien. At first she tried to resist his lips, but then her passion matched his, and he could feel a fire raging inside him, the desire for her was so strong that all caution was gone.

He was determined to be a good lover to make up for the past, so much of which was now a blur, but he was going to make this night memorable for them both. Sadie was the most alluring woman he had ever met, her beautiful breasts peeped out the top of her red dress, and he knew he was like a drowning man. She was using all her wiles to lure him on, and he was loving every second of it.

It wasn't long before they transferred to the back seat of the car. There was always a risk that a car driver might catch sight of their naked bodies in his headlights, but for Sadie that was all part of the fun of it. There was nothing more satisfying than having sex with someone you hated; the excitement and passion was so erotic. After the taster she had enjoyed with Sam on holiday, she now knew exactly what she wanted, and how convenient that Nathan was here to provide it. My God, she hadn't realised just how good he was; they might be in the back of a car and a bit cramped, but he had fulfilled his promise and given her something special to remember.

They were both panting when they hit the heights together, their frenzied bout of passion had shaken them both. For Nathan it was the proof that he loved this woman completely and utterly, no matter how many faults she had, she was the love of his life, and he never wanted to be without her.

For Sadie, she had expected a quick fumble on the back seat, because in the past she had never found Nathan that good at sex. But tonight he had alternated between passion and tenderness, and spent ages tenderly stroking her, making her feel good, most men didn't do that, they were all for their own pleasure.

Nathan wanted to hold her and stroke her hair afterwards to prolong that feeling of closeness between them. He knew he must not declare his love for her yet, he didn't want to scare her away, he mustn't be over the top, so he said lightly.

"So how was that then, did I redeem myself?"

Sadie could feel that warmth stealing over her again; that deadly warmth that each time she had succumbed to it, had caused her devastation in her life. Firstly at the age of thirteen, then with Danny, and now it was happening again, she had only wanted sex with him, she had wanted to seduce goody-goody reformed Nathan, and in some tangled and twisted way, his lovemaking had stirred something inside her she just did not understand.

"Not bad," she smiled. He had been bloody marvellous, and when his arm came round her, she just couldn't help herself, she snuggled against the warmth of his body.

"We'd better get dressed, you'll get cold."

They climbed over to the front. Sadie's red dress was crumpled but she didn't care, she wasn't going anywhere, she just wanted to sit here quietly with him. She was still in shock at the way he had made her feel. Nathan gently ran his fingers through her long tresses, her body felt relaxed.

"Sadie, something in your life has made you very angry, tell me what it is, maybe I can help."

She should have given him an angry retort and told him to mind his own business, but his fingers stroking her hair were soothing, and the closeness he had created inside her made her feel as if for once in her life she should bare her soul, and share her pain with him. Until now Sadie didn't know what honesty was, but for some reason she did not understand, Nathan inspired it from her.

"Where shall I start? My mother and I don't get on, I spent four years locked up for a crime I didn't do whilst Danny's killer went free, losing over four years of Danielle's life, and then there was Danny; I found love with him and he was murdered. Is that enough for you?"

Her tone had become harsh again, but he didn't care, there was more to it than added up, people who came from loving families just didn't carry that much hate around inside them.

"You say you don't get on with your mother, why? You both have similar natures, and your mother is a good strong woman with character. When I look at her, I see you in twenty years, and it's something to be proud of. I can't believe you are jealous of her?"

Sadie drew away from him, and he knew he had hit a nerve, he wanted to get right into her mind, to understand how she viewed life, he wanted so much to understand her.

"I don't know why I am telling you this Nathan, maybe because it's crucifying me, and I can never tell my father, I can never hurt him like that!"

There was a pause, and a break in her voice, and he knew it was hard for her to say it, so he gently stroked her fingers and this seemed to soothe her a little.

"Daddy is not my real father. I was born out of incest, my mother's brother was my father, and I can't forgive her for letting her own brother do that, and for deceiving Daddy."

Nathan had to use every bit of self control to stop his mouth from gaping open. This was the last thing he expected to hear, surely this wasn't one of Sadie's imaginings, but how could it be true? He couldn't believe it of honest upright Isabel, never in a million years!"

Sadie went on. "I have never told anyone, not even my closest friend Sunita, no one would believe me, but it is true and it still dominates my life."

"I see." Nathan was temporarily lost for words, and now Sadie continued, and it was plain to see, the way it all came tumbling out, what a relief it was for her to share it with someone.

"The story does not finish there. When I was thirteen, during the school holidays with Sunita, we met this boy about a year or so older than me, he was my first love if you like, although I can't really recognise love, and when I do, it does my head in! Anyway, I got pregnant and I didn't know what to do, then Mummy discovered me with a pregnancy testing kit in my bedroom. She went mad, so I told her he had raped me. I panicked, you see, and then she made me have an abortion."

Nathan had recovered his composure by now. This story was certainly not what he had been expecting, but he realised that sometimes truth is stranger than fiction.

"Were you given any options about keeping the baby? I know you were very young."

"This is the most amazing part of the story. My mother told me I must have an abortion because when she saw a photo of Matt, he was my long lost half brother, my real father had a girlfriend at uni, and she was his mother. That was when she told me who my real father was."

"Well it doesn't matter where the sperm came from, Philip will always be your father, he brought you up," said Nathan fervently, thinking about how Philip and Isabel were like the parents he never had. "Sadie, I think we need to find out more about this to put your mind at rest. Your mother would never do that, I know it, there is a big part of this missing, and when we can piece it together, I think your own self-esteem and your relationship with her will improve."

"Well, how can we? Daddy must never know, and if my mother knew I had told you, she wouldn't be happy."

Nothing was going to thwart Nathan now, he was getting somewhere near the truth, he knew it.

"I am going to speak to Isabel, with or without you. You only have half of a story and I think that is because of the shame this has created. Incest doesn't sit well with any of us, but I have faith in your mother, and I am sure she will explain herself. "

Sadie had an overwhelming desire to tell him why she had killed her brother; because she had always felt her mother had killed her baby by forcing her to abort it. Maybe thirteen had been too young to be a mother, but she hadn't even been given the choice. She felt like she needed to cleanse her soul, and she wanted for the first time in her life to have honesty, but something inside told her to hold back as yet, it was too soon.

"Am I the only person you have shared all this with?"

"Well I did have some counselling in which I mentioned about being pregnant at thirteen, but said I was raped."

"I see, and you had feelings for this boy, and you are now saying it wasn't rape."

"Yes I am. And do you know, when Mummy told me he was my half brother it explained why I had such an affinity with him; we looked alike and we were both like our father, who apparently had no scruples about getting his own sister pregnant."

"Sadie, this is why I am speaking to your mother. I know her, she's a good woman, and she deserves your support, too. You were too ready to judge and condemn her."

Sadie knew he was right. She also knew she couldn't stop him, his mind was made up. She did only have half of the story, so they would speak to her mother together because now she wanted to know the whole truth.

Later, in her bed, she thought about it all. What a messed up life she had, but already Nathan was helping her to confront all her demons. He was now a big part of her life whether she liked it or not, and she had to admit, to herself only, that she did like it.

Chapter Twelve

The next day was Saturday, and when Sadie woke up, she had to question herself as to whether she had taken leave of her senses. Last night she had enjoyed an amazing and passionate encounter with Nathan; she had thought she hated him, but now she was confused. Why on earth had she poured out everything to him, especially the truth about who her father was? It was obvious that Nathan would go straight to her mother. He had always been impulsive and stubborn, and no matter what she said to him, she knew he would still go his own way and she could not stop him.

The new Nathan, as she now thought of him, was totally unlike any boyfriend she had ever had. He was strong and determined, and if they did have a fling together, she knew without a shadow of doubt, he would wear the trousers. Sadie had been used to her men doing what she wanted, but with Nathan she wouldn't get away with it. But maybe he had earned her respect for all that.

Confronting her mother was going to dredge up a lot of unresolved pain for Sadie, and also keeping it from Daddy. He would be the only person who didn't know. Would that even be fair? So many questions without answers. For once in her life she didn't want to cause her mother anguish, but with the support of Nathan, she was going to face up to the truth and find out just what happened when she was conceived.

"Mummy, I can't find my ballet shoes."

"Danielle, you can never find anything, try a bit harder," she scolded lightly, then with a sigh she went to the closet where they would probably be under something. As far as Danielle was concerned, if she couldn't see it, then it wasn't there, and her mind was so easily distracted onto something else.

Sadie quickly got all of Danielle's kit together. It was almost time to leave, and her daughter had absolutely no sense of time or being late, and had now settled in front of the TV in her bedroom to watch Sponge Bob.

There was a tap at the door, and Sadie's heart did a double somersault. Would that be Nathan? She hadn't seen him yet this morning and was wondering when she would.

It was Philip offering to drop Danielle at ballet on his way to get the car serviced.

"Thanks Daddy," Sadie gave him a light kiss on the cheek, and he noticed how bright her eyes were. She looked happy, and she smiled. Sadie's smiles were rare, and therefore to him, quite precious.

"Come on Munchkin," he said as Sadie rounded up Danielle. "Nathan said he went to the Marlowe with you and he very much enjoyed the play."

Sadie couldn't help giggling, this was all so much fun. She remembered what they had agreed to say to stop her parents from prying. Now Nathan was beginning to realise why Sadie needed her own home.

"The play was great, I enjoyed it too," she murmured. Philip was pleased to see how she spoke without bitterness or anger. He couldn't think of anyone better than Nathan to take her out for the evening. He hadn't heard them come home, but it was nice to know that Nathan had brought her home safely.

After they had gone, the next knock on the door was Nathan. His grey eyes took in her flushed cheeks, but she wasn't smiling, her eyes looked deep and mysterious, so he was not sure what sort of welcome he would get. The closeness he had felt last night was not there, her body language was taut and cold, and he felt disappointment flood through him. Would he ever understand this woman?

He came straight to the point.

"Sadie, your father and Danielle are out and Ann has a day off, so now we must speak to your mother."

This was one of the few times in her life that Sadie was experiencing fear. Her mood was veering between extreme happiness after the closeness she had shared with Nathan, and

97

terror about what her mother would tell her about her father. She had always felt she was a bad person; and would her mother make her feel worthless? Could she even bear to listen?

"What will you say if she tells you it's none of your business?" her tone was harsh, and the old embittered Sadie had returned. He realised that getting through to her and giving her support was not going to be that easy, she had been so damaged by life. One day he would tell her that he would lay down his life for her, but not yet, he had to play it slowly, which for Nathan was so unusual, because he had always been a man of impulse.

He had thought about her a lot last night. She had dominated his mind, the way she had made him feel, and he was certain she had felt something too; that closeness afterwards, her confession, this had been more than just a frolic in the car. She was a complex woman to understand, but he was prepared to spend the rest of his life being bewitched and bemused by her. Life would never be dull with Sadie, that was for sure.

"Well I have broad shoulders, you know, it is my business because it affects you, and I want to help you to get the peace in your life that you deserve."

He could have told her that Isabel was close to him, and he could ask her anything, but that wouldn't have gone down well. He knew Sadie well enough to realise that life tended to revolve around her, so that answer would please her, but it was the truth anyway. He did care about her peace of mind.

Sadie had tried to put up a cold front towards him, but it was impossible. Even she had to admit she was enjoying having his support. Danny may have been the love of her life, but in his world it had been all about him. Danny had been selfish, she knew that, but it had not stopped her from falling heavily for him. When she realised she was having his child that love had grown to an obsession, she had to have him at any cost.

Nathan was so totally different. He was arrogant, impulsive and very decisive. He had made her laugh last night. She had felt close to him, and it was a good feeling, one which she had not experienced before. Nevertheless she was wary, she didn't want to go through the pain of loving and losing someone again, but she could not ignore Nathan. His loyalty was something she had never known with any man before.

She wondered if she should try and talk him out of this, but she could see by the look on his face it wasn't going to work. Please or offend, her mother was going to have to unveil her lurid past.

"OK, let's go," she said tersely, shutting the door firmly behind her.

Isabel was sitting in the conservatory enjoying a cup of coffee. Her dark hair was loose this morning, waving gently around her face. At fifty-two her face remained free from the ravages of time and stress. She had always been a beautiful and elegant woman and she still took great pride in her appearance. If she had any grey in her hair, one would never know, as she visited the hairdresser regularly, and today she had auburn lights amongst the dark tones.

She had worked hard to maintain her tall and slim frame; always eating organic food like Philip, there was a slight roundness to her stomach, but she still managed to fit into a size 12 in her clothes. Today she was wearing a pair of white slacks and a pale blue silk blouse.

The weather was a little hazy today, the sun had not yet come out from behind the clouds, and she was just wondering to herself if it would rain when the door opened to admit Sadie and Nathan. This in itself was surprising, because Sadie had not been friendly to Nathan, and Isabel had not got involved, she was wary of Sadie. She was surprised when Philip had told her earlier that Nathan and Sadie had gone to see the play at the Marlowe together last night, but she welcomed the idea that they might be getting on better.

"Good morning, I hear you enjoyed the play. What was it about? I was thinking of going if I can get your father to come along."

Sadie hesitated, she didn't have a clue, but Nathan produced a programme from his pocket, and gave it to Isabel, inviting her to read all about it. He was certainly on the ball in his efforts to keep their liaison a secret. Whilst Isabel was studying it, he gave her a broad wink and she stifled a giggle, it was partly because she could see the funny side of the situation, but also the fear of what was coming next.

Nathan led the conversation, and she was happy for him to do that, as she wouldn't have been able to discuss this subject calmly; it was something she had always felt unclean and ashamed about.

"Isabel, Sadie and I had a very personal discussion last night, and she told me something that no one else has ever known. She had to tell me because it has caused her so much pain, and we need your help so that she can come to terms with it."

Isabel put down the programme immediately. She could feel the blood rushing to her face. It didn't matter how time marched on, that stinking secret always caught up with her. Oh, how it had blighted her life!

"I hope you don't mind me knowing, it was crucifying her. If you can talk to her about her father it would help. If it's private, I can leave the two of you together to talk."

Isabel opened her mouth to speak, but no words would come. It had never occurred to her that Sadie had suffered. All these years she had carried the shock of what had happened to her, and now she felt ashamed that Sadie too, had suffered. She looked over at her daughter, who was standing there, her face completely impassive. It was always difficult to know exactly what Sadie was thinking, and now she wished she had tried harder to understand her.

They were all trying desperately to rebuild their lives now, and it was even more important than ever because Danielle was growing up. So many times she had wished she could share this mental torment that she'd kept hidden all these years with someone. It was almost a relief that Nathan knew, as long as Philip never did. She might appear mentally strong to everyone, but she knew if she lost Philip's love and respect, her life might as well be over.

Tears pricked at her eyelids, seeing her normally feisty and opinionated daughter lost for words, just standing awkwardly, and guilt flooded through her. She picked up a tissue, and to her amazement she saw tears in Sadie's eyes. A fear that some of the blame for her daughter's previous mental problems might rest with her flashed through her mind, so she knew she had to say something.

"Sadie, your father was my brother as you know," she paused giving a gulp at the mental pain this was causing her.

Sadie fidgeted, and Nathan touched Isabel's hand reassuringly. He could see how uncomfortable she was, but he totally trusted her character. "Go on, it's OK," he said gently.

Isabel took a deep breath and started talking; her words came out fast, and she explained everything about Joey. How he had been a loner and somehow different, but she had loved him anyway, and when he found out she was marrying Philip, his raging jealousy when he raped her that night.

Suddenly Sadie spoke, "Sorry, Mummy, that I didn't believe you when you said he raped you. I thought you had an incestuous relationship with him."

"Never! It pains me to talk about him at all. He was my kid brother, and I loved him, and even all these years later, I don't understand why he turned like that."

"It sounds like he was ill," suggested Nathan. He hoped that would make her feel better.

"What happened to him after that?" Sadie asked curiously. She could see her mother was suffering badly, and instinct told her Isabel was telling the truth, but whatever sort of pervert had her father been?

"He crashed his car into a wall that night and died," said Isabel feeling all that pain all over again. Would it never stop? She was waiting for some sort of angry retort from Sadie, but it didn't come; instead her daughter gave her the shock of her life when she came over and put her arms around her. Was this for real?

"I am going to leave you both to chat now, this is what you need," said Nathan, and he slipped away. Getting those two together after all the years of misery between them had been his intention. After all, when he became Isabels's son-in-law, he wanted to know that all the family were united. Nothing could ever change what had happened, but now they had to bury the past and move on together. Sadie didn't know it yet, but Nathan intended to marry her, and give Danielle some brothers and sisters; she needed to learn to share, being an only child with so many people doting on her might make her spoiled, and that would be a shame.

Sadie and Isabel spoke for a long time, and only ended their conversation when Danielle had been brought back from ballet by Nathan some two hours later. It was probably the first time in her life that Sadie had ever held a civil conversation with her mother. She had a desperate need to know about her blood father, and she realised that anger, spite and recriminations from her directed towards Isabel would achieve nothing. In the past she had punished her mother verbally for the hurt she felt Isabel had caused her. She should have realised her mother wouldn't have chosen to commit incest. Nathan had worked it out, and she now felt ashamed that she had always thought the worst of her mother. Her hatred had stemmed from that, especially after Mummy had insisted she have an abortion, but then she had been right, and Sadie realised she had only been protecting her.

Isabel was full of remorse at the way she had been towards Sadie, especially when she was pregnant. She had been just a young girl, and she hadn't given her enough support. She couldn't turn the clock back and change what had happened, but she could try to build a closer relationship with her now. Sadie had changed: Isabel saw a softer side to her since she had been re-united with Danielle, and this morning there had been tears in her eyes when they spoke about her father.

She decided to explain things in a way that would minimise Sadie's pain, so when she asked to know about her father and why he had behaved like that, Isabel explained that he was a very intelligent person, which had been true; so far above his peers, that he had made it to Oxford University, which only took a handful of the brightest students in the country.

She also explained that her brother was a loner, with not many friends because his superior intelligence made him stand out as different, so other students did not easily befriend him. This isolation, Isabel believed, caused Joey to have a breakdown which temporarily affected his mind. The remorse he suffered afterwards was proof his mind was disturbed at the time, so when he hit the wall, it may either have been an accident or suicide, but Isabel suspected that he had taken his own life.

This was all mind blowing information for Sadie to digest. The first time she had heard what sort of person her father had been; not a pervert, just a man who was mentally sick, and in a strange way she could feel an empathy for him. Sadie knew that she was different from her peers, and maybe she had inherited it from him, but she also knew she had lots of her mother's traits too; the dominant personality, the feisty nature. Daddy had always said this is why they clashed.

When they eventually parted there was a better understanding of each other, and Sadie marvelled that all the counselling and treatment she had received whilst in rehabilitation had not worked, but it seemed that, with a few well chosen words, Nathan had achieved what appeared to have been a goal that could never be reached. Sadie and Isabel had spent the last twenty-nine years bringing out the worst in each other, but this man had brought peace, and although she couldn't just put everything behind her in a flash, Sadie was determined, for the sake of Danielle, to make the best of her family roots, and try to be a better person. She had done some things in her life out of anger she was not proud of now, but she felt she wasn't that person any more, and she had changed for the better.

Isabel must never know that she had killed Jeremy. It was all so long ago, she now wondered how she could have done that. Philip must never know he was not her blood father; apart from maybe destroying his marriage, he might reject Sadie, and Sadie didn't do rejection. As for Nathan, he would say nothing if she asked him, even though he did have his own mind. His aim had been to make sure that Sadie and Isabel would bury the hatchet, and it had worked. It was impossible for Sadie to hate him any more, she could only be grateful to him for his support, and he had earned a new respect from her. Nathan had a strength of character that she admired, he was also a very fit man, and she hoped they could continue their secret liaison, because he had made her feel great.

In the past Sadie had always gone for men like herself, self centred and egotistical, the type that her family just would not approve of, but here in this house Nathan was loved by everyone, including Danielle, and no one would disapprove if they knew. As far as Sadie was concerned, she wanted him in her life, and not just at weekends either. She was hooked on Nathan, but certainly not ready to share her feelings with anyone else just yet.

Chapter Thirteen

It was now six weeks since Sadie had returned to her family, so Elizabeth came for a follow-up visit and what she saw was very heartening. Sadie and Danielle had bonded well, there was an atmosphere of warmth in the house. Sadie and her mother seemed to get on agreeably, and Isabel now appeared much more relaxed than when she had seen them last time.

Sadie smiled more and her expression was no longer blank and difficult to read. She was clearly proud of her little daughter, and the cheeky personality of Danielle brought many a smile to her face, and Elizabeth could see a softness in Sadie's demeanour that had been missing before. Alice the nanny had left; apparently she had another post to go to, and the family seemed to have managed without her. Elizabeth went away very happy, and subsequently wrote a glowing follow-up report about Sadie's rehabilitation. It was always nice to know that a former patient was thriving well in the outside community, especially when they blossomed amongst their own family.

Nathan was away on a business trip for two weeks, but he would be back in time for Danielle's birthday party, which was being held on the last Saturday of June. Sadie was secretly missing him a lot, but right now, together with Isabel, she was so busy with the arrangements for the party, the only time she could even think about it was in her bed at night.

Even the thought of going out and finding a man did not appeal to her, and Nathan had been right, she very much doubted that any woman could make her feel the way he had. Unlike Danny, he had been interested in her, not himself, and he had listened to her problems and fears and helped her.

Sadie could see another good reason why her parents had moved to Herne Bay. Situated where it was, in the far south eastern corner of England, it was difficult for the weatherman to predict an accurate weather forecast for this area. Most of the rain that was forecast petered out before it actually reached them, and the temperatures were amongst the highest in the country.

Living at the top of the downs meant they could catch the north wind in the winter, but in the summer, when the weather was very hot, they had the benefit of the gentle breezes from the sea, which helped them to remain cool. With all this in mind, they decided to hold Danielle's birthday party outside in the garden. The garden was large with splendid views of the surrounding area, so plans were put in place for a bouncy castle, a children's entertainer, and a marquee would be erected where the food would be served, just in case it did rain.

The whole of Danielle's class had been invited, and parents had the choice of leaving their children and having time to themselves, or staying and enjoying the fun. That meant there would be a lot of people in their garden, so Isabel was relieved they had the space to provide all this.

Danielle was excited that her real mummy had come to live with her again. She wanted all her friends to see Sadie, because her mummy was far more beautiful than any of their mummies. They had such fun together. They sang on the karaoke machine, Mummy painted her nails, which was something Alice would not have allowed, and she loved watching her mummy dress up in her beautiful clothes. Sometimes Danielle was even allowed to wear a bit of her makeup and perfume; Mummy had said it was just for fun, and it had to be washed off when she went to bed.

Danielle had been upset at first when Alice left so suddenly to work for another family. She hadn't told anyone how sad she was; but that sadness had not lasted long because life was so full of new and exciting things and she didn't have much time to think about it. Having her own mummy for her friends to see when they came to the party was really special for Danielle, and she intended to enjoy that moment.

Being a mother, and spending time with her daughter, gave Sadie a glow inside that she had never experienced before.

Somebody loved and needed her, thought the best of her, and didn't judge her. To one little girl, she was a good person, a loving mother, and she so wanted to live up to that ideal.

Every night when she put Danielle to bed they said their prayers together. At school Danielle had learned about Jesus and God. Sadie had found that, in prison, using religion had been a good way of making it clear she wanted to reform. In Danielle's world of a child, Jesus loved you, and you thanked him for things and asked him for help when you needed it, and he still loved you even when you had been naughty. Sadie was captivated by the simplicity of life through the eyes of a five year old, and the innocence of a child. It was heart warming, and she was more than happy to kneel with her, saying prayers before she tucked her into bed.

Then there were the stories, lovely bedtime stories, which Danielle listened to with rapt attention, her big dark eyes seemingly absorbing every detail and registering happiness or amazement when it ended.

Sadie and Isabel had been to an open evening very shortly after Danielle had started going to school full time. It had been mainly to reassure themselves that she was settling in all right and had friends. Her teacher, Miss Sanderson, had been so glowing about her, saying how bright she was; she could already read and write her name, and although she was inclined to chatter a bit too much, her infectious personality made her popular with the other children, and her sense of humour was a joy to experience. To hear from someone else that her daughter was special meant a lot. She didn't want to give Alice any credit for it, only Philip and Isabel. They had stepped in whilst she wasn't around, and thanks to their care, and a nursery class that worked with children before they went to school to perfect any early skills, it looked like Danielle would have a promising future.

Life seemed to have some meaning for Sadie now. She was recovering from the loss of Danny. It had taken her longer than Eleanor, who had since remarried to an actor, and was now pregnant with his child and living in New York. Sadie had no wish to stand outside Fosters Hall any more and leave flowers in his memory as others did. She was more interested in the present, that was what counted now.

Danielle did her usual run around before her bath. Sadie didn't mind, she had all the time in the world tonight, she wasn't going out anywhere. But she pretended to be cross, and reminded her if she wanted a story, she must get a move on. It would be so easy to spoil Danielle, and she mustn't; she didn't want her daughter growing up to be a brat.

"Mummy, can we read Harry Potter?" she asked after her bath.

Sadie did wonder at five, if it was a bit too grown up for her, but with help from her mum, Danielle managed to read the first couple of pages of the chapter. She was tired now, and beginning to flag, so Sadie took over and read her some more. Danielle was fascinated by spells and magic, her imaginative mind went into overdrive. So Sadie decided not to finish the chapter that night, it was too long.

After she had eventually settled Danielle she suddenly felt lonely, and she missed Nathan. Although he only came at weekends, his presence seemed to fill the house, and the thought of a repeat performance of that night with him was, as always, very much on her mind. Trouble is, all the while she lived with her parents, it was going to be hard, and how could she be sure he wanted to anyway, it had not been mentioned since and then he had gone away.

"Night night, Mummy."

"Goodnight sweetheart, sleep tight."

Sadie remembered how Philip had always said that to her when she was a little girl, and she had always felt safe. She was beginning to regret how she had shut her mother out of her life and caused her such misery. They had both suffered, and Sadie knew she had used her insecurities to do battle with Isabel in the past and now it must stop. She had always preferred to think the worst of her mother and that was because of the abortion, but she now realised that there had been no other choice. But the loss of that baby had made her unable to bond with Ricky's child. Danielle was different because of her feelings for Danny, but now that she was beginning to recover, she realised it would have never worked with Danny anyway, his character would not have been strong enough for her, and his vanity and need to always be centre stage would have clashed with hers. Sadie always wanted to be the centre of attention. That was why, if she had a fling with Nathan, that is all it could be. He had become a very assertive person, he wouldn't fall around her feet in submission, and Sadie had no desire to take orders from any man.

She went downstairs and into the lounge, yawning. Danielle wasn't the only one who was tired.

"Mummy, is everything sorted for the party now? Danielle can't stop talking about it," she enquired of her mother, who was sitting on the sofa with her iPad.

"Yes, most of them have replied by email, even though we sent out proper invitations. The whole class is coming."

Sadie didn't say what she was thinking. She would have done normally, but she was making a real effort to build a proper relationship with her mother, even if some of the views that Isabel held were different from her own.

If her mother wanted to believe that the whole class was coming because they all loved Danielle, that was fine, but Sadie thought it more likely they wanted to see the lovely house they lived in, and congregate in the garden, with their children enjoying everything on offer that day. In the short time she had been meeting Danielle from school she had noticed the clique of mothers. She was not a part of it herself. They were all busy competing against each other to prove their child was the best, and keeping in with one another, too. It was apparent that her parents had money, and Daddy didn't hesitate in splashing it around at times, so knowing the Morton Browns was probably some sort of status symbol to them.

Sadie's outlook on life had always been cynical, she could not change that, but for the sake of her daughter, she had to put the bitterness and hate behind her and make that family bond that was so important. Elizabeth had been pleased with the progress made when she called; and some of the time Sadie wasn't faking it, she did actually care, which bewildered her, because for her it was something new.

"Yes Mummy, emails have taken the place of letters now, and even Christmas cards are dying out. It's normal now for one to tweet Happy Christmas to your friends, and it goes straight onto your Facebook page, job done!"

"Facebook, the place where everyone tells you what they had for breakfast. Who cares?" joined in Philip, who had been resisting Sadie's attempts to have a page of his own.

Sadie had set her own page up; it was full of pictures of Danielle. She was so incredibly proud of her, she wanted to show the world. She had even found Sunita on there, and they had become friends and swopped photos. She was hoping to pay her a visit with Danielle in the holidays, just for old times' sake.

She went into the kitchen. In the fridge was an opened bottle of wine; she poured herself a glass and was about to take it into the lounge.

"Can you bring Daddy and I a glass of wine. The bottle is open?"

Sadie did so. She had been used to only thinking of herself, but now her world included Danielle, and although she didn't realise it, she was slowly changing and becoming less selfish. As she handed the glasses to her parents, even though it came from the top of the stairs on the first floor, the scream that Danielle let out was loud and piercing, followed by wails and sobs.

"Mummy, Grandma, help me, the witch is going to kill me!"

Sadie took the stairs two at a time, with Isabel in hot pursuit, visions of a stranger abducting or hurting Danielle were terrifying, and when she burst through the door it was to find her shaking with fear and hiding her face under her duvet.

"What's wrong sweetheart? What did you see?"

She wrapped her inside her arms, and Danielle clung to her and gradually her sobs became less.

"There was a witch. I saw her through the window, standing by the gate, with a black cloak and a hood, and she waved her arms at me!"

Her eyes were wide with fear, and Sadie looked over at the slight chink in the curtains where they had been parted. Had she seen someone, or was it just a bad dream?

Isabel strode over and looked out. It was dark by now, and the only sound that could be heard was the waves lapping against the beach, which somehow felt comforting.

"What were you doing out of bed in the first place? The street is deserted. It's too much Harry Potter at bedtime, it makes your imagination go overboard," decided Isabel. "Your mummy should be reading you Noddy or Postman Pat."

Sadie bit back a retort. Danielle referred to them as baby books. She loved Harry Potter, but maybe if it gave her bad dreams she would have to find something else. Enid Blyton books were perhaps more suitable and less frightening to a five year old.

"Grandma's right. You keep thinking about the witch and the spells, and when you go to sleep, you dream that the witch is there."

"She was there Mummy, I saw her, and when I screamed she ran away. She woke me up when she cast her spell."

Sadie came to a quick decision. Nothing was going to convince Danielle she had just had a bad dream. Herne Bay was the most unlikely place to have predators or thieves staring up at the window of a house with all the lights on, and the rest of the family not even in bed. It was a place where there was so little crime, people even went out and didn't lock their doors. The community was friendly, and even the neighbours had told her parents that the entry system set up to protect them was probably not needed.

"Come and sleep in my bed with me, and when that witch comes back we'll tell her to fly away on her broomstick!"

Danielle seemed quite impressed by this idea, and brightened considerably, so Sadie took her into the double bed she slept in next door and peace reigned once more. They all slept fitfully until the next morning, and by then the incident was forgotten. Danielle didn't mention it again, and although Sadie sat by her bed until she was asleep the next night, there were no more bad dreams, and Sadie started reading about the Famous Five to her, which Isabel thought was a very good idea.

Chapter Fourteen

"Bye sweetheart, have a great time."

Sadie waved to Danielle as the car drove away. She was going for a sleepover at her friend Laura's house. Her birthday was a week before Danielle's party, but unlike that party, only a few girls had been asked, Danielle and three others.

As Sadie shut the door, she realised she was alone and the quietness of the empty house seemed unnatural. Philip and Isabel had jetted off to the South of France. Their villa in Cannes had been leased out for three years, and now they had popped over for a few days just to see what redecorating was needed before they used it again themselves.

Nathan had rung her. He was back from his work trip to the Middle East, but Sadie had been too proud to admit she was on her own tonight and lonely. She had assumed he would come for the weekend, but it seemed he had stuff to catch up on. He was coming down on Friday, the day before the party, to lend his hand and help in any way that he could.

She had bitten down her disappointment at his words. Then all of a sudden it came to her; she would go to him, she would surprise him, and she could stay the night and drive back in time for Danielle's return tomorrow afternoon. Acting on impulse was a trait she shared with Nathan. In her opinion it made life more fun. So it wasn't long before she had packed a small bag and picked up a bottle of Philip's best Beaujolais, which they could enjoy later, and was driving up the M2 towards London.

When she arrived at his penthouse, the opulence of it was not lost on her, and the commanding view of the river Thames. If what Nathan said was true, and he had made his own way in life after her father had given him a helping hand, that would explain it. Her aim was to see Nathan, and as it wasn't often that Sadie went to her men, she questioned herself as to why she was doing it. There was something about Nathan she just could not resist. Maybe she was still fascinated by the change in him; the drunken, drug fuelled layabout had gone, and in his place was a fit and strong natured man who knew exactly where he was going in life. He had become a powerful figure, and Sadie could not help admiring that. Sadie believed that life was all about having power and using it. She was there now, so she found the private parking area and left the car.

She stiffened as she approached the main building, and she did not like what she saw. Nathan had his arms around a woman. All she could see of her was a mane of shining golden hair and a slim frame. She ducked hastily into the side; Nathan had not seen her, but she saw the look of tenderness on his face as he said goodbye to her, and it cut into her like the sharpest knife.

But just as quickly, that pain instantly became supplanted by a fierce red hot anger that knew no sense or reason. The other side of Sadie, that she had so desperately tried to suppress in her efforts to be a good mother, was challenging her, and such turmoil was going on inside her. This was followed by a deadly calm: her decision was made, she knew what she had to do.

Nathan waved once more to the blonde female, and he watched her walk across the parking area to her car before going back inside. This fuelled Sadie's rage even more; a cold calculating rage that had now taken over all her senses. She had to get this woman out of Nathan's life once and for all. She reasoned with herself that if obstacles block your way in life, they just have to be removed, whatever the cost.

The unknown woman was now in her car, and Sadie had to quickly return to her own car, which was parked near to the entrance. Sadie got a glimpse of her face as she drove past; it wasn't just her hair that was nice, she had a beautiful doll-like face, with big eyes, and a look of innocence about her, and, she thought bitterly, that was probably what had ensnared Nathan. She had put out a net and reeled him in, and now Sadie was going to have to save him from this manipulating woman.

Sadie slammed her car into gear and drove after her. During the journey, which took them round many roundabouts and through traffic lights, she was able to keep her in sight. They had crossed the River Thames and were now in Clapham, and when they reached Commonside, it was apparent that the woman had realised that Sadie was following her. Sadie carried on doggedly pursuing her. That voice inside her was telling Sadie that this woman was ruining her chance of happiness with Nathan, so she had to get rid of her.

She shot round the traffic lights, picking up the south circular which had two lanes. It was still light and, as much as she wanted to, she could not drive parallel with her, too many other cars were around. She continued to follow her. She was deadly calm, unlike her prey who was now weaving around her lane in an effort to shake Sadie off.

Now they were heading towards Dulwich Common, right out of town, and this is where the woman made her mistake. Instead of staying on the main road with other cars, she dodged down a side road close to the common, and Sadie exulted that it was empty. It was a no-through road, she had nowhere to go and was blocked in by Sadie's car. She locked her door as she watched Sadie get out of her car and approach her. Once Sadie was within earshot she threatened to call the police with her mobile phone.

"I don't know what you want from me but you were driving like a maniac, I am calling the police!"

"Oh, there's no need," purred Sadie; wasn't she loving this. "I have been trying to attract your attention, you have something hanging down underneath your car."

The woman hesitated. How stupid she had been. Why on earth would a strange woman have a grievance with her anyway? She'd never set eyes on her before. She put down her mobile and opened the car door.

"Oh, I see, thanks for telling me. Where?"

"There," said Sadie, and when the unsuspecting woman knelt down to take a look, her fingers tightened on the wine bottle, she lifted it and struck her from behind. She was glad she had brought it, and when her victim slumped forward, she rained a few more blows, marvelling that the glass had not broken. What a hard head she must have!

She had to be sure she had done it properly. Luckily she had her white summer gloves on so was not concerned when she turned the body over. She could scarcely believe she was still alive, but a low moaning sound confirmed it. In her anger she dashed the bottle against the side of the car, and watched as the red wine dripped down onto her victim's head.

She was beginning to panic now. It was still light, someone could come along at any minute, and she needed to get out of here. She jumped into her car and rammed it into reverse, driving furiously back over the prostrate body, and then she drove forward again just to make sure. Now the eyes stared back at her, lifeless, and blood was gushing out of the woman's mouth. She had fixed her for good, and she had saved Nathan from this scheming female. But two things worried Sadie, the loss of a good bottle of wine, and not being able to see Nathan tonight. She could not be linked with being in that area when they found the body. Regretfully she would have to drive back to Herne Bay and make sure someone saw her, being at home would be her alibi.

Nathan was glad to be back, and he wondered wistfully if Sadie had missed him. My God, he had got it bad, he knew it, this woman totally dominated his mind and his senses. He had tried to get her out of his mind, and in so doing he had met Melissa, a very attractive blonde with big blue eyes, so different from Sadie, the complete opposite in fact. But try as he might, being with her did nothing to assuage his longing for Sadie.

He felt a heel for sleeping with her. It had meant nothing to him, but obviously it had to her. Whilst he was away, his thoughts were totally centred on Sadie; how unpredictable she was, and how very alluring. He had planned to come and see her as soon as he got back, but Melissa was there, waiting for him, and he knew he must not lead her on any more. She thought they were an item, but he had used her and he felt bad. He didn't usually treat women that way, but he had to know if anyone other than Sadie could evoke such feelings inside him, and she hadn't even come close.

She had shed a few tears when he told her; that made him feel worse, but he had wiped them away and told her she deserved better than him and, with her looks, he was sure she'd have men queuing up to take her out. When she turned back towards him, as they stood at the entrance to the apartments, she looked so heartbroken and vulnerable he had put his arms round her and wished her a happy life, and he truly meant it. He had waited until she reached her car and then, with a sigh of relief, gone inside and up in the lift to his own apartment.

The urge to be with Sadie was engulfing him. He had phoned her as soon as he got home, and she seemed fine, and her voice gave no hint as to whether she had missed him. He had resisted the urge to go to her that weekend. He was fighting his own feelings, but he had to see whether she seemed upset when he said he was too busy. Her voice gave nothing away. She didn't seem bothered, and disappointment flooded through him. How long would it take to win her over?

He tossed and turned in bed that night, wondering how he was going to resist the urge to get into his car on Saturday and drive to her. Sleep was evading him, so he got up early at 7 o'clock, and after a shower he felt better. To hell with it, life was too short to waste any of it, he would go and surprise her; but first he would have some breakfast and coffee to wake himself up properly.

He dressed casually, and when the buzzer went on the intercom, he was surprised. It was still only 8 o'clock. He spoke into the mike.

"Yes, who is it?"

"Mr Nathan Edwards, it's the district police here, can we have a word please?"

Now he wondered what was going on, and fear flooded through him; surely nothing had happened at Herne Bay. Sadie and Danielle were both so precious to him.

He let them in. Two officers in uniform with very grave faces. So it was serious then.

"The body of Melissa Cooper has been found in a country road near Dulwich. She had been run down by a car it would seem. Your name and address were in her handbag. Was she your girlfriend?"

"Only very briefly. But she was here yesterday evening. I saw her into her car and she drove off. She was fine then."

He had tried to be honest, but the shock of their words had totally taken him by surprise. Poor Melissa, she had everything to live for! He felt angry to think that she had been knocked down by a hit and run driver who hadn't had the guts to stay and see if they could help her.

115

But as the conversation progressed, it was clear to see the police believed she had been deliberately knocked down. Disbelief flooded through him, why would anyone do that to Melissa? It was in his own interest to explain the events as it appeared that he might have been the last person to see her.

Nathan was horrified when he realised he was under suspicion. What a nightmare this was. The shock of hearing Melissa had died was the last thing he had been expecting. It was taking a while to get his head around it. He gave a statement of his movements last night, and confirmed his car had not left its parking place. Once they had examined the car he knew he would be in the clear, and he was relieved when they finally went. He might be in the clear, but they believed that the killer was lurking somewhere in London, and they were prepared to do a house to house search to find whoever had done this horrific crime.

He was feeling even more in need of Sadie after this shock, so he got in the car and drove down to Herne Bay. Sadie was surprised to see him. He had not realised her parents were away, and it seemed that Danielle was not due home from her sleepover for a couple of hours. Because he needed a shoulder to cry on, he told Sadie all about the tragedy involving Melissa. He was even honest enough to explain that she had been serious and he had not.

Sadie had sympathised with his loss and her arms had been there to comfort him. She was still in her dressing gown, and when it slipped to the side, exposing her beautiful legs, he just couldn't help himself, his fingers stroked their way up her legs and by the time they reached her thighs, he knew that it was not just comfort he needed but passion. Sadie sensed his desperate need of her to assuage his misery, and her body responded to his caresses, but on this occasion she took charge.

"Let's go to bed, I know how to comfort you," she murmured, springing from the sofa in a graceful cat-like movement, her eyes gleaming with passion.

Nathan allowed her to lead him up the stairs to her bedroom, she dropped her dressing gown onto the floor, and he gulped at the sight of her enticing body. When he joined her on the bed, his lips found her nipples and his fingers stroked her intimately, she was wet and ready for him, and he felt that when he entered her, it was like two souls joining together, sharing their grief. Making

116

love to Sadie helped to lift his spirits and bound him to her even more. How could people think she had no emotions? Right now she was his rock.

"Thank you, that was amazing," he whispered to her, and Sadie's eyes gleamed with satisfaction. No one could possibly connect her with the murder. Thank goodness Nathan was in the clear as his car had not left the premises, and as for Sadie herself, she had disposed of a nuisance. Nathan had admitted the girl had wanted more than a friendship. That voice in her head had been right telling her what to do, thank goodness she had listened.

But even as they lay together on Sadie's bed, a feeling of unrest swept through her, she felt as though someone was watching her; she couldn't put a finger on what it was, but it was enough to take the edge off her happiness. Sadie sensed something was wrong; it was a weird feeling. Maybe it was just her imagination.

She'd driven her car through the car wash this morning, just in case there had been any blood left on the tyres, and thrown the white gloves away; they were in a bush at Dulwich. And as Nathan had assumed she had spent yesterday evening here on her own, she couldn't see how she could be linked with the murder in any way.

This was yet another example of the power she had. None of her murders had ever led back to her, and it was ironic that the only one she hadn't done, was the one she had been blamed for. She had Alice to thank for that, but now Alice was gone her life had been spared; because Sadie would have had no qualms about removing the woman who had spent five years with Danielle and deprived her own mother of that same time. She could feel the anger rise inside her at the injustice of it. So many things in her life had not been fair, so it had been up to her to act to make it right.

Nathan was making coffee. It was only a few minutes before Danielle was due back, so Sadie gave her rumpled hair a quick brush, then slipped into jeans and a T-shirt. His voice floated up the stairs.

"Do you know where Ann keeps the coffee?"

"I haven't a clue," said Sadie as she ran down the stairs and into the lounge.

"Got it!" Nathan's voice was triumphant. When Ann had a day

off the family had to fend for themselves, so no wonder Sadie didn't know. But when they got married, Sadie would have to find her way around a kitchen; Nathan had no intention of having a housekeeper.

"Oh dear, it's raining. It had better not next Saturday!" Sadie heard the raindrops pattering against the window, so she looked over, and then let out a loud scream, causing Nathan to drop the cup of coffee he had lovingly made for her.

"Nathan, someone is spying on us, quickly, it's spooky!"

He would have moved faster if he hadn't got boiling coffee on his hands. He grabbed a kitchen towel, and his long legs covered the distance from the hall to the lounge in maybe three seconds.

But Sadie wasn't crying. Once she had got over the shock of being spied on, she was at the window, banging angrily on the pane. By the time he looked there was no one in sight.

"Who was it?"

"Oh, some nutter with a black hooded raincoat. They didn't scare me, but this must be the one that scared Danielle. What a saddo with nothing better to do than peer in windows and frighten people!"

"We ought to mention it to the police, in case they do it to someone else."

"Yes, they don't frighten me, I just say get a life, but Danielle is another thing, she's a young child and it's a lousy thing to do to her!"

Sadie's face was dark with anger and her black eyes glittered, of all the places for crazy people to hang out, she wasn't expecting it to be Herne Bay. Nathan couldn't help admiring her spirit. She was much tougher than your average female. She was a force to be reckoned with, and didn't he just love that about her, and the way it set her apart from other women. Sadie was unique.

He rang the local police station and spoke to them, explaining the two incidents and suggesting they might be linked. When he came off the telephone he spoke soothingly.

"They haven't had any other reports of this happening, but now we have told them, they are gonna keep an eye on this house."

"No one can get in here unless we want them to, Daddy was right to have security; but a spooky black figure at the lounge window is terrifying for Danielle. I am so glad she's not here. The gates to the drive don't open unless the button is pressed, but the garden gate that leads to the downs can be opened, we have to have that so the postman can get to the post box by the door. That saddo came through it and peered through the lounge window, we can't stop that!"

"I am sure it will be OK, Sadie."

Nathan was not sure he had convinced her, and he could see she was angry. God help the nutter if Sadie got hold of them. He reckoned she could pack a punch. He went back into the kitchen to clear up the spilled coffee, then made her another one, and himself as well. Sadie was very thoughtful whilst she was drinking her coffee, because she had a very strong suspicion who that figure might be but she wasn't ready to share it with Nathan. There was only one person who would want to hang around this house, and that was Alice. Sadie had not believed she would leave Danielle that easily and forget her. The silly cow had now taken to spying on them; how pathetic was that!

But Sadie was going to make sure she was right out of their lives for good. There would be a time when she would slip up, and that is when Sadie would strike; she would take advantage of the situation when it presented itself to her, as she had always done with such great results so far. Sadie believed she was invincible. If Alice didn't creep away and hide under the stone she came from, then Sadie would take care of her.

They both sat there absorbed in their thoughts. Nathan was still coming to terms with the news of Melissa's death. He read about it all the time in the newspapers, but he didn't expect it to happen to someone he knew. Was there a jealous ex-boyfriend, who saw her with him and then chased after her? Guilt flooded through him that she might have lost her life because of him. But then he rebuked himself for being ridiculous, she had come to see him uninvited. But still he felt bad that this had happened so soon after she had been to see him.

Sadie felt that Nathan being there was right. Her parents were still away, and tonight there could be no jiggy jigs, Danielle was in the habit of coming into her mother's bed in the middle of the night, and what a shock she would have if Nathan was there too. She explained that to Nathan, who grinned.

"I will be a very good boy and stay in the guest room, even though the thought of your delicious body between the sheets, just along the hall, will be such a temptation!"

119

Her body pulsated rapidly, and she could feel herself flushing at the thought of being ravaged by him again; was there time before Danielle came home? She turned towards Nathan, and it was as if he read her thoughts, as he quickly peeled off her clothes.

"You sexy little minx," he murmured. "If we can't do it then, let's do it now."

"Mm, no time like the present," she whispered, closing her eyes with rapture at his touch.

Chapter Fifteen

The day of the party dawned sunny and bright, just as Sadie and Isabel had so fervently hoped it would. In the garden, apart from the swing, climbing frame and Wendy house, which were permanent fixtures, there was a big bouncy castle, music, puppets, and an entertainer who did magic tricks. A marquee had been erected, where all the food and drink would be served.

Philip and Isabel had done it all properly, and no expense was spared. As well as all the food that children love, such as peanut butter sandwiches, sausages, jellies and ice cream, for the adults there was smoked salmon, salad, prawns, Chinese and Indian food, a huge birthday cake, and Kentish strawberries with clotted cream.

The children had soft drinks or milkshakes, for the adults there was beer, wine, and even a few bottles of champagne. Philip and Nathan were not particularly looking forward to spending the afternoon with about thirty five year olds, but it was Danielle's day, so for her sake they would stay and drink a beer or two.

Sadie had been running round like a headless chicken, making absolutely sure that everything would be in place for 3 o'clock that afternoon. Danielle had a new pink lacy dress, her black hair shone with vitality, and she was wearing a pretty pink hair band. She had even managed to wheedle a tiny touch of very pale lipstick from Sadie to match her pale pink nail varnish.

Isabel came to inspect her. "Very nice, but how long will her dress stay like that?" She enquired, watching her granddaughter skipping excitedly round the room, waiting for that magic time to come.

121

f

"It doesn't matter. This is her day, let her enjoy herself with all her friends," said Sadie firmly. Chances were, after playing in the garden, the dress might not be wearable any more, it might get stained or ripped, but it had been bought for the party, and Daddy could easily buy another for her. Sadie didn't really think it mattered that much.

Isabel sighed to herself and said nothing. Shorts and T-shirt were best for playing in the garden. If she had got her way, Danielle would have put her dress on to cut her cake and have the photos done, but she knew that with Sadie it was easy come, easy go, and Philip was her money tree. But then she chided herself. If Sadie's only fault was selfishness, and not valuing money, then she had much to be grateful for. No one could fault Sadie as a mother, coming home to care for her daughter had been the making of her.

Sadie and Isabel had both worn sundresses. It was a very hot day and there was no need for tights, so they looked cool and smart without going over the top. When the guests started to arrive, most of them were in shorts and T-shirts. Sadie had debated about wearing shorts, mainly so Nathan could see how good her legs were, but then she decided she didn't want to look the same as the others. Her sundress was a vivid pinkish mauve, it had thin straps and was full length, whereas Isabel had opted for a sundress with thicker straps and tiny blue flowers on a white background, which came just below her knee.

Nathan gave a low whistle when he saw them both with Danielle.

"Well, here I am surrounded by three beautiful women. Life couldn't get much better than that."

Isabel accepted the compliment graciously, and Danielle did a final twirl before running off to play with her friends. The man who had been hired for the occasion was organising musical bumps, and Isabel had got a big parcel together for pass the parcel, which would be the next game.

Nathan stood there with Sadie, smiling at her. Inside he was still wondering why poor Melissa had been murdered, it continued to haunt him, but he could put on a good front. Nothing was going to spoil this party. He now felt so much a part of this family. All he could do was to bide his time until Sadie realised how much he loved her, and his one hope was that she could forget the excuse for a man that he had been and warm towards the man he was now.

Taking that psychology course and getting a degree in it had given him more of an insight into how people reacted in situations, and how their minds worked. Having been given a chance in life after his bad start had made him feel he wanted to give something back, so he had toyed with the idea of being a counsellor, but then the chance of a career in computers, which were now such an important part of everyday life, had made him change his mind. When his true potential had been realised, he had very quickly climbed the ladder to success. But he still cared about people, and the satisfaction he had got from helping Sadie and Isabel sort out their problems, just by getting them together and paving the way for them to call a truce, had made him happy. He wanted as much harmony as possible in the future within this family that he had become a part of.

Sadie returned his smile. She was glad Nathan was here; she needed to know what was happening in London, just to make sure her movements were covered. She had seen all the news coverage, and the papers, even Philip and Isabel were aware that someone Nathan knew had been murdered in Dulwich, and how shaken he had been, and yet he had still come down to see them all and be a part of Danielle's birthday celebrations.

She injected a sympathetic tone into her voice, and a softness into her dark eyes which Nathan noticed and was relieved by. She did understand how bad he felt.

"I have been thinking about poor Melissa. How old was she, do you know? I hope you are not blaming yourself for her death, you were not the last person to see her obviously, the unknown car driver was."

"Oh Sadie, I am glad you understand. I was trying to forget about it 'cos it's Danielle's day, but I sent her away unhappy, and it haunts me. But we would never have been a couple; for a start she was only twenty-two, too young for me, I knew that."

Sadie looked into his grey eyes and saw sincerity; so Melissa had not meant anything to him. She felt glad, she couldn't share her boyfriends. Was he her boyfriend again? She really wasn't sure. She knew he liked sleeping with her, like many others before him, but then he might have liked sleeping with a young one like Melissa too. Her jealousy rose inside her like a deadly poison, and that voice reassured her she had done the right thing by removing Melissa.

"Oh dear, such a young age to die," she murmured. "I hope the police didn't give you a bad time over it, I know only too well how they can jump to conclusions and bully people when they want to solve a crime."

Nathan pressed her fingers and she didn't remove them from his touch, and then he put his arms about her and hugged her briefly. Sadie felt a warm glow of satisfaction inside, she liked the feeling of closeness from him; something she would have spurned in the past.

"Oh babe, you went through so much; you are such a very strong woman. I am so proud of you! As for me, they did interview me, and my car was throughly examined, but it hadn't left the parking spot for days. They gave me the all clear, and the first thing I did was jump into it and come down to see you."

"I know, and I am glad they are not bothering you any more. Do you think they will catch whoever it was?"

"God knows, they are concentrating their search all around London, house to house enquiries, that is where she lived, and her friends and family are there."

Sadie smiled to herself inwardly. She had done it again, removed someone who was a threat to her happiness with Nathan, and even got him feeling sorry for her. She was beginning to think Sadie Morton Brown was invincible, and it was a great feeling.

Philip wasn't greatly impressed with seeing thirty or so lively five year olds running all over the place, but he kept a bright smile on his face, and circulated amongst his guests, handing out the occasional beer if the bar man they had hired was busy elsewhere. He had been hoping to disappear off to the Herne Bay Angling Club, of which he was a member, and pop down there for a quick pint with Nathan. It was very pleasant sitting at the tables outside looking over towards the clock tower and the bandstand with the sea shimmering behind it.

But when he looked over, Nathan was in earnest conversation with Sadie. He had even hugged her, and he was amazed, one minute Sadie was just being Sadie towards Nathan, but now they seemed to have developed a closeness, and that was not a bad thing at all. A man like Nathan would be good for Sadie, he wouldn't indulge her as much as he, her father, had. Philip knew his faults, but the money was always there, and who else could he spend it on if not his own family?

It seemed ever since they went to that play at the Marlowe together, they had become closer. Sadie was a nicer and softer person since she had come back home and picked up her life with Danielle again. All she needed now was to marry the right person, and could he dare hope it might be Nathan? One thing was for sure, Philip was going to leave them both to get on with it all. Poor Nathan had suffered a nasty shock last week when that girl he knew a bit had died. But here he was, supporting Danielle, and it looked like Sadie might be commiserating with him. Anyone who thought Sadie was devoid of all emotion was wrong, she did care, but just found it hard to show her emotions. He abandoned his former idea of going down the road; what was it Isabel had asked him to do? Oh yes, where was that new phone of his? He picked it up, and made his way across the garden, he had some videoing to do.

Sadie had mingled just to please Mummy. She wasn't interested in any of these parents, they all thought their children were the best, and they boasted about everything they could do. How stupid they were, Danielle was head and shoulders above all of them! But she didn't need to stand there and convince them, she just spoke a few words and passed onto the next one. She could have done with Nathan's wit and charm, having him beside her felt good, but he had managed to collect a group of boys together and taken them down the far end of the garden to play a game of football.

He had seen the boys getting restless, pass the parcel and other games were not for them, and as they started to get bored, they were running about and bumping into people. He figured if he took them away for an energetic game of football, then the party could go on as planned. All the girls were enjoying the games, and then the entertainer had started doing magic tricks, and they still had the puppet show to come.

Danielle was having the time of her life. She was a little excited, her cheeks were flushed and her eyes were bright. She thought her mummy looked beautiful in her bright sundress, and she made sure all her friends knew who she was. She was enjoying the games. Pass the parcel had been fun, and musical bumps, her pink dress now had some grass stains on it and her hair had escaped from its band. She had been enthralled by the magic man, as had all her friends; she couldn't believe those silly boys had gone off to play football and missed it all, but then it was with Uncle Nathan, and he was always fun to be with.

Isabel was helping the caterers to round up everyone to come into the marquee and sit down to eat. A special place had been left for Danielle, with her mother and grandmother sitting on either side of her. Nathan had brought his band of dishevelled but happy boys back, and Philip was at the ready to take photographs of Danielle cutting her cake.

After running around and playing for a couple of hours, the children tucked in, parents were enjoying helping themselves as well, and the barman was going round topping up glasses. There was a rumble of happy voices, and Sadie and Isabel exchanged glances, it was going well. The party continued after everyone had eaten; music was playing, and now the parents were settling into little groups.

Nathan couldn't resist looking at Sadie. She was turned to the side, discussing something with her mother, and didn't realise his eyes were on her. But then she turned and their eyes met, and he gave her a wink. If only she knew that she was the main focus of his life. She smiled at him and he felt his heart glow, no longer did she bristle up when he tried to be nice to her; were her defences down? She was still very much her own woman, but that is what fascinated him, her strong character. He felt that no one understood Sadie like he did, she was like a precious bird with a damaged wing. Once that wing was mended, then that bird was complete, and could fly. His heart went out to her for all that she had been through. Prison must have been horrendous, and the bullying, her true identity was not her fault and it had affected her for all of her life. He wanted to spend his life making it up to her.

His heart quickened as she got up and came over to him.

"Nathan, Daddy is videoing Danielle cutting her cake, can you take some photos, we have that new camera and I know you are good at photography."

"Certainly." He went to get the camera. She was asking him to do something; she needed him, he felt pleased.

After the cake was cut, plates with slices were taken round, although many of the guests opted to wrap their slice in a napkin and take it home. Gradually people collected their children and started to leave. There was just a small group of them left sitting in the garden. Nathan was sitting next to Sadie and Isabel, then Isabel sprang from her chair to shake hands with some guests who were going.

"How about we go for a quiet drink later?" ventured Nathan, he had spent all day with her and now he wanted to make love to her.

Sadie eyed him pensively. For the first time in her life she didn't want her encounter with him to just be about sex. She had no doubt they would end up in the back seat of his car. It wouldn't be quite like last Saturday, when she had comforted him when he was so distressed about Melissa. She had just spent a whole day with him, and her body ached to feel his gentle hands on her.

"Maybe. After Danielle is asleep," she said. But who was she kidding? After Danielle was in bed she was longing to spend some private time with him. She looked around for her daughter. "Where is she, anyway?"

"Oh, she popped inside a few minutes ago."

Sadie got up and went to find Danielle, but as she searched the house, and called her, there was no response. She must be out in the garden. She searched every part of the garden, and by now she was joined by Nathan and her parents, and they all kept saying, "She won't be far."

But Sadie wasn't listening to anyone; panic was sweeping through her, where could she be? She wouldn't have gone with any of her friends and she never left the house without her family. She felt sick and ill, and was totally distraught.

But then it hit her like a very heavy sledge hammer. What a fool she had been! Mad Alice had been spying on them; she wanted Danielle, she always had, so she had kidnapped her. Now she felt a mixture of anger and anguish rise inside her. That bitch had her daughter. She was so mad, she might even harm her!

"She's been kidnapped. It's Alice, I know it is. She's been spying on us."

"Are you sure?" said Isabel. She couldn't stop shaking,

Danielle spending time with that unstable woman did not sit well with her.

Philip tried to be the voice of reason. "We need to call the police. She can't have gone far, it's only a few minutes since we saw her." He picked up the telephone.

"Daddy, I can't wait that long, I need to find her myself. She's not safe with Alice."

Nathan looked at her set face; what a brave woman she was. No histrionics from Sadie, just a deadly calm, she didn't waste her time weeping and wailing, she did what she had to.

"I will come with you," he said, grabbing her arm. "Quick let's get in the car!"

He could see by their faces that Philip and Isabel were about to tell them to wait for the police and not to do anything stupid, and they were probably right, but nothing was going to stop Sadie, and he wanted to be right by her side giving his support. He quickly picked up his car keys, and by the time they had exited the drive, Sadie was pointing along the road towards Beltinge.

"Go that way, I think she would have headed away from the town. Just a gut feeling, you know!"

"We'll find them, don't worry." He pressed her fingers for the second time today.

"We will," said Sadie, her dark eyes showing her anger, "and when we do, Alice is in big trouble."

"Yes she is!" echoed Nathan. "If it's Alice she's a fool, she can't get away with it."

Chapter Sixteen

When Alice left the Morton Brown family, and Danielle, it had devastated her. Putting on a bold front, and appearing not to care when she was with Philip and Isabel, had been hard but necessary for the sake of her pride. But when she got in the car and drove away, the tears had blinded her and she couldn't stop sobbing, so she had pulled into a quiet car park at the top of Bishopstone Glen, and then given vent to her emotions.

She didn't know or care if anyone sitting in the other two cars parked there could see her, and eventually when all her tears had been shed, she found some tissues, wiped her face and blew her nose. The thought of never seeing Danielle again, the little girl who had come to mean so much to her, was overwhelming, and she felt totally unable to cope with life, even wondering whether suicide would be the answer.

But then jealousy and hatred towards Sadie stirred inside her, it was totally overwhelming, and her thoughts turned to everything that had happened since she met Sadie. She remembered how she had planned to use Sadie to get revenge on Danny for dumping her. But in the end the thought of them both together had crucified her, she couldn't bear it. And then Sadie had borne his child, which made it even worse.

Sadie was completely evil, she had got away with killing her own brother, and it was Sadie's fault that her beloved twin Sarah had taken her own life, so Alice decided she had to pay, and it had been so easy to pin the blame on her for the murder of Danny. But she hadn't reckoned on there not being conclusive evidence that

Danny had been murdered, or the second twist when it had been decided that Sadie was insane and she would be locked away and unable to harm anyone.

That had been the best news that Alice could hear and, just to make sure she had revenge on her, she had become a nanny to Danielle, her daughter, how it would hurt Sadie to know that. But Alice hadn't reckoned on the overwhelming love she would feel for that little girl, a love so strong she could almost believe she had given birth to her. She had none of her mother's evil inside her. She might resemble her in looks, but her nature was sunny and uncomplicated. The last five years had been happy for Alice, with Sadie out of the way, and watching Danielle grow into a cheeky, feisty, but totally loveable child had been so rewarding. But then that evil bitch had returned, and it had all been taken away from her.

But she knew what she must do. Sadie's parents were blind and stupid. They might have money, but they didn't have a brain cell between them if they thought they could all play happy families. It was clear in Alice's mind that she had to remove Danielle from that house and take her away to somewhere safe, and then she could grow up away from the evil influence of her mad mother.

She decided to stay close by. She owed it to Danielle not to be too far away from her. So she spent the first couple of weeks at a local Premier Inn. It was close to the house, so she drove past at least once a day, but never saw anyone. Philip had stuck to his word, and money was paid into her bank account regularly.

Then she took her car over to a garage at Ashford and traded it in for another one. They would not recognise the red Ford Fiesta, as before she had had a blue Renault Clio. Next she moved into the disused caravan on the farm, which was situated halfway between Bishopstone and Reculver. The farmer and his wife had taken a long holiday in Australia for some six weeks or more and their son was care taking the farm. He had told Alice all about it in the local pub one evening. The field where the caravan was situated held no interest for him, it had no crops or animals in it, so she had parked her car up a lane, bought some cleaning products, and made the caravan habitable for the short time she would need it.

Now she was no longer working she had a lot of time on her hands. After buying a few new clothes and shoes she became bored. She was so drawn to the house, and her longing to see Danielle welled up inside and almost choked her. She tried to subdue the feeling, but it was enveloping her like a big blanket. She didn't feel complete without Danielle, and as each day passed, she was finding it hard to eat or sleep. Common sense and logic had long since deserted her, all she knew was that she needed to get Danielle away from her evil mother and they could start a new life together.

One evening, as dusk was falling, she parked her car in a side street and crept up to the wooden gate that led out to the downs. She stood there looking longingly up at Danielle's bedroom window. Her baby would be in there getting ready for bed, and she wasn't there to read her bedtime story to her. The tide had come in, bringing some wind with it, so she pulled the black jacket around her and buttoned the hood. There was a slight chink in the curtains, and suddenly there was Danielle's face peering out, and Alice's heart turned over with emotion. Without even thinking, she raised her hand in greeting to her, but as soon as she heard the scream she realised that she might have frightened her, because Danielle wouldn't have known it was Alice.

She vanished as quickly as she had appeared, it wouldn't do for anyone to see her; knowing Sadie she would have the police after her saying she had been hassling them. But the urge to see Danielle only got stronger. Her baby was living her life without Mama Alice, and that had to be put right. She knew Saturday was a day when Danielle went to ballet, so this time she sat in her new car on a rainy day, waiting for someone to sweep past with the little girl inside the car.

But when it didn't happen, she was overcome with curiosity to satisfy herself that everything was all right. Her jacket concealed most of her and the road was deserted, and as she approached the wooden gate, she quickly glanced around her, but the road remained empty. Without even thinking about it, she scaled the low gate, it might be padlocked, but if they thought that would keep her out they had another think coming.

She crept towards the lounge window without thinking about the huge risk she was taking. When she peered in there was no sign of Danielle, only Sadie and, as she turned to flee, her foot touched against a rock, dislodging it, and the noise it made caused Sadie to scream out. She had to run fast. She found her car, jumped in and left the scene, but all the while she was wondering what Sadie had done with her daughter, and her imagination was working overtime. Was her baby even safe any more. After that she had hung around outside her school a couple of times, and was relieved to see Danielle arrive at school with her mother one morning. She had to duck down as they walked past, so as not to be recognised, and it was all she could do to squash down the raging jealousy inside her when she saw Danielle clutching trustingly at her mother's hand, just like she had done in the past with Alice.

She decided that the day of the party would be the time to put her plan into action, so she was up early that hot day. She put her long hair back from her face, and found some dark glasses and a straw sun hat, so her appearance would not be glaringly obvious to anyone who might spot her.

She was sitting in her car when the guests started to arrive, and to her great satisfaction it was as she expected, the iron gates remained open, and the little wooden gate leading to the front door was not padlocked. With so many people coming in and out, security had to be relaxed, so she was able to slip inside unseen and watch what was going on.

But watching didn't do her any good. Seeing Danielle playing with her friends was OK, but when she was with her grandparents, Sadie, and Nathan, then it caused Alice insane jealousy, growing like a cancer inside her, and multiplying, totally destroying any rational thoughts. Sadie was the main focus of her hatred, and her closeness to Nathan was apparent, which only fuelled Alice's hatred more; Sadie had succeeded with him, whereas Alice had failed.

As the afternoon wore on, she changed her position several times, and by the time the guests were leaving, she was pleased to see that Danielle had left the family group to go indoors to the bathroom. Alice did not even think about the risk she was taking. This might be the only chance to reach her darling child, so she took it, and followed her in.

As Danielle came out of the bathroom, she stiffened, wide-eyed with surprise at seeing Alice standing there with her arms outstretched to her, and she suddenly realised how much she had missed her. She ran to hug her.

"Mama Alice, I've missed you. Why did you leave us?"

132

Alice ignored the accusing tone of her voice. These cruel people had probably turned Danielle's mind of course, but once she was with her, she would be OK.

"I had to leave you, baby. Your mother came home to take care of you."

"Granny said you had gone to look after a baby."

"You are my baby. How about you and I going on holiday?" Danielle studied her, and thought intently.

"We need to ask Mummy, she will miss me."

Alice choked back the anger that raged through her. She had to tell her something quickly to get out of here before they were discovered.

"I have sorted it with your mummy, it's OK, baby. I am going to buy you some new things and then we can go, and guess what, tonight we are going to sleep in a caravan."

Danielle liked the idea of sleeping in a caravan, she never had before, and all her life she had trusted Alice, there was no reason not to, and if her mummy approved, then why not?

"Shall we go and say goodbye to them?"

"Oh, they just popped out, but we can Skype them later."

Once they were in the car she relaxed a bit more; her mission was accomplished. The caravan was only five minutes drive from the house, and Danielle was very excited. Alice had bought her some clothes and shoes, so once she had parked the car and taken her into the caravan, she showed them to her, and also two cases that were already packed. Alice planned to take her back to Spain. She knew she could rent an inexpensive apartment, then find a school for Danielle, and start a new life.

Luckily Danielle's passport was still stored in the drawer of the bureau in the lounge, along with all the others. Alice had rejoiced that they still hadn't locked them in a secure place. She had plane tickets for the next day, but in the meantime she had to make it seem like a game to Danielle, and she had to get her through that airport, onto the plane, and into Spain whilst her family were looking for her in England. She hoped they wouldn't immediately spot the missing passport.

Danielle slept fitfully that night, it had been a very exciting day, and she was exhausted. Alice was relieved, tomorrow they would drive to the airport and get the afternoon flight. Her car was going to have to be left at the airport, she would have to buy another one in Spain, but Philip's money would be funding that. Her hope was that Danielle would settle into her new way of life and go to a new school, and leave all her roots behind her. To Alice it felt wonderful to be reunited with her, but now she had to convince Danielle that only she, Alice, truly loved her, which should not be too hard because that is what Alice herself believed.

When Danielle woke up the next morning, the thrill of sleeping in a caravan was beginning to wear off. When she asked Alice if she could Skype Mummy on her iPad, Alice said Mummy was out, and so were her grandma and grandad. There was something different about Alice that made Danielle miss her family even more. She seemed edgy and in a hurry and, although only five, she could sense there was something wrong. When she found out they were going to Spain she wasn't sure she wanted to. All the glamour of leaving the house last night had vanished and now she wanted to go home.

"I went to Portugal with Mummy, but flying is boring."

Alice was finding this all very traumatic. In just a few weeks her control over Danielle had gone. She kept hankering for her family, and she didn't want to go to Spain. How could she make her happy and win her back?

"I tell you what, we are not leaving just yet and our fairy godmother says she will grant you one wish."

She hoped it was something that she could give her, but at least it was distracting her from asking to go home.

"My wish is to go to the Fairy Glen, stand on the bridge, and see if we can see any fairies."

Ever since she was a tiny baby, Alice had taken her to the Fairy Glen. It was Danielle's favourite place, and she still believed in fairies, and had a vivid imagination, so the idea of fairies hiding under that bridge and only coming out at night, really appealed to her.

Alice relaxed a bit. Bishopstone Glen was less than a mile up the road; it had once housed gypsy caravans, but now it was a local beauty spot with an abundance of birds and wildlife. Danielle would want to stand on the little wooden bridge, and maybe after she could walk her round the winding path which led around the headland, and she could hold her hand whilst they looked down the rugged cliffs onto the beach below.

When they got there, Alice was wondering whether it was such a good idea. A fine Sunday meant the car park was full, and on the beach there were families picnicking, barbecuing sausages, the occasional swimmer could be seen, and dogs everywhere. But sometimes there is safety in numbers. Alice had watched Meridian News reporting on Danielle's disappearance last night when Danielle was asleep, they had even showed a picture of herself and asked if she would come forward to help them with their enquiries.

Alice pulled her sun hat a bit lower; she had also bought one for Danielle, and tied her beautiful black hair back into a ponytail. Holding hands they tiptoed onto the little bridge with the water gushing below on its way to the beach. A couple of cyclists had dismounted to walk their cycles over the bridge in obedience to the sign which said 'No cycling'; they were deep in conversation, and barely noticed them. Alice stood there, whilst Danielle's eyes widened with excitement and her imagination took over. She clapped her hands over her mouth to show how quiet she was being, and it lasted all of two minutes before she whispered into Alice's ear.

"I saw a fairy over there, but she's gone under the bridge."

Alice played along with it, pretending to look along the river bank, and as she could see a group coming from the beach, she managed to edge Danielle around to the 'fairy path', as they called it; it was quite overgrown now, and the long grass shielded them from view. She was planning to walk around the headland before getting Danielle into the car and driving to the airport. Glancing back, she heard the shout, and saw Sadie and Nathan crossing the bridge.

Chapter Seventeen

Nathan drove all around the area, and Sadie was hoping for a sight of Alice's blue car. They scoured the beach and cliffs, then tried Bishopstone Glen, even venturing along the clifftop path, which was now vastly overgrown. They asked at the local general store if anyone had seen a woman with reddish brown hair accompanied by a five year old girl with black hair, but no one had. It was as if Alice and Danielle had just vanished into thin air.

After an hour of fruitless searching, Nathan suggested they return home. He was as angry and concerned as Sadie was, silently wishing that they had all listened to Sadie more. He had believed her when she said that Alice was mad and dangerous, but he wasn't sure her parents knew what to believe, and none of them had even contemplated that Alice would do this.

At home detective inspector Ryan Jones was questioning her parents. Did they think Alice was holding Danielle for ransom? But Sadie firmly assured him that it was not as simple as that. Alice wanted Danielle, she had taken her somewhere where they couldn't find her, so they could start a new life.

Ryan eyed her with interest. He knew the story, but what a turn up for the books. Whilst they were all keeping an eye on Sadie, it was Alice who had flouted the law and kidnapped the very child she had cared for during the last five years. Sadie's sultry beauty did not escape his attention, and he saw anxiety and concern in those dark eyes of hers, and anger when she spoke of Alice, but could he blame her? She had come home to build a new life, and look what had happened to her.

"Don't worry, Miss Morton Brown, we will find her. They can't have gone far yet, we have a description of the car, and the number plates."

Sadie was not so convinced. Damn the police, they took their time, they didn't know what the word emergency meant.

"She's with a mad woman, and you expect me to not be worried. My daughter is everything to me!" The passion and emotion in her voice was not lost on Nathan. He put an arm protectively around her shoulder and she didn't resist him.

"We are grateful for your help, but time is of the essence; Alice may not be responsible for her own actions."

Isabel was twisting her hands together, not knowing what to say, she had always trusted Alice with Danielle. Even when Nathan had told them about Alice apparently trying to frame Sadie for the murder of Danny, they hadn't been sure. There had been so many different accounts of things, in the end they didn't know who to believe.

Philip had taken the precaution of checking the passports, and his heart lurched when he realised Danielle's was not there. He came into the lounge to deliver the bad news.

"I am afraid Danielle's passport has gone."

There was a moment of silence, whilst everyone realised just what this meant. They could escape to anywhere in the world and never be traced. Sadie turned to Ryan, there was desperation in her voice. Danielle was everything to her, she could not bear to lose her.

"Please find her before she goes to the other side of the world. I can't live without her, she is my everything!"

"Don't worry, all the ports and air terminals will be checked, we will put out a message on the local news, they won't get far. But are you absolutely sure it's Alice Lorenzo who has taken her? We have no proof as yet."

Nathan felt Sadie's body tense with indignation, and he cut in quickly, anxious to ensure there were no harsh words said. He was only too aware that Sadie sometimes gave people the wrong impression of her.

"You are right inspector, we don't have any proof. But Alice has been spying on the house, and she has an unbalanced mind, and we always knew how much she had come to believe Danielle was her own child, so it's highly likely she has taken matters into her own hands."

137

Ryan left them promising to pull out all the stops to try and return Danielle safely to her family. He realised it was a delicate situation, they must hurry, maybe the local news wasn't enough, this needed to go nationwide.

Sadie didn't even try to go to bed, she spent the whole night pacing up and down. She was like a caged lion, wanting to escape, but where to? She had no idea what was in Alice's mind, or where she might have taken Danielle. Was Spain a possibility? Alice had connections there, and had lived there, but surely the mad cow would realise that Danielle would tell people who she was and ask for her family. But then the cold finger of doubt clutched at her heart; would Alice be enough for Danielle, and would she turn Danielle's mind against her family? The pain this caused wrenched at her stomach, and she ran into the cloakroom, and was just in time to stop herself vomiting all over the floor.

Nathan and her parents watched with horror, realising just how much this had devastated Sadie. She may have usually hidden her emotions but where Danielle was concerned she was all over the place. Isabel tried to be practical by making tea, something she usually left to Ann, but it was evening now and Ann had gone home.

Philip and Nathan dutifully sipped at theirs, but Sadie's remained untouched. Eventually Nathan persuaded her parents to get some sleep, promising to let them know if there was any news. They had all seen the local news, the photograph of Danielle smiling happily, and the request for Alice to contact them to help with the enquiries. Sadie and Isabel had said that tomorrow they would both make a plea on the national news, asking for the safe return of Danielle if nothing had happened.

Nathan watched her pacing up and down. He knew nothing he could say would make her sit down and relax, so he poured her a brandy and one for himself too. He watched her knock it back in one gulp; had it even touched the sides? He drank his more slowly; drink no longer dominated him, he was now the master of it.

It was close to dawn when she collapsed onto the sofa next to him and he stroked her hair until she fell into an exhausted sleep. They stayed like this until the sound of the telephone roused, not only them, but also Philip and Isabel who appeared at the door, their faces creased with worry and concern.

It was the police telling them that Alice's car had been traced to a garage at Ashford and the owner had told them she now had a red Fiesta, and Sadie wrote down the registration number. The police promised them the car description and registration would be circulated everywhere. Sadie just about remembered to thank them before replacing the receiver, and explaining this new development.

Ann had arrived and she carried on regardless making breakfast, then it was all laid out in the sunny breakfast room and Nathan put his foot down. Sadie was to eat some toast to help settle her stomach, the vomiting last night had left her looking pale and fragile. Her normal feisty attitude of not doing anything unless she wanted to was missing, she seemed like a zombie, this worried Nathan, he preferred it when Sadie argued with him: where was her spirit?

Sadie went through the motions of eating her toast and sipping a little orange juice; at this time she needed Nathan's strength. It felt like an earthquake was taking place inside her stomach. The warm sensation as the toast went down was soothing, she started to feel almost human again, and a new strength flooded through her; she couldn't give up, she must find her daughter.

"The police are busy looking all over the country you know, but they may not have even left this area yet. After all, if Alice saw the regional news, she might be too scared of being discovered to leave England."

Hope flooded through Sadie. Nathan spoke a lot of common sense, maybe Danielle wasn't too far away. She suddenly felt the urge to go into the Glen. It was a place where Danielle's imagination took over. She had enjoyed standing on that wooden bridge and seeing, through the eyes of a child, something as simple as fairies. In Danielle's mind, they were hidden underneath, and only came out when it was very quiet, with no one around.

"Nathan, let's go up to the Glen, it's her favourite place."

Looking at her pale face and haunting dark eyes, which looked even blacker against the pallor of her skin, Nathan realised she needed peace, and going somewhere that reminded her of Danielle might just help.

"Well OK, but don't forget that at midday you have to be around in case the police want you and Isabel to do your appeal," he reminded her.

Sadie nodded agreement, and after a hot shower and a change of clothes she felt a bit better. The toast had stayed down and she steeled herself to keep calm. Visiting the Glen would help, it was full of happy memories. When they were in the car she found herself squeezing Nathan's arm in a rare gesture of affection; his strength and solidarity were just what she needed, he was there beside her at one of the worst and most traumatic times of her life.

As they pulled into the car park overlooking the clifftop, Sadie's eyes travelled along the parked cars, and then to her amazement she saw the red Fiesta parked at the end. The registration was a combination she would never forget, MAD, an apt number for Alice she had thought at the time, and here was the very car, right under their noses whilst the police searched everywhere else.

"Nathan, it's the car, they are here!"

"Are you sure?"

"Certain!"

He screeched to a halt, and they both jumped out. Sadie was scouring the car park, and then she saw them, just above the long grass of the clifftop path. Her fury rose as she saw Alice, as bold as brass, urging Danielle along the path. How dare she, in broad daylight, entice her daughter along the headland, away from her family!

"There they are, we can stop them!"

Nathan had also spotted them, and he realised that Alice had looked back and seen them, which made her quicken her pace. He thought quickly about how dangerous the situation was. They were heading along a narrow path with a steep drop towards the sea from the rugged cliffs, emotions were running high between Alice and Sadie, any wrong move could prove fatal for Danielle.

"Sadie, let me talk to her. Don't try to chase her, we mustn't put Danielle in danger!"

But once she had spotted them, Alice panicked; Danielle had seen them and cried out with happiness, "It's mummy and Nathan!" which only fuelled Alice's desperation. She had grabbed the little girl's hand and was dragging her away from them, even though she was crying and begging her to stop.

Nathan and Sadie ran after them. In her haste, Sadie had tripped and fallen in the long grass and Nathan stopped to help her up. She was angry with herself, Alice had rounded the headland now, she was at the top on a narrow strip of overgrown grass with the cliffs falling away behind them and the waves crashing on the rocks below as the tide came in. They rounded the final bend in the path, and her heart turned over as she saw Alice right at the edge, her eyes blazing, clutching her weeping daughter. The look in her eyes prohibited them coming any nearer, and Nathan put himself protectively in front of Sadie to try and calm the situation. He spoke calmly and slowly.

"Alice, you are frightening Danielle. This is silly, you know, please let her go."

Alice ignored him, her voice full of bitterness and hate as she flung her words at Sadie.

"You thought you had won, bitch, but I've got your most precious possession! You turned her against me, you and your pathetic excuse for a family!"

Danielle was sobbing and screaming with fear, but for the first time in her life, Alice was ignoring her. She didn't want to go anywhere with Alice any more. This was a side of her that was very frightening. When she had seen her mummy and Nathan she had felt safe, and she wanted to go home with them, but Alice wouldn't let her. She was being so nasty to mummy, and they were standing right near to the edge of the cliff, it was really scary. Alice was holding her so tightly, and all she wanted to do was run to the safety of her mother's arms.

For the first time in her life, Sadie kept her temper under control. She could see there was no reasoning with Alice. Her fear that Alice might harm her daughter completely overrode anything else, so she spoke calmly and reasonably to her, whilst keeping her hatred hidden inside.

"Alice, of course she doesn't hate you, none of us do. Let her go and we can work things out."

Alice was completely knocked off guard by the softness of Sadie's words, it was the opposite of what she had been expecting, and she momentarily relaxed her iron grip on Danielle. The little girl made a dash into Nathan's arms, sobbing with relief, and Sadie was able to take her away from the edge of the cliffs to the safety of the path.

Sadie hugged her with such relief. She didn't give a damn what happened to Alice, the mad cow had certainly shown them all how crazy she was! But she might have known that Nathan would try and calm the situation. Alice was right on the edge now, one step back and she would be gone, and Nathan was holding his hands out to her, trying to bring her back, all the while speaking calmly to her, promising they could help her.

But Alice wasn't finished yet. She wanted to make Sadie squirm; she may have lost Danielle, but Sadie wouldn't keep her either when they caught up with her.

"You think you are so smart Sadie, but I've always been one step ahead of you! You can't hurt me any more, you've done your worst, but they will catch up with you and then you will rot in jail, but this time I won't be there for Danielle, she only has your parents left."

Nathan was not quick enough to reach her. He watched with horror as Alice turned, and gave a blood curdling scream as she dived over the cliff; but instead of falling straight down, her body hit overhanging rocks, and bounced over and over until it finally came to rest on the beach below.

Sadie had managed to shield Danielle's face from the grim scene. There would be time enough later to explain that Alice had tripped and fallen over the cliff, and she had behaved that way because she wasn't very well. She would allow Danielle to remember Alice with fondness, not for Alice's sake, but for Danielle's, her daughter must be spared the pain. They were free of mad Alice.

Chapter Eighteen

Sadie was now entering a very contented period of her life. She no longer had the desire to move from one place to another. Canterbury was as far away as she wanted to be from her family, she was finally realising how important her family was to her. She felt guilty about the way she had misjudged her mother. She had wanted to believe her mother was bad, that might explain why Sadie had her own bad feelings inside her, and she had avoided the truth until Nathan had made her face up to it.

But now she was a mother, so bitterness and hate had no place in her life if she was to be an example to Danielle, and allow her daughter to grow up with the right values in life. She now had a warm relationship with both of her parents, not just Daddy, and it felt good. But she had an even stronger relationship with Nathan. He had been there for her when Alice had tried to do her worst, and afterwards, at the police inquiry, he had kept her calm during endless questions and insinuations. Then followed the post mortem, and as both Nathan and Sadie had said that Alice appeared to slip over the cliff, it was inevitable that the result would be an open verdict. Whether Alice meant it or not, no one except them knew, and it was a secret that would bind them together forever. Alice had proved by her actions that she was not sane, and both of Sadie's parents now wished they had listened to her more. They now believed it was Alice, and not Sadie, who had done the evil acts.

Nathan was falling more under Sadie's spell. If she was a witch, she was a good one in his opinion. She was an excellent mother, and her relationship with her parents was going from strength to strength. Whatever she may or may not have done in the past was really of no interest to him, it was the person she was now that he loved, and he knew she cared about him too. Now that everything had calmed down since the distressing death of Alice, he planned to ask her to marry him. She would have her wish to go and live in Canterbury; he would work from home, and visit the office maybe one day a week. That would work, and he wouldn't be sorry to leave the hubbub of London behind him. He was looking forward to going house hunting with Sadie. If she turned him down the first time he would try again until she said yes. He could see their life of happiness and excitement stretching out in front of them. Sadie was unique, fascinating and enigmatic, and he wanted to spend his whole life taming her, and understanding those hidden depths of her personality. Life with Sadie would never be dull.

Sadie had managed to put Alice's traumatic death behind her. In her eyes, without Alice, she was now free. But she had been concerned for Danielle. Alice had suffered a very violent end to her life, and Danielle had been a spectator to that, even though Sadie had shielded her eyes at the worst moment.

But it seemed that Alice's behaviour had frightened her, and Danielle was relieved to be back with her mother and grandparents in the place she felt safe. She accepted that Alice wasn't well and she had gone to heaven, and it was only a couple of weeks before she seemed to have moved on. Sadie was relieved that she hadn't suffered any lasting effects. Even after having Alice in her life for five years, Danielle had accepted her mother back willingly, and this gave Sadie the chance she wanted to prove she was worthy to care for her daughter. Everyone was so supportive, and life had never felt so good.

Nathan now came down every weekend, and she hadn't been able to stop herself from falling deeply in love with him. He had been at her side just when she needed him. His loyalty and strength had got her through a very difficult time, and loving him had changed her, there was a softness that was not just reserved for Danielle, she had finally put her bitter attitude behind her.

Sadie had always been the one who men came to, she attracted them like moths to a flame, and the power this gave her enabled her to control the relationship and end it when it suited her. But with Nathan it was different, he had always been his own person. In the beginning it had infuriated her, but now she liked his strength, and was happy for him to wear the trousers. Even she was surprised at how she had changed, but love does change everything.

Would she ever know peace through loving him so much? When they were apart she missed him, and she wondered who he was with and what he was doing. It wasn't that she didn't trust him, it was other women she didn't trust, and try as she might to subdue that other side of herself, she knew that if any woman showed any interest in him at all she would have to remove them from his life; that voice inside told her so frequently. Loving Nathan came at a price.

She wondered if anything would change between them if they lived together, but why would it? The trauma they had been through had only bound them closer together. She knew Nathan could be a bit bossy at times, but she could give as good back. She enjoyed their bantering as much as he did and, if she capitulated to his ideas, it was because she wanted to, it was just that he had thought of it first.

Tonight, after he arrived from London, they were going for a quiet drink and a meal in Canterbury. It was now mid-September, three months since that fateful day in the Glen. The school holidays were over and the weather was still mild and pleasant. Danielle seemed to like the idea of her mummy and Nathan being close, as did Isabel and Philip. In the past Sadie, out of sheer defiance, would have done the opposite of what they expected, but this was Nathan, and she liked the idea that everyone approved.

She had to control herself from running out when she heard his car come through the iron gates and up the drive. But it didn't stop Danielle, and when he came in, she was clutching his hand excitedly, asking him endless questions, and he was grinning and teasing her by giving silly answers which made her laugh.

After they had put Danielle to bed and read to her, they checked with Isabel that she was happy to babysit. Philip had gone down to the angling club for a drink, but Isabel had declined to accompany him.

"I hope it wasn't because of us, we can always have a drink here and an Indian takeaway," said Nathan, noting that Isabel looked a little pale and tired tonight.

g

"No, it's fine. I have a headache, so I won't be up late," said Isabel. "You go out and have a good time, we will be OK."

"If you are sure," said Sadie. "Danielle is already asleep, she was tired."

The restaurant that Nathan had booked was fairly full. Its Indian cuisine was well known, so there was no way he was going to pop the question in front of the rest of the world. They both enjoyed a tasty meal and drank a bottle of wine between them. Nathan was glad they had taken a taxi. When they reached the Ship Inn on the seafront, he got the driver to drop them there for a night cap. The house was just a short walk up the hill.

Although the locals were in there, he managed to find a quiet corner, and this time they ordered coffee. His days of over indulging on alcohol were way behind him now, he didn't need drink to stimulate him, just having Sadie by his side did that. He felt drunk with love, but he wasn't a romantic sort of person, and found the thought of going on one knee a bit old fashioned and embarrassing. He wondered whether Sadie could sense his awkwardness; to him it was glaringly obvious. But Sadie had other thoughts on her mind.

"Now that things have calmed down, I might talk to Daddy about moving to Canterbury."

He wasn't sure if she was deliberately being provocative. Sadie was feisty, and she loved to wind him up, but this time she had given him the perfect opportunity to say his piece.

"Why don't you move to Canterbury with me? I am buying a house there."

Sadie looked surprised, but she couldn't help a thrill of excitement going through her at the thought of him living so close. This was like a bolt out of the blue.

"You never said! You want me to move in with you, and Danielle, of course?"

"Well that's what people do when they get married."

He heard his voice saying these words, and then there was silence; and he watched Sadie take a slow sip of her coffee, and her face was completely impassive. My God, what was wrong with this woman, did she have no feelings for him?

Sadie kept her feelings in. Her heart was singing, but Nathan joked about so many things. He had once told her many years ago that he wasn't the marrying kind, and she reminded him of this.

146

"Sadie, I am not that person any more, you know that! You're a beautiful witch, and I want to spend my life with you and Danielle."

He was relieved it was finally out. The joy on her face was apparent, and when he slipped the diamond ring on her finger, that he had taken so long to choose in an effort to get it right, he could have sworn he saw tears shimmering in her eyes.

They were both on a high when they left the pub, and throwing caution to the winds, they crept down onto the beach and stripped naked, then jumped in the sea, laughing like children as the waves broke against their bare flesh. After they came out of the water, they lay panting on the beach, and then he made love to her. For Sadie this was the most poignant lovemaking yet; she had his ring on her finger, so he didn't just think of her as a good lay. This was one time in her life, as it had been with Ricky, of course, a man respected her, and it felt good.

Nathan looked at this woman who had come to mean everything to him. Oh, how everyone had misjudged her. She was a loving mother, a good daughter, and would make a fascinating wife. There was no one quite like Sadie, and he was so grateful that he had been given another chance with her, because he had certainly messed it up big time on the first occasion. She might be a little selfish, and spoiled, but with him she wouldn't get away with it. Perhaps he had better warn her.

"Well, Miss Morton Brown, your life with me will be very different. No housekeepers or nannies, just you, me and Danielle, plus as many kids as we can make together."

At one time Sadie would have rejected this suggestion, but she wanted to be a proper wife. She had learned a bit about cooking in America, thanks to Colleen, and the thought of cleaning her own house and making it nice appealed to her. She might even get a part time job whilst Danielle was at school; nothing fancy, maybe working in a clothes or shoe shop. A brother and sister for Danielle was an exciting thought. Could her life get any better?

"OK," she smiled at his cheekiness, what this guy could get away with was unbelievable! "Let's go and break the news to my parents. We have a wedding to plan."

But even as she said these words, a feeling of uneasiness swept through her. She felt the presence of Alice, even though her mind was unwilling to let her in. She remembered Alice's last words before she plunged over the clifftop:

". . .they will catch up with you and then you will rot in jail, but this time I won't be there for Danielle, she only has your parents left."

What had Alice meant by those words? Who would catch up with her, the police? She had always covered her tracks well, and felt she was invincible. Did Alice know something she didn't? So many questions with no answers. Nathan had dismissed her words as the ramblings of a mad and obsessed woman, but then Nathan had never delved into Sadie's past. He said it didn't matter to him, it was the woman she was now that counted.

Remembering this gave her some comfort, and she spoke sternly to herself for allowing something like this to spoil her moment of happiness. She suddenly realised they were still naked.

"Well, let's get dressed and then go and see them, I don't think somehow Mummy would approve."

Nathan tweaked her bare boob and picked up his clothes.

"Come on sexy, bet I can get dressed before you."

Isabel was glad everyone had left her tonight. She had so much on her mind, and keeping up a pretence that everything was all right would be impossible for her. She had been given the worst news ever earlier today, she wanted to share it with Philip before anyone, and she wondered how he would cope with it.

For over thirty years now, there had been so many traumas to cope with. Being raped by her brother, and then keeping it from Philip. The loss of her beautiful son Jeremy. Sadie's behaviour as a child, then her arrest and the possibility that she might be a very evil woman. Then recently the realisation that they had allowed an insane person to care for their precious Danielle, and the shock of her untimely death. No one could wish that on another person. If only Alice could have got the help she needed, it was incredibly sad. .

But then it seemed as if life was getting better for all of them. Sadie had become warmer and softer, and Isabel had been amazed at the change in her character. Being a mother to Danielle had brought out a different side to her, one that Isabel could love, and

148

then there was Nathan, it was clear how much respect Sadie had for him, it showed in her eyes.

When Isabel had found the lump on her breast she had been a bit worried, but she knew that nine out of ten of these were often nothing, and she didn't feel ill, nor have any pain. She had gone to the doctor feeling fairly confident that his diagnosis would be a non malignant growth. He had been very kind, and gently told her not to worry. The good thing about having a private doctor was she could be seen immediately, so he had done a biopsy that same day, and she had waited the required time, and then phoned up for her result.

But the receptionist had refused to discuss the results with her, which put her in a panic, so she had insisted that she speak to the doctor. But he had been just as secretive, just asking her to come and see him, and she knew then, instinctively, that something was wrong.

She was filled with horror, and she couldn't bear to tell anyone. It took all of Isabel's courage to go to the doctor. She had faced so many crises in her life, and somehow coped, but this time it was too much. She didn't want to believe the words he said with a grave face. They were the words that no woman wants to hear, and now it seemed her life was over. But before she departed this world she wanted to cleanse her mind of the terrible secret she had kept from Philip all these years. She could not go to her maker without being honest with him. Philip had always been, and would remain, her inspiration in life. He had helped her deal with the loss of Jeremy, and everything else that life threw at them. His calmness had been balm to her emotional nature, and she could never imagine life without him. Even though she was of a stronger nature, he was her rock and her safe haven, and now she needed him even more than ever before.

Whilst Danielle was sleeping and the house was quiet she took a bath. She deliberately kept her eyes away from the disgusting lump that had done its worst, and ruined her life. It might only be small, but it was toxic, and she hated the poison it was spreading inside her.

When Philip arrived home she was sitting in the lounge waiting for him, dressed in her night clothes and dressing gown. He knew straightaway by the bleak expression on her face that something was very wrong. He went over to her and gently touched her hand. He could see she wasn't angry; on her face was a look of resignation, which scared him, this just was not his feisty wife Isabel.

"Philip, I am going to die, but before I go, I want to share something with you I have carried around for years."

In all their years together, Isabel had always been a bit on the dramatic side, as was Sadie, it was something he believed that women liked to do to get your attention, but this last statement surely must be a joke? There she sat, maybe a little pale, but still very beautiful, how could she possibly be about to die?

"Don't say such a thing, how can you?"

The anguish in his eyes cut through her like a razor blade. She didn't want to hurt him, but she so needed his quiet strength!

"I have breast cancer."

"But that does not mean you are going to die. I will get the best Harley Street specialists. Lots of women have treatment and survive."

Philip had tears in his eyes as he said it. They had been through so much over the years, and just as life seemed to be getting better this cruel thing had happened. He couldn't lose her now. He didn't care right now what she had to tell him, he just wanted to give her and himself some hope.

He knelt in front of her chair, cupping her tear-stained face gently.

"I am going to be here for you all the way; we will beat it you know. How far advanced is it?"

He held his breath waiting for her answer, and inwardly praying it was not as bad as she had made it sound.

Isabel wiped her eyes with a tissue. She was feeling a bit better now she had told him.

"The surgeon says they can operate, but I may lose my left breast, then I have to have radiotherapy afterwards, and chemotherapy too. I won't be a woman any more, I won't be whole, and I am not sure I have the courage to go through with it. If I decline the treatment it will spread and I will die."

"Isabel, losing a breast does in no way compare to losing your life, and it will make no difference to me. I have always loved you, and I always will, with or without it!"

His words were so comforting. She had worried that he would no longer find her attractive, he might even find himself another woman. Maybe she was being ridiculous, but at the moment she was all over the place. She hugged him to her, his strength gave her new hope.

"I have to give the surgeon my decision by tomorrow. Oh Philip, I am so scared."

"Of course you are, but I will come with you to the surgery, we will find out exactly what we need to know, and I will support you all the way! Now what did you want to share with me that is worrying you?"

His words had inspired her, perhaps she wasn't going to die. But it made no difference, it was time Philip knew the truth about what had happened that terrible night, now over thirty years ago, but still imprinted in her mind. So she explained everything, how her brother had come to see her in such an angry mood, then he had raped her. Her shock when she was pregnant, and although she should have maybe had an abortion, she had thought it would hurt Philip if he thought it was his child. Then she finished off by saying that although she had never done a DNA test, she believed her brother was Sadie's biological father.

Whilst she sat there holding his hand explaining everything, she noticed that Philip's demeanour did not change. There was no expression of shock and horror on his face, which really surprised her, and when she had finished, she sat there waiting for some sort of reaction from him.

He was calmly stroking her fingers now, and he digested her words before he replied to her.

"You are not the only person who has kept a secret my love, and as we are having complete honesty, I can only hope you will forgive, and still love me after I have confessed."

Isabel was visibly surprised, and she gave him her full attention. Her news hadn't caused him to bat an eyelid. What confession could he possibly have to make?

"I was passing your house that night on my way home. If you remember after so long, we had agreed that I wouldn't see you, you were tired and wanted an early night."

Isabel nodded, and he continued.

"Joey came out. He was very angry and he swore at me, then he told me what he had done. He was laughing and mocking, and I was incensed with rage. It was obvious he was drunk, but I knew at that moment he was not in his right mind. Anyone who can do

151

that to their sister and then jeer about it is not right in the head. I lost my temper and knocked him to the ground, and believe me it took all my will power not to knock on your door and come and see you."

"What happened after that. . ?"

"He got up, then got in his car and drove furiously away. I should have stopped him, he was drunk, a liability on the road, but my anger overtook any rational feelings I might have had, so I just let him go. I wanted him out of my sight."

"You knew, but you never told me," said Isabel wonderingly. "Joey was responsible for his own death, not you, he should not have been driving, and I don't want you to blame yourself. Your reaction was normal."

"When you said you were pregnant I always knew there was a chance Sadie might not be mine. But Isabel, I never cared, a drop of sperm doesn't make a father. It's the years you spend bringing up the child that count, so Sadie was always going to be mine, I held your hand when she was born. We will never know for sure, but it doesn't matter, Sadie is our daughter."

Isabel leaned against his shoulder shedding tears for all those years she had struggled to keep a secret from Philip that he already knew. But now that they had spoken about that traumatic night she felt as though the weight of the whole world had been lifted from her shoulders. Then she remembered, these revelations would not take her cancer away. The thought of the operation and the treatment was very daunting, but Philip made her feel safe, and his support and strength would help her to fight it. She wasn't ready to give up on life yet, she wanted to see Danielle grow up, and now that her relationship with Sadie had changed, she wanted to savour that too.

All those years of not understanding her daughter, and not being able to love her, had been firmly put behind her. Sadie was turning into a daughter they could be proud of and, as Philip said, it was best not to know who had fathered her, because he had brought her up, and was her father in every sense of the word.

Chapter Nineteen

"Mummy and Daddy, what's wrong, you look so serious?"

Sadie was just about to deliver their exciting news, but Nathan touched her arm gently in an effort to suppress her. Isabel and Philip sat with very sober faces in the lounge. There were streaks on her mother's face and it was clear to see she had been crying.

Philip was sitting beside her, but he looked very anxious and he was patting her hand in an effort to comfort her. He spoke slowly: "Your mother has been diagnosed with breast cancer, it is treatable, but she needs our support."

"Oh no, Mummy! I am so sorry."

Sadie was astounded; this was a huge shock, Mummy had always been so healthy. She really did care, and she wondered why it had to happen to them. This family just seemed to stagger from one crisis to another. She wanted to make up for the lost years when she had been warring with Isabel.

"I am seeing the surgeon tomorrow," said Isabel.

"Yes, and I am going too," Philip reminded her.

Suddenly Sadie's mind was working overtime. If her mother was having an operation, she would need time to get well, and there would probably be more treatment after. There was no way she could even think about planning a wedding, it would have to be put on hold until her mother was well enough to take an active role in the whole thing. For the first time in her life, Sadie thought about someone other than herself.

"Mummy, don't worry, I will support you all the way; so will Nathan."

To which Nathan nodded his agreement.

Sadie tried to sound casual when she made the announcement: "Nathan and I just got engaged."

Isabel temporarily forgot her woes. "Oh, that is wonderful, we are thrilled for you, aren't we, Philip?"

Philip enthusiastically nodded his agreement, if he could have chosen a husband for Sadie he would not have hesitated to choose Nathan, especially as he was already part of the family. The Sadie of old would not have done anything her parents approved of, as the rebel in her would make her prove she had her own mind. He was so relieved she had finally grown up.

But this happy news had come at the wrong time, because Isabel would be laid up for a while and wouldn't need the extra stress that planning a wedding would mean. He hoped his next question didn't sound off-putting.

"So when do you plan to finally tie the knot?"

"Oh, there's no rush," Sadie said airily, "probably no sooner than next year."

Inside she was agonising. The idea of being married to Nathan, having her own home and more babies gave her a wonderful feeling of security. She would have liked it to happen as soon as possible but, in this instance, her mother came first. She would need help and support over the next few months, maybe even longer, so no way was Sadie going to give her extra worry. Even with a wedding planner, it was still time consuming and stressful. Her mother needed to attend this wedding in the best possible health. She might even lose her hair when she had the treatment, so until she was well, regrettably, the wedding had to be put on hold.

"I hope it's not because I am ill," said Isabel anxiously.

"Not at all. We want to be engaged for a while," said Nathan, very convincingly. He wanted to make Isabel feel better. He knew how excited Sadie had been about planning the wedding, and now it was clear she was putting her mother first this time. His admiration of her grew even more; the selfish Sadie had gone, and in her place was someone who really cared. It was amazing how she was changing. She was a great mother and she would make a very caring wife.

He winked at Sadie. It was as though she had read his thoughts. They both knew why they were pretending there was no rush; for

Isabel's sake, but they didn't need to admit it and make her feel bad about it. So Nathan made one of his cheeky remarks.

"Well, when Sadie finds out that I snore, she might wish she hadn't married me, so I might as well enjoy being engaged first."

Sadie laughed and dug him playfully, and the mood lightened. They steered the conversation away from Isabel's distressing news; but even though they all made banter to keep Isabel's spirits up, it remained very much in their minds.

It wasn't long before they all retired to bed, and Philip promised that they would know what was happening the moment they returned from their appointment with the surgeon. Philip was not at all keen on anything medical; he never went to the doctor himself unless it was absolutely necessary, and steered clear of hospitals, but for Isabel he would make the exception, she was his love and his life.

Later the next morning they all sat down as a family whilst Philip and Isabel explained what was going to happen. The surgeon had suggested that as her lump was in the early stages, it could be operated on right now without removing her breast, and then a course of radiotherapy and chemo would follow. The prognosis was good, and her surgeon had applauded her for going to him so early and avoiding the operation to have one or both breasts removed. He did explain that chemotherapy would make her feel unwell, but there was plenty of support to help her cope. He had also been pleased to see that Philip had come with her.

"Oh Mummy, that is good. If you want me to come with you when you have the chemo, I don't mind," said Sadie.

Philip shot her a grateful look. If Sadie also wanted to be involved it would take quite a weight off his shoulders, he didn't do hospitals that well. The surgeon had explained that the chemotherapy would take place at a local cottage hospital, and that the treatment was intense and Isabel would not feel at all well afterwards. Seeing Isabel suffering would be hard for Philip, he was used to his wife being strong, healthy and in control of herself and her life. He knew he was being cowardly, he would always stick by her, but having the support of Sadie as well meant a lot.

Isabel took her mind off her own predicament, remembering what the doctor had said.

"Sadie, they have now discovered a gene that causes cancer and it can run in families, so you and Danielle have to be tested to make sure you are not carrying it."

Sadie looked at her in horror. She had never really thought about her health, she was rarely ill.

She always thought that cancer was something other people got, and as for little Danielle, the thought that she might develop it later made her feel sick inside; nothing nasty must ever touch her precious daughter.

"OK Mummy, we will take the test."

She knew she could not refuse. Apparently the sooner they knew, the more they could do about it. The thought of losing her breasts filled her with dread. She wanted to be sexy and attractive for Nathan for as long as she could. If she needed cosmetic surgery in later years, to improve herself, she would not hesitate, but the possibility of going under the surgeon's knife to have her breasts removed reminded her that she was not invincible, she could be touched by cancer too, and the thought of it made her shudder.

Nathan hid his anguish from them. Not Sadie too, his love, hadn't she been touched by enough tragedy in her short twenty-nine years? He spoke confidently, hoping his words would come true.

"Thank you for telling us, Isabel. Of course they have to do that, but I am sure it's just a precaution. Nowadays prevention is better than ever."

He put his arm protectively around Sadie's shoulders. Her courage in supporting her mother was so unselfish, and he would support her in the same way, whatever the outcome of the tests.

Isabel's surgery took place on the following Tuesday. It all went as planned and she was allowed home very quickly. Because they had left her breasts intact her recovery was quick, and after a couple of weeks, the surgeon decided she was fit enough to start on her treatment sessions. Sadie and Danielle had taken the test, and to Sadie's immense relief, the results came back that neither of them had the cancer gene. Danielle didn't fully understand the concept of this illness, so Sadie had said that God was taking care of them both, and when she put Danielle to bed that night, they both knelt in prayer to thank God for being spared from carrying the cancer gene.

Sadie kept her word, and attended every single session with her mother. She had to remain outside whilst her mother was having the treatment, but she was there when Isabel came out, to support her and drive her home. Sometimes they had to stop on the road whilst her mother got out, and then Sadie had to hold Isabel's hair back from her face whilst she vomited in the kerb. It made Isabel feel as though she had lost all her dignity, and she frequently felt glad that Philip wasn't there to see her like this. No woman would like her husband to see her in this sort of state, and she was worried that anyone passing would think she was drunk. But when people stared, Sadie soon sorted them out, and angrily told them to walk on because her mother was ill.

Most of them did, but on one occasion a nurse stopped on her way home. She realised that something was wrong and came over to them. Sadie had explained that her mother had just had a session of chemotherapy, and the young nurse had expressed her sympathy, which was of comfort to Isabel; she really didn't want to be like this, but she had no control over it. The nurse had advised Sadie to get her home as soon as possible, and then Isabel should rest, and whilst she was receiving this treatment, do very little and take life easy.

Luckily for Isabel, because she had a housekeeper, and money was not a problem, she was able to do all this. Her constant feelings of nausea forced her to lie down a lot when she wasn't visiting the hospital, and she started to lose weight because she couldn't eat much. Sadie was alarmed to see her mother apparently fading away. Her face looked gaunt and the illness had aged her. One morning when she went into her room, it was to find Isabel had not got out of bed.

"Come on Mummy, you have a session today," she said, wondering why Isabel was not up. Was all this medication affecting her mother's memory?

Isabel covered her face and her body racked with sobs.

"I can't get up, I haven't got the strength, and now my hair is falling out. Sadie, I can't deal with it any more, leave me alone."

Sadie became angry because she knew that sympathy was not going to work.

"No I won't leave you alone. You will get out of bed, I will help you to dress, and then we are going to the hospital. As for your hair, the surgeon said it would fall out, but when you are better, it will grow back. In the meantime we'll find you a wig, any colour or style you fancy."

Isabel looked at her daughter and saw the determination in her eyes. She didn't want to give up and die, but the months of continual nausea had weakened her body and her spirit. Sadie's anger somehow inspired her. So after being helped to wash and dress, she allowed Sadie to take her for her session, and then afterwards they went to choose a black wig, which was very similar to her own hair.

Sadie felt very sad to see her mother declining. Her weight loss didn't suit her. It went from her face and neck, which aged her, and she looked gaunt. Then she lost her hair, which was her crowning glory, and she was left with thin little wisps like a baby. She very bravely had them shaved off, and with the encouragement of Sadie, Philip and Nathan, wore her new wig.

It was a huge surprise to Sadie just how ill she was, because she had thought that, as her mother was in the early stages, she would be OK. She frequently reminded herself how glad she was that they had put the wedding on hold; Mummy had to come first, and she must help her to get well.

Nathan had been great. He still continued to visit every weekend, but knowing that she loved him was enough, and he made no mention of house hunting at this time, realising that Isabel needed Sadie right there with her, encouraging and inspiring her to get on with her life and fight the deadly adversary that cancer was.

Sadie realised how precious life was. Until now she had taken it for granted, but she had often wondered if she had been in her mother's place, would she have been able to cope? Illness is not kind to anyone; it robs the most beautiful of their looks and their hair, apart from leaving them feeling that everything is such a huge effort. Sadie had never had to deal with anything like that in her life, and her looks and her sexuality had been what she had relied on to get her through life.

Philip had watched his wife losing weight and hair, and declining before his eyes, and tried very hard to hide his heartbreak. He kept up a cheerful front with her, constantly speaking about taking her on a nice cruise when she felt better. But deep inside he couldn't help wondering if that day would ever come. The Isabel who was always so strong and determined, and grasped life with both hands was gone, and in her place was this frail little person, who had to spend more time in bed than out of it. He treated her like porcelain china, always afraid she might break.

Nathan was concerned too. He spent time trying to bring a smile to her wan face; which was not easy, as Isabel was very depressed that she couldn't do much. She frequently spoke about, "If I don't make it, please take care of Sadie," only to him, of course, but he found that chilling, and he told her to stop being ridiculous, it wouldn't be long before she was buying a new hat for their wedding.

Sadie had seen that her father's way had not worked, so she tried tough love to encourage her mother to pick up her life again. She had spent the last few months devoting her time to Isabel, so much so that her mother developed panic attacks whenever she left her side. Sadie spoke sternly to her, telling her not to be a drama queen, and get out of bed. "You are not dying, Mummy, pick up your life and get on with it!" she said vehemently on more than one occasion, and at the time, it usually inspired Isabel to make an effort, but even Sadie was now wondering if her mother could ever be well again. She felt exhausted from all the stress, especially as she had to keep telling Danielle that Granny would soon be well again.

Isabel finished her treatment, and the surgeon was then satisfied, after various tests, that the cancer was in remission. Philip had gone with her that day and he came home full of hope; after all, the surgeon should know. Isabel did not respond immediately to this news, but gradually, over the course of about six weeks, lots of things started to change. First of all the nausea went and she started to eat again, then she began to feel stronger, and there was positive joy on her face when she looked in the mirror and saw tufts of hair beginning to sprout again from her bald scalp.

"Sadie, come here. My hair is growing again!"

Sadie rushed into the room and hugged her mother. They had done it, they had turned the corner, Mummy was going to get well again! All the gloom that had settled over the whole house had been lifted, and during the next three months Isabel's health improved rapidly. Her hair grew again thick and lustrous, though Sadie teased her to hurry up and put some colour on it as it was grey. Isabel couldn't wait to go to the hairdresser again and have the whole treatment; she felt like a woman again.

With her mother's new found confidence back again, Sadie realised just how much her mother's presence in the house counted. She was the focal point of all their lives, and when she had temporarily left the helm, they had all been lost. Philip and Nathan relaxed again. They had not known much about women's illnesses, and realised they could not give her the help that Sadie had. They both realised what a rock Sadie had been to her mother, and a lot of her recovery could be attributed to Sadie's help and encouragement. Philip, in particular, saw how much she had changed. She was a daughter to be proud of.

One day Isabel got up with a spring in her step. It was so great to be alive, even the thought of going back for a check-up didn't scare her; she was convinced she had beaten the cancer. So when the surgeon confirmed it was still in remission, and he now didn't want to see her for six months, she said what she had wanted to say for a long time.

"Philip, it's time we got together with Sadie and Nathan to plan their wedding, and I want it to be very special. After what Sadie did for me, it's the very least we can do!"

"Of course, my love, we'll make it the happiest day of her life!"

Philip had finally got his wife back. Life was sweet, and he would agree to anything.

Chapter Twenty

One year later...

"Sadie, how beautiful you look, and Danielle too!" It was an emotional moment for Isabel, and she stood there with tears shimmering in her eyes. Not only had she never imagined she could possibly have a proper mother and daughter relationship with Sadie, but up until twelve months ago, she had not been sure she would live long enough to even go to her daughter's wedding.

The ivory coloured dress with the long train, scooped neckline, and lace bodice, which showed her small waist off to perfection, was a one-off, having been made especially for Sadie, who had been very particular with the dressmaker about how she wanted it to fit. Isabel had kept out of that discussion, knowing that her daughter knew exactly what she wanted, but she had been allowed some input into Danielle's dress. Lemon was an unusual colour for a bridesmaid, but it worked, the pale colouring against Danielle's very dark hair and peachy skin looked very striking and blended perfectly with her mother's dress.

Sunita's daughter Jasmine, also very dark haired, was the other bridesmaid, and Sunita herself was matron of honour. Nathan had struck up a friendship with Sunita's husband Peter, so it seemed a good idea to ask him to be best man. Nathan had no family to invite to the wedding, but Isabel and Philip were his family now anyway, and they had to invite their own family, which was diminishing rapidly, as both sets of Sadie's grandparents were no longer alive, so it was Sadie's uncles and aunts, and cousins, whom they had not seen for years. There would also be quite a few of the friends and associates that Isabel and Philip had made over the years, so it was going to be quite a grand affair.

Sadie smiled back at her mother, whilst Danielle clutched at her hand wonderingly; she had such a beautiful Mummy. She felt so proud, and her own lemon dress was made from a heavy brocade that had little tiny embroidered flowers on it, and a lemon sash; and she loved her new cream shoes, and she remembered what Mummy and Grandma had said about walking carefully and not scuffing the toes. She felt like a princess, and she couldn't wait to walk behind her mother down the aisle next to Jasmine. It would be so exciting.

At one time Sadie would have thought her mother was being ridiculous, because emotion was something she had lacked. But after helping her mother fight cancer, and now seeing her return to her former good health, it was a moment to be savoured and enjoyed. Mummy was well again. She had a new gold coloured outfit, and a very in your face big hat, but what the hell, this wedding was going to be the happiest day of her life. She really wanted to be 'happy ever after' with Nathan. It may have taken her to reach thirty before she met the right man; and thank goodness he had changed, but now so had she, and for Sadie, life could not get any better.

She gave her mother a reassuring hug, noticing how thick and lustrous her hair had grown. It was long enough now for Isabel to wear piled on top of her head, and it really suited her. She had now put weight back on, those lines on her face had disappeared, she looked easily ten years younger, and her spirit and drive had returned, which, sometimes Sadie had to admit to herself, she could have done without. Mummy worried about everything, and there was no need. Sadie felt calm and relaxed; to her, right now life was perfect.

Today was the last fitting of their dresses and nothing needed to be altered, and tonight was her hen night. The only problem with that was that during her life Sadie had never made many friends other than Sunita, who would obviously be there. Peter, Sunita and the children were staying at the local Premier Inn; they had even laid on a babysitter for tonight from a local agency, which Philip had paid for as well as their rooms at the inn. Philip and Isabel had paid for everything and, as usual, no expense was spared. He had offered to put Peter and Sunita in the classy hotel at Whitstable with the rest of the family, but Sunita had felt they might be out of their depth, and anyway the Premier Inn was near to the house, and the beautiful little church at Reculver.

Sadie had cousins who were twins. Their names were Mia and Myra, and she had never particularly liked them, or had anything in common with them; they were a bit too prim and proper for her, but maybe if they got some wine inside them they might be more fun. They were about size twenty, and frequently told everyone that big is beautiful, whilst looking at Sadie, in her size ten clothes, with disdain. At one time she would not have bothered with them at all, but she knew Mummy and Daddy would be pleased if she made the effort, and after all the money that Daddy had shelved out, she had to do it. If she had reverted to her selfish ways Nathan would have had something to say about it, and for him she wanted to be the perfect wife.

Nathan was staying at their new home tonight, which they had chosen together. It was a town house set on three floors, and although it was very near to the heart of Canterbury, its situation overlooked some of the most beautiful ancient architecture, with the river Stour flowing right through the heart of it. Instead of a garden they had an area of decking with fantastic views, and pots of flowers and shrubs adorned it, with seating and a barbecue area. There was plenty of room for Danielle to play out there. Sadie was happy there was no garden, as it would have meant hiring a gardener. She was not into gardening and Nathan probably wouldn't have the time.

The house was less than two years old, and inside it had the most modern of kitchens and beautiful bathrooms, the carpet was still fresh and new, so they had not bothered to redecorate, and most of the very tasteful furniture from Nathan's penthouse went in there perfectly, although they had bought a new bed and furniture for Danielle's room.

The thing that had attracted Sadie to Canterbury in the first place had been the busy night life, the clubs, and the amount of tourists that passed through the city, but now she would be living there with Nathan as her husband, it was the sheer convenience of being so near to such a vast selection of shops. She would have her own night life at home with Nathan; her wanderlust had ceased to exist. Something had always been driving her on to find a better life, but now she had it. As for her parents, Herne Bay was a ten minute drive from Canterbury, so the ties would remain, and her parents would always be part of Danielle's life.

As she got ready to go out, Sadie smiled to herself when she remembered the look of amazement on Philip and Isabel's faces when she came home and told them she had a part-time job at Fenwick's in the ladies' fashion department. She had decided to get a job, not because they needed the money; after all, the house they were about to live in had cost Nathan over a million pounds, and he had put down a substantial amount of his own cash as a deposit, firmly and politely refusing any financial help from Philip. She knew that he wanted to prove to her that he wasn't using her parents as a meal ticket, he could stand on his own two feet, and in return she wanted to show him she could be independent, so she had gone out and got the job, which she intended to keep until she had their first baby.

When she told Nathan about the job he had acted as though it was a normal thing to do whether you came from a rich family or not. She had not enjoyed being a nanny in America, and all that pretence that she liked children, but it had been a means to an end. She now knew there was nothing like having your own child. Danielle meant the world to her, and although she squashed it down firmly, there was even a feeling of guilt about what she had done to that family. At the time she had not cared, but she was no longer that person any more. Sadie didn't want to spoil her feelings of happiness by dwelling on any of her past deeds; that voice inside her had always dictated what she should do, and right now the voice was quiet, which gave her a chance to savour her happiness.

She was ready now. The weather was surprisingly mild for April, so she put on a light dress and sandals, wore her hair loose because tomorrow the hairdresser was going to dress it on top of her head in a very sophisticated style and set her headdress and veil on it, so tonight was going to be a very free and easy night. Sadie planned to have some champagne and get a bit merry, but no way was she going to get wasted, because she wanted to enjoy every single second of her wedding day.

The taxi had arrived. It had done a round trip, first picking up her cousins Mia and Myra, and then Sunita, so she ran down and squeezed in next to them. There was a pub in Canterbury that did the best fish and chips in the whole city, it was even warm enough

164

to sit outside and eat. Their table was booked and the champagne already ordered.

"Drive on," she ordered the taxi driver, who was giving her an approving look. Maybe he did fancy her: tough, she was taken, Nathan was enough for her.

Myra was the more effervescent of her cousins, if she could call her that. In the beginning they had been a bit of a bore, but after some champagne Myra had loosened up a bit and told them about a fling she had with someone from work. Sadie would have regaled them with tales of her experiences in the past, she had so many, but she had been careful not to overdo the drinking, sometimes being an audience to someone who is drunk can be quite entertaining.

"Yes, we had it off in the stationery cupboard," said Myra, her eyes gleaming with pleasure at the memory. Sadie couldn't help wondering how her size twenty frame fitted inside a cupboard, and how big the man was, but perhaps she'd better not ask.

"Did you get found out?" she asked mildly. It must have been a noisy encounter.

"Yes, she lost her job over it," said Mia, to everyone's surprise. Until then she had appeared to be mute. She glared at her twin with obvious disapproval.

"Oh, but it was worth it," smiled Myra.

"Well it wasn't, you are still unemployed," Mia reminded her.

"I have a job," said Sadie, changing the subject back to herself.

Sunita was impressed. She had known Sadie ever since she could remember. They had both been a bit wild when they were children. Sunita had chosen to grow up when she met Peter, but the last time she had seen Sadie she had despaired of what would happen to her. She'd had an affair and a love child with Danny Foster, then been accused of his murder and locked up.

During their years together Sunita had learned not to take Sadie's stories too seriously, and she had never believed that Sadie had murdered her own brother, but had realised she was jealous of him. All the while she had vehemently denied killing Danny, and in the end had been locked up for nothing because it had been Alice. It was a shame, in her opinion, that Sadie had got involved with Alice because she had not been a nice person. Maybe that wasn't a fair thing to think, maybe she had been mentally sick, but she had certainly put Sadie and her family through a lot of stress before her untimely death. Now that Sadie had Nathan she had become a different person. All the spite and sarcasm had gone. She was happy, and no one was more pleased for her than Sunita. As for getting a job, especially, as they mayhem so rich anyway, it was very impressive.

"Well done you!" she said warmly.

Mia now had another reason to berate her twin for losing her job, and she cut in spitefully.

"It's OK for you, Sadie. With your looks you could get a job anywhere, especially if it's a man hiring you. My sister isn't so lucky. She goes around saying big is beautiful, and most men are intimidated by her, they think she's bossy, and right now she sits at home eating doughnuts."

"I do not. I've been on the computer looking!" said Myra angrily.

Sadie bit back a bitchy comment; it was boring being good all the time, and these two were something else. This was her hen party, not theirs, and the way that Mia was carrying on she guessed was jealousy, she had probably never had a man. She was glad she had not asked them to be bridesmaids, they would have made two of slender Sunita. Big might be beautiful, but not at her wedding.

"Well, I have to work to keep like this you know. I am thirty now; not too many takeaways, exercise, and in the summer I have to stay away from Herne Bay seafront because I love ninety-nines."

Obviously, although Sadie had thought that was quite tactful, it did not go down well with her cousins, as they both glared at her. They didn't want to be reminded of what they should be doing to look like her.

Sunita had used her tact to steer them onto a different subject, saying how happy she was for Sadie that this time she had made a go of it with Nathan.

"Yes, I am looking forward to spending my life with him," agreed Sadie, but Mia was not finished yet.

"Life is not all hearts and roses, you know, Sadie. Beware, after a few years, a handsome man like Nathan can have his pick of anyone, so don't let yourself go, otherwise he will go out and get himself a younger model!"

This was too much for Sadie, that voice was causing mayhem

in her head, telling her that no one could get away with telling her things like that. Her upstart of a cousin suggesting that Nathan would ever stop loving her. Her anger rose like a torrent, but the conflict inside her was threatening to choke her, nice Sadie battled with nasty Sadie, whilst Sunita looked on nervously.

"Oh, don't worry Mia, I will take care of myself, just like you have, and Nathan won't leave me. Now let's have another bottle of champagne."

Sunita blinked, was that it! She had got the hidden meaning, but it was no more than Mia deserved. In the past Sadie would have probably given her a tirade of abuse, every swear word she could think of, and might have even finished off by giving her a black eye. My goodness, love does conquer all, Nathan was obviously the best thing that ever happened to Sadie.

Sadie encouraged both of her cousins to drink as much as possible, and was quietly delighted when they both vomited in the ladies' room later, before they went back in the taxi. That served them right, the rotten bitches had ruined her evening! But Mia, in particular, had crossed her once too often. That voice was urging her on. Mia had to be removed from her life, just to keep it perfect, but it could not be yet, nothing was going to spoil her wedding tomorrow. With that thought occupying her mind, Sadie went to bed and slept fitfully. Mia had it coming later, but right now it was Sadie and Nathan's time.

Chapter Twenty-one

When Sadie woke up the next morning she was disappointed to find it had been raining. But as she was not getting married until 2 o'clock, there was time for the weather to change. At first it was misty, the sun seemed reluctant to come out, but by midday the sky was blue and the ground was drying out.

Everybody was busy, and Sadie didn't have to go anywhere. First of all the hairdresser came, then she had her nails done; and Isabel also, and even Danielle had special treatment and was allowed some nail varnish and a very light peach lipstick.

Sunita and Jasmine arrived at midday, because everyone was getting dressed together at the house. Peter had stayed over with Nathan. Apparently the stag do had been a bit messy, but after taking some headache tablets, they were now fully recovered. Peter had the ring safe and ready, and he was making sure that Nathan would get to the church on time.

Sadie was relieved to hear this. Typical men, they had to behave like little boys, and then wonder why they had a hangover afterwards. For the first time in her life she had done something sensible so she could enjoy her special day. Not so her stupid cousins, she could tell they were not used to drinking. Sunita had only had one glass of champagne, it was not encouraged in her religion, but she had wanted to raise her glass and wish her best friend well for the future.

They had nearly two hours to get dressed, and Sadie put her dress on last. She was making sure that everyone else looked right; after all, they would be walking behind her. Then there was

Mummy. Sadie could see her mother was all over the place emotionally and worrying about everything, so she suggested that Isabel got dressed and then she would be around to check that Sadie looked OK before she left the house.

Danielle and Jasmine were still running round with excitement, so it was decided to dress them and then let them go on ahead with Sunita, she could take care of them. Isabel would go and look after their guests whilst Philip, who had left them all to it, and gone to sit in the conservatory until he was needed, would be ready to give Sadie away. Like all men, it had not taken him long to dress. His top and tails suited him well. He was still a very striking man, and his breeding showed in the way he wore his clothes and the manner in which he behaved. Philip was a man of class.

When Sadie was finally ready, her mother left for the church. As was the custom, she would arrive a little late. Isabel could feel the butterflies inside her, she so wanted this day to go right. The sight of her daughter looking so radiant and beautiful, and yet unbelievably calm, had moved her so much. Now she must go and make sure all the guests were in the right places, and also that Peter and Nathan were there.

She didn't need to worry, Nathan was already inside, standing nervously, but when he saw her his face broke into a wide smile and he gently hugged her.

"There you are Isabel, looking lovely. Is my bride on her way?"

Isabel beamed at his compliment, and reassured him that Sadie would not be long. Nathan was like a breath of spring. His bright temperament, and cheery attitude to life was always uplifting, and to know that he was going to be Sadie's husband had delighted both herself and Philip. When she looked back on it all, if Sadie hadn't gone to America and left Nathan in the flat, Philip would never have gone over and found him, and not only would he not be a part of their lives, also he might be dead by now from drug addiction and alcoholism. What a waste of a good man that would have been; he only needed a chance in life. It must have been fate that had brought him into their lives.

She glanced around at the guests, the church was full, mainly with the contacts they had made over the years. Because of their wealth you were someone if you knew the Morton Browns, and

h

you certainly would attend a wedding if they asked you to. She went over to greet some that she knew, remembering to speak to Henry and Doris, and their twin daughters Myra and Mia, who she knew had gone out with Sadie and Sunita the night before. Isabel had also been asked to go, but she had preferred to leave the younger ones to enjoy themselves, Sadie didn't need her mother tagging along.

The organ was playing, so she took her place in the front pew. This could well be the sign that Sadie was arriving; and it was, the bride appeared at the door on the arm of her father, and they started to walk slowly down the aisle whilst the congregation turned to get a glimpse of them.

Nathan turned to see his bride. He knew she would look beautiful, Sadie could wear a bin liner and still look sexy, but it was more than beauty that shone from Sadie, it was a radiance that he had never seen before. She glided along on the arm of her father, who looked incredibly proud, her dark eyes sparkled, her smile was all encompassing, showing her beautiful white teeth, and her happiness was so apparent it filled the whole room. My God, what a lucky man he was!

Philip was so proud to be giving his daughter away on this very special day. All the preparations had been a bit overwhelming, he had kept out of that, and Isabel had done her usual panicking, wanting everything to be just right, but Sadie had been as cool as a cucumber, and even her hand linked through his arm was relaxed and in control. As they made their way towards the altar, and he saw the look of love and respect of Sadie in Nathan's eyes, he felt very happy that Nathan was going to be her husband.

Sadie's day was as perfect as she had hoped it would be. Sunita and the bridesmaids complemented her beautifully, and the sight of Danielle dressed like a princess, and loving it, gave her so much pleasure. Nathan, her handsome groom, gazing at her with such love in his eyes, could this happiness be for real? Those vows they exchanged meant everything to her this time. Nathan was her soulmate, and the love of her life, and when she promised to be faithful to him she meant it from the very bottom of her heart.

The rest of the day was just a blur of happiness. Talking to the guests at the reception, Daddy's speech, and Peter's too. Then they ate, but she couldn't remember what she had. She did remember being in her new husband's arms when they led the dancing, and his intoxicating nearness, so when he whispered in her ear that it was time to go and get changed for their honeymoon, and how much he fancied her, she sprang into action. Regretfully releasing herself from his arms, she went outside to find the chauffeur to ask him to take her back to the house so she could get changed and he could pick up their cases.

She smiled to herself when she found the chauffeur having a crafty fag. He dropped it guiltily when he saw her, but such was Sadie's happiness, she didn't care. She had just signed the register, and was now about to start a new life as Mrs Sadie Edwards. There was going to be no double barrelled surname for her, she wanted to have the same name as Nathan, her maiden name was now long gone.

Everything went according to plan at the house. She changed into her going away outfit, a striking red two piece with black patent and very high stilettos; but then she wasn't planning on doing much walking, she just wanted to look good. Their flight to Los Angeles took off in three hours, and although they could have stayed in a hotel overnight and gone tomorrow, Sadie had said she wanted to go the same day. Their wedding night would take place when they reached their hotel as it would still be night time there. They were flying first class, but she wasn't sure how well the other passengers would react if they celebrated their marriage on the flight with an audience. Sadie thought it might be fun, but her days of doing stuff like that had to be over now, she was a responsible wife and mother.

Eric the chauffeur stole a quick glance at her whilst he was driving her back to the reception venue. This woman oozed class, as did the whole family, they were so rich it was obvious; expensive clothes, and what a looker, she was like a film star! He couldn't help wondering if he would get a tip. His money wasn't that high as a chauffeur, and these people had so much they didn't know what to do with it. His wife was due with their first baby pretty shortly now, and he had taken extra shifts to try and make ends meet. But it wasn't easy, and after her maternity leave, regrettably, she would have to return to work.

As they drew up in the courtyard, the music could be clearly heard, people were having fun, and the drinks had been flowing for some time now. Sadie had been intending to go straight in and let Nathan see she was back, and then they could head for Heathrow airport. But then she saw the sight of her cousin Mia once again the worse for wear. She was heading out towards the little wooden bridge that stood over the gushing stream, but as she staggered across, it was apparent that she had not seen Sadie.

Mia's words from last night came to Sadie: "Be careful that Nathan doesn't leave you for a new model!" and instantly, like a pin to a balloon, Sadie felt her bubble of happiness burst. But she was not going to let Mia spoil her happiness. That voice inside her told her what to do, and Sadie listened, because she knew was right.

She smiled ingratiatingly at Eric, then feeling in her bag, she slipped him a fifty pound note. There were plenty more where that came from, and she needed to get him on side.

"If you want to go and have another smoke it's fine. I will get Nathan, and in about ten minutes, you can take us to the airport."

Eric was delighted, a tip and permission to smoke, what an understanding young woman she was! His wife had been trying to get him to give up smoking before their baby was born, and he had tried, but they had so much stress that he was finding it impossible. He was left with a feeling of guilt, so when someone didn't seem to mind, it made it a whole lot better.

"Yes Mrs Edwards, thank you so much."

He shuffled round the corner where no one could see him as he rolled his own. That fifty pounds would feed them for a week, and it might even stretch to a haircut; his brown hair straggled beneath his chauffeur cap. At twenty-eight his skin had prematurely aged because of his habit, and his face was small and monkey like, with piercing blue eyes.

With Eric now out of sight, Sadie moved over towards the shadowy bridge where Mia was standing. She could feel the adrenalin pumping through her veins. That bitch had given her the perfect opportunity, as she stood there in her bright orange dress which Sadie had thought looked atrocious on her. It was loud and cheap looking, just like the wearer, and as she sidled towards her she noticed Mia was also smoking. What a laugh, goody two-shoes Mia puffing away, no wonder no man came anywhere near her. Sadie may have been a lot of things in her life, but never a smoker. She hated the smell of it, and a woman doing it was even more repulsive, especially one who pretended to be so good.

172

Mia stepped off the end of the little bridge, and immediately Sadie saw her chance. She came up behind her and pushed with all her might, only too glad she was not still wearing her wedding dress with its cumbersome skirts. The edge of the bank loomed near, and in slow motion Sadie watched fascinated, as the cumbersome figure of her cousin flopped head first into the water with her orange outfit spread out around her soaking up water. She looked like a huge man-eating goldfish, and if it hadn't been so necessary to get rid of her, Sadie would have wanted to laugh.

She knew that the water was not that deep, but she could also tell that Mia was very drunk, as she floundered in the water, unable to bring herself upright. The only sounds she made were choking noises, so Sadie assumed she must have swallowed her cigarette.

Sadie knew she didn't have long before Myra appeared. They might argue, but those two were joined at the hip. So to make sure she had done the job properly, she picked up a rock and smashed it against the back of Mia's head. She was relieved to see her head turn to the side in submission, and there was blood oozing from the back of her neck. Satisfied that she had fixed her now, Sadie straightened up. That had taken a lot of effort in her high heels, but she had managed to stay dry at least. She dropped the rock into the space next to her. The water would wash her prints off, and they would assume Mia had hit her head on a rock and suffocated. As she sped round the corner to go and find Nathan, her last thought about Mia was a contemptuous one, those words on her cigarette packet were certainly true, smoking does kill.

Chapter Twenty-two

Myra had a love-hate relationship with her twin Mia; she could not live with, or without her. They frequently clashed. She was the one who enjoyed life in her own way, and Mia was the one who never approved of anything, who always seemed jealous. And yet she loved her, she was her best friend at times, and her worst enemy at others.

The argument had started over nothing. Mia had declined to dance with her cousin when he came over and asked. Myra, on the other hand, had got up and danced. She liked having fun, and when she came back to the table, Mia had a face as long as a poker, she didn't think Myra should have danced with him.

Myra had a mind of her own, and would not allow her twin to dictate to her, and she had told her so. Mia then seemed to knock back the vino a bit too quickly and went outside to clear her head.

Whilst she was gone, Myra wondered if she had been a bit too harsh with her, but she didn't want to be ruled by her sister, so it was a few minutes before she buried her pride and went to find her. When she found her twin laying face down in the water, even though it was shallow, at first she thought she was dead and she screamed at the top of her voice for some help.

She stood there helplessly watching whilst one of the guests who was a doctor, got to work on her, and gave her the kiss of life.

"Phone for an ambulance," he said curtly, as her sister started to cough and splutter. So it had worked, he had saved Mia's life.

She did as she was told, and by now many of the guests had collected around the still body, and Mia had slipped into a coma, so she realised they were not out of the woods yet; anything could happen.

When the ambulance came the paramedics wasted very little time, being anxious to get Mia to hospital. After some fruitless attempts to wake her up, they soon had her on a stretcher inside the ambulance. Her mother was in a bad way, she was convinced Mia wasn't going to make it, and her father had his work cut out to try and keep her calm. Just as they loaded Mia inside the ambulance, the paramedic turned to ask who was coming, and Myra was not going to miss supporting her twin, so she stepped forward and made herself available. Her distraught parents went too.

As the ambulance raced along with its blue light flashing, it was obvious just how serious it was; Mia might die. Myra said every prayer she could think of to have her sister back. If only she had known, she would not have argued with her, then Mia would not have gone out there and fallen into the stream. To Myra it seemed simple: her sister had drunk too much, couldn't stand up straight, so she'd taken a tumble in the stream.

When they reached the hospital, no time was lost in getting Mia on the stretcher into a special unit, and they were kept hanging about for a long time. During this time Myra did her best to console her weeping mother, telling her to not give up hope. Life without Mia was unthinkable, she knew if she was given another chance, she would be a bit more tolerant in the future.

The doctor came out eventually and told them that Mia was as comfortable as they could make her, but the blow on the back of her head had caused some damage and she was in a coma. They couldn't know for sure, when she woke up, if there would be any permanent brain damage.

"Blow on the back of her head," repeated Myra. "But I thought she just fell in the water."

"Well the police will want to speak to you. It appears that some heavy object was used to hit her from behind."

Myra and her parents were in disbelief. Who would want to harm Mia, it just didn't make sense. What sort of person would creep up to her at a wedding reception and do such a thing? Mia didn't know that many people outside her family, just the other women at the library where she worked, and Battersea was a long way from Herne Bay. It seemed more likely that someone had entered the hotel grounds illegally. It surely could not be anyone from the wedding party.

When the police arrived, after realising Mia was not conscious enough to speak to them, they asked Myra if she could help them. She felt so guilty about her sister's predicament and it weighed heavily on her conscience, so she blurted everything out to the constable and his companion. If she was hoping it would make her feel better, she was wrong. They latched onto the fact that she was angry with her sister, and before she knew it, she was virtually being accused of slipping out quietly and hitting Mia on the back of her head. This made her angry.

"Why do you have to twist everything? Yes, we had a row, we often do, but I love my sister. We are twins, but that doesn't mean we have to agree about everything!"

Constable Blake looked at Myra, so obviously very distressed, and decided she was telling the truth.

"Thank you for your help, we will do our utmost to find the person who did this."

He then shook hands with her father, nodded at her mother, and left the hospital with his companion.

Sadie and Nathan sat in the back of the taxi, arms entwined around each other, they were off to Heathrow and their honeymoon.

"I've switched off my mobile, and it's not going on until we get back!" Nathan said firmly.

"Me too, I've promised to Skype Danielle, but at least for tonight, it's just us."

"It's a shame we haven't got a private jet, but you wait until I get you to our hotel!"

Sadie felt her body respond to his words; that tingling sensation that swept through her like a very strong electric current. She knew it would be worth waiting for, the way he made her feel, he had taken over her heart and her body. Nathan had captured her very soul.

Her mobile hadn't been on at all today, and she was relieved he had switched his off. She had wanted him to in case they were contacted before they got on the plane, when Mia's body was found. She didn't want anything to spoil their honeymoon, but if they had not taken off, maybe they would be expected to return. Of course, when she Skyped Danielle tomorrow they would hear all about it, and thank goodness they would be away from it. Mia had said things she shouldn't, so in Sadie's mind removing her from their lives was justified, and even now when she thought about what Mia had said, it made her feel very angry. Her life without Nathan would be nothing, and anyone who suggested that could happen did not deserve to live.

"Oh, I can't wait for that," she said, kissing his cheek tenderly.

Nathan found her lips and gave her a long lingering kiss. Two heavenly weeks with Sadie; every day he spent with her she became more loving and demonstrative. Now she seemed to have put all her demons behind her, he was looking forward to an exciting life with her. More children, and together they would get through anything that life threw at them because they had each other, and in his mind, that was all they needed.

Isabel and Philip were very upset when they found out what had happened to Mia. What a terrible accident to have at a wedding reception, and as it was their reception they felt very responsible. Isabel wished they had chosen a venue without a stream, then the worst that could have happened to Mia is that she just fell over.

Later that night, after Isabel had put Danielle to bed, Doris phoned to give them an update. She was sobbing down the phone when she gave Isabel the news.

"My poor Mia is in a coma. Somebody hit her over the head, they tried to kill her. What sort of evil person would do that? My Mia wouldn't harm a fly, she's a good girl!"

Isabel gasped with horror, surely it couldn't be true?

"I am so sorry Doris, but maybe it was just someone a bit drunk messing around? No one would deliberately hurt Mia. Please come and stay with us whilst she is in hospital, we want to support you."

She felt inviting them to stay was the least they could do. Poor Mia, what a dreadful ending to what had been such a happy day. Now they would all be worrying about whether she would suffer any brain damage.

Tomorrow, when Sadie Skyped Danielle, she would have to tell them. There was no point now, they would be on the plane, and it wasn't as if they could do anything about it. There was no reason to spoil the first night of their honeymoon, tomorrow evening would be soon enough for them to know.

Doris, Henry and Myra arrived soon after, they were too upset to stay at the hotel for what should have been their last night. They felt they wanted to be with family, and Isabel and Philip were more than willing to extend their hospitality to them. They would stay for however long Mia remained in hospital. They could visit her every day. Isabel prayed with all her heart that Mia would soon wake up unaffected, and hopefully she would tell them what had happened. Maybe she had been fooling around with someone, having a laugh. But surely no one would have wanted to harm her, it was just too distressing to even contemplate, and once again she wished there had been no water for her to fall in, what a terrible tragedy it was!

None of them slept well that night, all the excitement and happiness of the wedding had been totally destroyed by this event. Isabel was wondering how she would explain yet another tragedy to Danielle. She was only six years old, and this was the second bizarre incident in a year. Tragedies like this seemed to follow their family around, and it was especially upsetting after such a very beautiful wedding and a happy day.

On Sunday Mia's family went to see her. There was no change in her condition, she remained in a coma, and the doctors explained that her body was in shock, so at the moment they had no plans to try and rouse her from it.

It was late on Sunday afternoon that the police came round to interview them, and to get details of all their friends and family at the wedding, so they could all account for their movements the previous night.

"Oh dear, this is so shocking!" exclaimed Isabel. "Our beautiful wedding will now be remembered for all the wrong reasons."

"You must stop blaming yourself. Mia is an adult, she went outside of her own free will, Isabel," Philip gently reminded her. He could have added that no one asked her to get drunk either; it was true, but it would sound callous. He just didn't want Isabel to carry the weight of the world's problems on her shoulders. She had done that for years in the past, and since she had suffered cancer, he was even more anxious to ensure that his wife didn't have any more stress than was necessary.

"Well I am afraid that somebody must have come up behind Mia whilst she was in the water and hit her with a rock which we found in the water next to her. It still had traces of her blood on it," said constable Blake gravely. "Do you happen to know if there was anyone absent from the party at the time when Mia went out?"

Philip took over. "I am sorry, there was music going. We didn't even know Mia had gone outside, we knew nothing about it until Myra discovered her and raised the alarm."

Isabel joined in: "I remember that Sadie and Nathan were just about to go to catch their flight, and Sadie didn't want to leave Danielle, so her goodbye was a bit prolonged, and in the end I took Danielle home, as it was getting on a bit, and she's only six."

Constable Blake considered her words, and then said slowly.

"So you left the reception then?"

"Yes, I took Danielle home, but we had arranged a babysitter, and our chauffeur brought me back within about half an hour."

She flushed, realising that constable Blake was implying she was a suspect. Philip was not happy about the policeman's assumption. They did have a job to do, but to suspect Isabel was the most ludicrous idea ever and he wasn't going to stand for it.

"Constable, my wife was accompanied by my chauffeur at all times, if you have any doubts at all just ask him."

"I am sorry sir, it's my job to be suspicious, no offence meant," said Blake. It didn't take long to upset people, the price one had to pay when entering the police force.

"We went outside at the same time as Sadie and Nathan because Danielle wanted to wave goodbye to them. They slipped away quietly because they didn't want to be held up by over excited guests and tin cans hanging from the car, and all the other things that can happen. The cars are parked at the front of the reception hall, and Mia must have been round the back by the little bridge where she was found."

Constable Blake's companion busied himself writing as Isabel explained. Then she added.

"When we got outside, our chauffeur was by the car, but Eric, the one that was taking Sadie and Nathan to Heathrow, appeared from round the corner a minute or so later. I didn't take much notice at the time, but I still can't see why he would harm Mia, if indeed he did."

"Well, I will see him so we can eliminate him from our enquiries," said Blake. "Do you have his contact details?"

Philip was relieved that the heat was now off Isabel. Just about everyone interviewed would be a suspect now, this was how the police did their job. The whole sorry business was very strange. He went over to the bureau where he had Eric's contact details.

"It may not have been any of your guests, someone might have got in unseen from outside. But mugging Mia would not have been an option, as her handbag was left where she had been sitting."

"Well, constable, anything we can do to help, we will," said Philip, politely shaking Blake's hand, hoping they would take the hint and go soon. He felt Isabel had suffered enough since yesterday, and now it was time this interview was over. He was glad when they closed the door on them, and also glad that the police had not wanted to interview Mia's family again; that was the last thing they needed right now, and it was a good thing they were in the guest wing when the police arrived. No doubt they had seen the car but had chosen to remain where they were, away from all the incessant questions.

Danielle arrived home at 6pm. She had been at her friend's house all day. When she had been invited yesterday, Isabel wasn't sure, but today, with all this new drama going on, it had been a relief to let her go and have fun with her friend.

At 6.30pm on the dot, Sadie Skyped Danielle, just as she had promised she would. She knew her mother would speak to her first, but being well versed as an actress, she was ready to give a believable performance, not only for the benefit of her parents, but Nathan too.

"Sadie and Nathan, I am so sorry to spoil your honeymoon, but you have to know that somebody, during the reception yesterday, attacked your cousin Mia, and she's now in hospital in a coma. Her parents and Myra are in bits, and we don't know for sure that she will live, and even if she does, she may have permanent brain damage. "

This news was a surprise to Sadie. Mia not dead; she thought she had fixed her. Suddenly the seriousness of the situation hit her and fear flooded through her. Mia was alive, and she might have seen her. Her mouth said the next words, but her heart was filled with dread.

"Nathan, this is terrible. Mia has been attacked. Who was it?"

Nathan came over to hear about it, this was news he hadn't been expecting. Whatever was going on? He had only met Sadie's cousin briefly, but it seemed unbelievable that someone had put her in hospital whilst they were all at the reception. He expressed his concern to Isabel.

"We have no idea who did it. All we know is she went outside, possibly to clear her head, as according to Myra she had a few drinks, she was by the little bridge over the stream, then she tripped and fell into the water."

"I thought you said she was attacked," said Sadie, her heart was pounding with fear; for the first time ever she had failed to finish the job properly. She had so much to lose if she were found out: Nathan, Danielle, the love and respect of her parents and her freedom. Desperation set in, she couldn't bear to go back inside again, and all sorts of thoughts were raging through her head, maybe she should feign illness to get back home, and then go to the hospital and smother Mia before she could talk.

"Well yes, we thought at first she had just fallen face down into the water, but the police discovered an injury on the back of her head, and a rock nearby with traces of blood on it, so they know someone attacked her."

Sadie was silently cursing herself for leaving that rock around, but there had been so little time, and Eric was around the corner smoking and could have walked round and seen her.

"Mummy, that sounds so awful, and at our wedding, too. Do the police have any suspects?" She then held her breath for Isabel's answer.

"Not at the moment. You wouldn't believe it, I mentioned taking Danielle home, and I was cross examined. Still I know it's their job."

Nathan voiced his concern. "Isabel, that was ridiculous to suspect you, perhaps someone came in from outside. We wouldn't like to think that anyone who was at our wedding, either a friend or relative, would do such a thing!"

"This is what I thought, and I am sad that your special day will be remembered for all the wrong reasons."

"She has to recover!" said Nathan stoutly. The thought of Mia suffering brain damage inflicted by an unknown psycho at their wedding did not sit easy with him. It was funny how these tragedies seemed to follow him around. He had never felt comfortable at his flat after Melissa had been run down by an unknown car. It was true that it wasn't at the flats that it happened, but he had been the last person to see her alive. Then poor mad Alice had plunged over the cliff before his very eyes, and now this. But this seemed to have happened after they left. Who would do such an evil act?

"Well the only people who were outside at the time was apparently the two chauffeurs. If you remember, our family one was waiting at the car for me, but Eric, the one that we hired, was round the corner, apparently smoking," said Isabel.

Sadie saw a way out of her predicament, silently thanking her mother for providing it.

"Mummy, I think you should tell the police about him. Even though he was hired to take me to and from the wedding, it didn't stop him leering at me. I wouldn't trust him with any woman, he made me feel uncomfortable."

"You never said," remarked Nathan, putting a protective arm around her.

"Why spoil our day," she murmured, her dark eyes meeting his. He couldn't really blame any bloke for being stirred by her, but a chauffeur had to be trusted, he had a very precious cargo to take care of, and this man had fallen short of what was expected of him.

"I will lodge a complaint when we get home," he said grimly.

"Yes, and I will make sure the police know about that," said Isabel.

Sadie smiled to herself. They were so easy to manipulate, and she was certain that Mia had not seen her when she thought about it, she had never turned round. She was off the hook again.

"If you have to," she murmured. "Now how is my baby Danielle? Can you put her on."

Chapter Twenty-three

Ricky had made huge progress in the last year. Thanks to various sources, he had finally tracked down Simon and Jill Hopkins. They were living in a small apartment in the Bronx area of New York. He had taken the first steps to contact them by writing and explaining that he was a member of the FBI, and would very much like to meet up with them when it was convenient.

He didn't mention anything about his son. It was only hearsay, there was no record of them adopting a child, and his biggest fear had been that Sadie might have killed her own son. Even though she had been released, and was apparently cured of her mental problems, Ricky was used to being suspicious about everything, it came with the job.

He had been sad to hear about Alice's premature death. She had seemed a nice enough person when they met, but no blame had been laid at the door of Nathan or Sadie. He had become used to calling her Sadie now, but when they were together she had been Marina. Alice appeared to have fallen over the cliff, whether it was an accident or not, no one could be sure, and for all he knew, this Nathan that Sadie was now involved with, and had in fact now married, could be as scheming as she was.

The other side of the coin was that maybe Sadie had done nothing except take him for a ride financially, all her lies and boasting were to give herself illusions of grandeur, and she had dumped her son on the Hopkins because having a baby cramped her style. The fact that she had made a shed load of money from it, and crippled them financially, was typical Sadie style, but he needed them to tell him it was true, Alice's word alone was not enough.

Obviously Sadie and Alice's mutual hate had stemmed from both wanting the same man. Again, there was no proof that he had been murdered, but her boasting about her brother had got her arrested as a suspect, and then committed as insane.

In the beginning, coming so soon after the death of Amy, what Sadie had done to his family, particularly his three princesses, had been devastating, and he had felt so much anger towards her. He had been deceived by her, and had thought she was a decent woman to entrust with his precious daughters. How wrong he had been, and the heartbreak she had left behind her when she took off had been very emotionally damaging to both the girls and himself.

But time is a great healer and his plucky girls had picked themselves up, and after a while their faith in women was restored. It had taken a few years, because as far as they were concerned, first their mother had left them, and then Sadie, and women were not to be trusted. Going to heaven, to them at that time, was like their mother moving to another country, death was not something they understood.

Brenda was now sixteen, and very mature, Kathy fourteen, and Maria eleven. Initially they had not trusted Kirsty, but she had been very patient with them. After a while, she became a great friend and confidante to them, just at the time when they needed the support of a woman in their teenage years to understand what was happening to their bodies. It was not something they wanted to share with dad, but all part of growing up.

Nowadays the two families got on great. He didn't live with Kirsty. His girls would come first always, but as she also had teenage children, they had fun hanging out together, and that dreadful loneliness he had suffered when Amy died had gone, he could live, and feel and love again, he had his life back.

When he had seen Sadie in prison, he had been shocked at the change in her appearance. This thin and gaunt woman looked old and he could see she had suffered, and his hate and anger had evaporated in an instant. The only worrying thing was that she didn't appear to know him, or even realise she had a son.

So this had made his task much harder. But thanks to Alice telling him about the Hopkins, he had tracked them down, and he was about to find out whether his son did live with them, and was still alive. The fact he might not be was a chilling thought, but at least he would have peace of mind if he found out the truth.

His original plan had been to track down the Hopkins and get proof that Sadie had sold her baby, then pass the arrest over to Dave. But although in his eyes what she had done was shocking, revenge was no longer his sole motive, he wanted to meet his son at last.

When Simon opened the letter his heart skipped a beat. His immediate thought was that the FBI had found out about them. They had moved about a bit during the last eight years, with his job at CNN there had been opportunities, which he had been glad to take. Not only did he hope that Marina would never change her mind and want her son back, but also there was always the fear at the back of his mind that the law would hunt them down. After all, buying a baby was illegal. He knew if Jill found out she would be very upset, young Billy meant everything to her. In fact, she did spoil him a little, but then Simon excused that because her longing for a child had been so immense. She had gone through the heartbreak of miscarriages, and then finally, like an answer to their prayers, Marina had been there, a single mother who could not cope with her baby.

The letter didn't actually mention what it was about, so maybe he could set up a meeting when Jill wasn't there. During the day Billy would be at school. Well, that is if they didn't have any more bother with him. He blamed living in the tough Bronx area; bad people and bad influences. Most of their money had been spent on getting Billy, and ever since then they had to take the cheapest lodgings in the areas that were less sought after.

Billy was a bright and intelligent boy, but he had this tendency to bully other children. He didn't have many friends, was in fact a loner, and he couldn't count the number of times they had been called to the school to discuss his behaviour with the teachers. Last month he had been suspended for fighting and injuring another pupil, in an apparently unprovoked attack, but now he was back at school and under strict instructions to shape up or else risk expulsion.

Simon and Jill had been devastated by his behaviour. If they had more money, they would have arranged for him to see a child psychologist, but they could not afford that. This last time, Simon had a very strict word with him, telling him how serious his behaviour was, and he felt he might have got through to him and maybe he was just going through a phase like kids did sometimes. He didn't want to think it was anything to do with the fact they had told him he was adopted. That was the word they used, although it had never been made official. They had wanted to be honest with him right from the beginning, so Jill had explained to him how special he was because they had chosen him when they could not have a baby of their own. His birth certificate had his mother's name on it, and when he was older he would have found out anyway. He had asked once where his mother was and why she had not wanted him, and Jill had said his mother was on her own and she couldn't look after him, and now she was his mum and proud to be.

Ricky had put his email address on the letter, so with a sigh, Simon sent him an email, so much quicker than a letter, arranging for their meeting the next day. He knew Billy was on a school trip tomorrow, and Jill was going shopping. This was going to prey on his mind all night, but he would see this FBI man tomorrow, and see what he could do to make sure that they didn't lose Billy. No matter how tough the going was, for Jill's sake, he had to see it through.

Jill was having a pamper day today. She had seen Billy onto the yellow school bus, kissed Simon goodbye, and was now on her way to the beauty parlour. First she was having her hair and nails done, and then she was going shopping. Simon had said it was time for her to have some new clothes and shoes, and he had given her some money. She was touched because they were not wealthy, and she knew he would have worked extra to get that especially for her.

Since Billy had gone to school she had taken a part-time job at the local grocery store. It was not highly paid, but the extra did help, especially if she wanted to spend it on Billy. She would have let Billy have the moon if he wanted it, so she knew it was a good thing that Simon put his foot down sometimes and told her to spend a bit on herself. He thought Billy had enough money spent on him, and she deserved to have a treat sometimes.

Billy had been a bit difficult lately and she hoped it was just a phase. They had banned him from watching anything violent on TV, and made sure the parental controls were in place on the computer, limiting him to what sites he could go on. There were so many things on the Internet that could disturb a child's mind.

When he was a baby, he had been so placid and contented, rarely crying, even when he had been parted from his mother, but since he had been at school he seemed to change, he didn't like other children, and seemed to have issues with them. They had both tried to talk to him and find out what was wrong, but he had not said much, so they had hoped it was just growing pains.

Today he had gone on a school trip, they were going canoeing, which Billy loved, so they were not anticipating any trouble. Jill planned to sit down with him this evening and ask him all about his day. He would be full of excitement and ready to share it with them.

Although Billy had a high IQ, he was quite happy to spend time on his own, he didn't seem to need friends. Jill had not always understood that, and in spite of all the difficulties with him right now, she had never regretted for an instant having him in their lives.

She parked her car on the parking lot outside the beauty parlour. It was only early May, but already very hot. In the car she had air conditioning, but when she stepped outside, with the full sun beating down mercilessly on her, it made her feel dizzy and sick. It was only a short walk into the shop, but a wave of nausea swept through her and she wasn't sure she could make it.

This was silly, the sun didn't usually bother her like this, whatever was wrong? She clutched at the outside of the door, and Ruth, who was booked to take care of her, noticing that something was wrong, gently pulled the door open and supported her.

"Are you OK, honey? I saw you hanging onto the door like you might take a tumble at any time."

Jill clutched at her as dizziness assailed her body. This was awful, she felt like she was going to throw up. "I need the bathroom!" she gasped, and then running past Ruth, she just made it in time.

She felt wretched afterwards, weak and dizzy, and also very embarrassed, but Ruth took care of her, helping her over to a chair, and holding a glass of water in her hand which she encouraged Jill to sip.

"I am so sorry. I think I must have a bug," she gasped between sips of water.

"No need to worry honey, that heat is something else. Would you like one of us to drive you home?"

Jill felt so angry with herself. Her first pamper day for ages and it was all messed up, all she wanted to do now was go home and flop on the couch. Simon had said he was working from home today, so he would be there. She had to forget looking good, and any new clothes, but at least now she had thrown up the dizziness had gone.

"No, it's OK, Ruth, you've been so good to me, and I'm so sorry I can't keep my appointment today. I will rebook when I am feeling better."

"No worries honey," said Ruth sympathetically. She looked very white, thank goodness she had made it into the bathroom. Bugs could be nasty when they came over you so suddenly like that. She was glad to hear her husband would be at home, then if she did need to go to the hospital, he could take care of her.

Jill could feel a headache coming on now, but she didn't say. Maybe if she went home, took some pills and had a lie down, she would feel better. She left the salon, walking slowly through the intense heat to her car. Switching on the engine and air conditioning she waited until she felt the cool air coming through before getting in, and then she drove home slowly.

When she reached their home, which was shabby and could do with a lick of paint, she noticed the drunk flopped in the kerb, his empty bottle laying beside him. He muttered something incoherent at her, and she wondered how he could lay there and survive this heat. If only they could afford to move to a better area. Seeing stuff like this wasn't good for Billy, and she wanted him to grow up to be a responsible person.

As she got out of the car, another equally dishevelled drunk lurched up to the first one, and their voices were raised as they babbled obscenities at each other. But they were cut short by a car containing law enforcement officers, who without ceremony, hauled them both protesting into the car and left the scene.

This had totally captured Jill's attention. It had happened so quickly, she didn't notice the other police car immediately. It was parked in the street outside their house, and because it was new and shiny, it looked totally out of place in the scruffy surroundings. For a moment her heart lurched with fear. Surely not Billy, he couldn't be in trouble, and then common sense took over. He was out with his school, not hanging around the streets.

But as she entered the house she could hear voices talking, and when she went into their small parlour she saw the FBI man in uniform talking to Simon, and her fear returned. What was he doing here?

Simon stiffened with surprise, but kept his voice calm, not wanting to distress her.

"You're back so soon honey, what happened to the trip to the beauty parlour?" and then without waiting for her answer he carried on. "Mr Scott from the FBI is here to see us, this is my wife Jill."

Jill shook hands tentatively wondering what was wrong, her stomach and head were aching, and all she wanted to do was lie down, but she didn't want to leave Simon. Her conscience reared its ugly head, as she remembered what they had done eight years ago; bought a child.

Ricky shook hands with her. Both these folks were looking very uneasy, and although this visit was unofficial, they didn't know. He wasn't really permitted to investigate people connected with his past life or even the present one. If it was official it had to be handed over to someone else, and he would have to keep out of it, but all he wanted to do was to find out if they had his son, and if the boy was still alive. Fear gripped at his insides if that was not true, but at least it would put his thoughts to rest.

"Do you have a son called Ricky."

His question was like a bolt out of the blue, but he had meant to catch them unawares, he wanted the truth.

Simon swallowed awkwardly, he could have said no, because their boy was Billy, but he was not in the habit of lying to the law. He glanced at Jill,who reacted exactly as he knew she would.

"We have a son, but his name is Billy."

She walked over towards the display unit, which was quite grand, and oddly out of place in such shabby surroundings. On the top shelf was a photo of Billy taken quite recently, and she silently handed it to Ricky.

Ricky studied it. He was a tall and sturdy boy, his hair was the same colour as Ricky's and he had the same long face, but his eyes were Sadie's, dark and unfathomable. He felt a huge surge of emotion looking at the son he had never known. He had missed the first eight years of his life but he had an overwhelming desire to know him now.

Nevertheless he realised that as far as this couple were concerned, Billy was their son, and why on earth was he called Billy now?

"Can I see his birth certificate?"

Jill and Simon exchanged worried glances, which were noticed by Ricky. Jill felt even more sick than she had before. They were just about to be found out. Panic set in that she might lose Billy, and she could feel tears pricking at her eyelids.

Simon was trying to think of a way out, but there was none, so he got up and walked slowly to the bureau. He opened a drawer and found the offending document, then handed it to Ricky for his perusal.

Ricky read it swiftly. Mother's name Marina Virdini, father Ricky Scott. The only reason she had named him as the father was so she could get child support off him, but surely an attorney would say that gave him rights.

"I see the mother is Marina Virdini, so you have adopted him then?"

"Not exactly," said Simon. This was awful, and he could see Jill was close to tears.

"His mother had just separated from her husband," then realisation struck home. "It's you, isn't it? He whispered with disbelief. "I can see the likenss, you are his natural father."

"I am!" said Ricky very firmly. "His mother left me, and I never saw him, nor was given the choice of caring for him. All she wanted was a huge pay off from me, which she got, and she obviously didn't want our son either. I know you haven't adopted him, there is no record of it, but as you can see from the birth certificate, his real name was Ricky."

"You aren't the only one. We sold our house to pay her off, then she vanished without trace, and we have never been able to contact her to make an adoption legal."

"You paid for the baby!" So it was true, Alice had got it spot on. Ricky could, even now, scarcely believe what he was hearing. Surely no woman in her right mind could sell her own baby, and he felt a wave of pity for his son, that she hadn't wanted. How cruel she was.

Jill burst in emotionally. "So now you know. We were so desperate, we wanted a baby, and she said she couldn't cope. So we bought him, and this is why we have to live in such a run down area amongst alcoholics, druggies and prostitutes. She bled us dry, and now I suppose you are going to arrest us."

Now a lot of things made sense to Ricky. They had once had a comfortable life, with nice furniture which didn't look right here. Sadie had ruined them financially, and this was why they were living in this run down area. What a place to bring up a child! But at least young Ricky, or Billy as he was now known, was alive and well. It was obvious to him that they were suffering now, so he intended to put their minds at rest in a way where maybe they could all benefit.

"Don't worry, that was not on my mind. I know you have broken the law, but I understand why you did it. All I want is to meet my son. I won't try and take him from you, but maybe I could play some small part in his life?"

He had often wondered what he would do if he ever tracked his son down. It didn't seem fair to the girls to move him in with them, it would be a huge adjustment for them to make, and would remind them of his mother and what she had done. But he was Ricky's flesh and blood, so first he would get to know him, and then maybe Billy could visit his home sometimes, and meet his three half sisters.

Jill sobbed with relief. She wasn't going to lose Billy. Both Jill and Simon were glad now that their secret was out; no more pretence and anguish.

"Thank you so much. You don't know how glad we are to hear that. We will certainly let you be a part of his life, as he knows we are not his natural parents."

Then they all sat down together, with one common aim, to put the welfare and interests of Billy first, because they all realised that none of this was his fault. Ricky suggested that if Simon could get a transfer with his job, moving down south might be a good option. There was plenty of building going on around the Greenview area, and it was a nice neighbourhood with very little crime.

Simon and Jill liked the sound of that, and they explained to

Ricky that they were going through a difficult patch with Billy; and having looked around the neighbourhood, he was not at all surprised. This was a no hopers' area, so between them they must give Billy an environment that he could thrive in.

When he left them, a meeting had been set up with Billy for the following week. The Hopkins had promised Ricky they would pave the way by explaining that he had been looking for Billy for a very long time, and he did care about his son.

Jill explained why she was home early, and then took the rest that she needed to rid herself of the bug. She rested for the day, and was able to get up and fix some dinner when Billy returned. The relief that she felt that she was not losing her son, or being arrested, was tremendous.

Ricky was thinking on his journey back; after eight years his search for his son was over, it had haunted him for such a long time. Life was getting better for all of them, and although the thought of Sadie selling her own baby was repugnant to him, he still felt guilty that he had imagined that she might have killed him.

Sadie was a complex woman to understand. It was clear she had issues to behave like that, but he forgave her, because his family had moved on from the grief, and he was about to meet his son.

Chapter Twenty-four

Sadie and Nathan had a very memorable honeymoon. It was a time when they were able to devote themselves exclusively to each other, and they made the most of it. It wouldn't have mattered if their honeymoon had been spent in a less exotic location, as they rarely left the bridal suite, and opted for room service, rather than eating downstairs with the rest of the guests.

They simply couldn't keep their hands off each other. They had both had other partners in the past, but this feeling they shared was of complete happiness and fulfilment with each other. For Sadie it was a completely new experience. Nathan brought out everything that was good in her, and she so wanted to be the woman he would look up to and love and respect.

When everything was going along so well, that voice remained silent inside her and she felt free to make her own choices. Nathan had not just captured her heart, he had got right through to her soul, and being with him, with a future stretching out in front of them, was wonderful.

They Skyped Danielle every day, and at the end of the first week, Isabel had reported that Mia had woken up, apparently without any brain damage, to the relief of everyone. A few days later she was able to leave hospital, and the day before they were due to fly home, the whole family had left Herne Bay and gone home to Battersea.

The police had interviewed her, but all she could remember was tripping off the end of the bridge, and then blackness, until she woke up in hospital feeling very confused. She had not

j

noticed anyone outside, and as her assailant had come from behind, she didn't know anything about that either.

Sadie silently hugged herself with glee when she heard all this. It had been a bit tight this time, but once again she had got away with it. Then the voice had reminded her that Mia was still alive and didn't deserve to be; she had suggested that Nathan would leave Sadie, and that was unthinkable. But this time the voice didn't win. Sadie was so totally in love with Nathan and she knew he was with her too, which made her feel safe and secure in his love, and she didn't think anyone could spoil that. Mia had escaped this time, but if her cruel tongue should ever threaten their happiness, then Sadie would have to dispose of her, and properly next time. She hadn't seen her for years before the wedding, so it was likely she wouldn't see her for years after. By that time Mia would have become an old maid, and Sadie and Nathan would have had more children. The thought of that was very satisfying to Sadie.

They made an effort to breakfast with the rest of the guests on their last morning. They were checking out, and then Nathan was driving to the airport, where they had to leave the car and pick up the overnight flight.

Nathan could not disguise the love in his eyes as he looked across the table at his new bride. He had never been a hearts and flowers man, but Sadie had done something to him; she had softened him up, and he liked the feeling.

When he first knew Sadie she had been self centred and hard, but he had sensed underneath that tough exterior there was a vulnerable person who needed love. Then gradually she had started to change, and after reuniting with her daughter and her mother she had become loving and caring. When her mother was so ill she had nursed her back to health, encouraging her to pick up her life again when the cruel cancer seemed to have defeated her. No wonder he cared so deeply for her, she was a woman of strong character, and he was proud to call her his wife. Whatever she had done in the past was of no interest to him, it was the person she was now that counted.

Later, as he drove to the airport, she lay in the passenger seat, her eyes closed, and he was content to watch those beautiful lashes framing her cheeks. No wonder she was tired, they had spent the last two weeks in each other's arms all night every night, and he hoped that already she might be pregnant. To have a child with her would be the ultimate joy of their union, a brother or sister for Danielle.

When they arrived home in England it was early morning, so they got a cab back to their home in Canterbury. Isabel had arranged to pick up Danielle from school, allowing them to sleep off their jet lag, and then they would go over to Herne Bay to pick her up and have dinner with her parents. It felt good to be in their own home. He had his whole life with Sadie ahead of him, and he knew it would be exciting and unpredictable, just as she was, but that was just why he loved her, because Sadie was unique.

Constable Blake was getting very frustrated with this investigation. The local police in Whitstable were putting pressure on him to make an arrest. This part of Kent was a happy seaside area, and the news that there was a person who had attempted to kill someone at a wedding reception had not gone down well.

He had interviewed every guest and drawn a blank, nobody appeared to be outside when the young woman was attacked, nor did they hear any screams. He decided to go back and speak to Mr and Mrs Morton Brown once more. He was glad the young lady in question had made a good recovery, but that didn't make it less of a crime, it was attempted murder. But he could find no reason for it. She didn't have a boyfriend, no one appeared to dislike her, and she had no money on her to steal.

When he arrived at the house, he was shown into the hall by the housekeeper, and then Isabel came in and took over. They went into the lounge, where Philip was reading a newspaper, but he got up and shook hands with him politely.

"Good morning Constable Blake, what can we do for you today?"

"I just came to make sure you had nothing to add to what you told me before. To be honest with you sir, we have no witnesses to the attack and the young lady can't remember anything. There is someone out there who tried to murder her, and it has obviously made the locals feel very nervous."

Philip and Isabel exchanged glances. After speaking with Sadie about her driver Eric, who they believed had been disrespectful towards her, Philip had asked Isabel not to mention it to the police. He said he would speak to him himself.

As much as he loved his daughter, Philip was aware that she sometimes exaggerated, and when he had first met Eric he had made up his own mind about him. The man was very respectful and in awe of the whole family, not at all the type to leer at Sadie. He also knew that Eric's wife was due to give birth at any time now, so he certainly didn't need the stress of being a suspect. The police had already interviewed him, and the fact that he had been driving Sadie and Nathan to the airport during the time it was all happening made the police assume he was not a suspect.

But Philip also didn't like to think there was a would-be killer at large. He may have misjudged Sadie, and Eric might have fooled him, so he decided to tell Constable Blake what he knew, then it was up to the police to sort it out.

"There were two people outside about the time it happened: our chauffeur, who was sitting in the car when Isabel came out to take Danielle home, and the other chauffeur appeared from round the corner a minute or two later to take my daughter and Nathan to Heathrow."

Isabel was relieved that Philip had obviously had a change of heart. It was never a good idea, in her opinion, to hide anything from the police.

"I see, round the corner being the direction of the bridge then? I wonder what he was doing there."

"Having a smoke apparently," said Isabel. This was all a bit sick really. She saw how Blake's face lit up, he had a suspect. If the chauffeur was innocent, then he had a lot of aggravation now to put up with. She felt sorry for him.

"Well thank you very much. I have his contact details, so now I will go and speak to him again."

He shook hands with Philip and Isabel, then left. He had come in looking really defeated, and now he was going out like a man with a mission to fulfil. Isabel became worried.

"I hope he doesn't tell Eric that we said anything, because it looks like we dropped him in it."

"I know," sighed Philip, "but if he's done nothing wrong, then there is no problem."

"True," said Isabel. "Now I am off to pick up Danielle from school."

196

"I think I will come with you. After all, she's leaving us tonight after dinner to go and live in Canterbury, so let's make the most of her now."

Isabel patted his hand, she felt the same. After six years Danielle was going to live with her mother, but wasn't that normal? Living with her natural mother was much more preferable than having a nanny and no mother. It wasn't as if they would be living that far away, and they would certainly need a babysitter at times. It might bring a lump to their throats to think about it, but they had to do what was best for Danielle and Sadie, and not be selfish. She would never forget Sadie's unselfishness towards her when she was ill. They had done their bit when Sadie was not around, but now it was time to take a back seat, and let go of Danielle.

Eric had taken a day off work today. It was Evelyn's due date, and although her labour had not started yet, she had a hospital appointment and he was going with her. She was big now and he didn't want her driving; her stomach didn't fit easily behind the steering wheel, so he could take her there himself.

She had not had an easy time of it, there was sickness at the beginning of the pregnancy, which seemed to last a long time, and now her ankles had swollen, so it would be a good thing when the little one arrived and she was able to get back to normal.

Just as they were about to leave the house, there was a knock at the door. Who could it be now? They didn't really have time to see anyone, or else they would be late. Eric was slightly irritated when he opened the door to find Constable Blake and his trusty companion on the doorstep. He had already been interviewed by him, and he needed to get Evelyn to her appointment.

"Good morning, sir, may we come in?"

They stepped inside, and he wondered why they had even bothered to ask. Police always did what they wanted anyway, whether you liked it or not. Blake's next words took him totally by surprise.

"I would like you to come along to the police station and help us with our enquiries, if you don't mind, sir."

"I can't, I am taking my wife to the hospital; and anyway, I already told you everything I know," he said wildly. This couldn't be happening, not today!

197

"Not quite everything it seems. Especially not that you were outside on your own at the same time that Mia was attacked!"

"But I was nowhere near her, I was a few yards away from the car having a smoke."

His look of anguish towards Evelyn was partly because he knew she would be disappointed in him; he had promised to quit now the baby was coming. Then his guilt because today she needed him so much, and this damn policeman was not interested in them, all he wanted to do was question him, and not even at home, it was at the station.

Evelyn spoke quietly, which he thought surprising in the circumstances.

"Eric, you go to the police station, and I will ring Hetty, she won't mind taking me to the hospital."

"But I wanted to be with you. The baby might come."

"It won't come that quickly. I am sure once you have answered all the questions, Constable Blake will release you and you can join us later."

Eric looked at her admiringly, this was probably the time in her life when she needed him most of all, and she was being so brave. Her friend Hetty would help out, they both knew that. There was a part of him that was disappointed that she could manage without him, and as for the damn police, your whole life had to stop when they came round barking orders, they were like little gods, or they thought they were! All this tumbled through his head, but he said nothing, he was always courteous and respectful to everyone, you had to be if you were a chauffeur or else you would not keep your job.

He reluctantly allowed himself to be ushered out to the police car. One look at Evelyn confirmed she was not happy with him, but she was too polite to let it show in front of the police. He felt miserable and hopeless, especially as he couldn't be with her now, at a time when their first child was about to be born.

Whilst he was sitting in the police car, it suddenly occurred to him that he was in a difficult situation here. If he was the only person outside when Mia was attacked, he could not prove it wasn't him. Surely they were not going to charge him, and lock him up. He covered his face with his hands, overcome with emotion. He couldn't even kill a fly, but he wasn't sure they would believe that, and a feeling of fear swept over him.

When they reached the police station, he was taken into an interview room. Constable Blake had left him by now, and a man who introduced himself as Detective Inspector Palmer arrived with a companion to interview him. He switched on the recorder, stated the time and date, and then his first words totally took Eric by surprise.

"Did you enjoy driving Sadie around?"

"Sadie?"

Palmer smiled cynically, he was a grey haired man with an air of arrogance about him. Eric guessed him to be about fifty, and there was something about his attitude he did not like, but he knew he had to put up with it.

"Of course, she's not Sadie to you. Miss Morton Brown, who became Mrs Edwards."

"Yes, it's a job, the whole family are kind to work for."

"Way out of your league though, Eric."

Eric wondered where this was leading, so he explained how kind she had been giving him a large tip that day. Palmer curled his lip sardonically.

"Mrs Edwards is a very attractive woman Eric, you must have noticed that?"

"Well I did, but I am paid to drive her, that's all, so even if she was not beautiful it would make no difference to me, as long as I get her to her destination."

Palmer eyed him superciliously. He had given the right answers, so now he would try rattling his cage.

"I put it to you, that when Mrs Edwards gave you that tip you thought you were well in with her, and you became too familiar with her, and she rebuffed you. So when no one was around you tried your luck with her cousin, who also was not interested, and in getting away from you she tripped over into the water, and in a fit of anger you picked up the rock and hit her over the head."

Eric sat there, his mouth opening and closing like a gold fish. So flabbergasted was he by these fanciful imaginings, he was unable to speak. He so wished he had never told them about the tip.

There was no one else to fight his corner except himself, and he wasn't going to allow them to try and pin anything on him, so he took a deep breath and was relieved to find his voice had returned.

"Inspector, I would never try to be familiar with anyone I work for. They have their own class, and I always treat them all with respect. Please let me go, my wife is in hospital, and I need to be with her."

But Palmer had not finished with him yet. He could see the little runt couldn't cope under pressure, so his questions and insinuations came thick and fast. They had to pin this crime on someone, or else questions about how the investigation was being handled would be asked.

Eric could see which way this was heading, and he was absolutely determined that he was not going to take the rap for someone else's crime. This man's bullying attitude was getting right under his skin, and he was angry because he was being denied the right to spend time with his wife when she needed him so much. He continued to politely answer questions, keeping his anger under control and remaining respectful, which totally floored Palmer.

What did it take to wind this bloke up? The more Palmer continued with his line of questioning, the more convinced he became that Eric was blameless in all this, and regretfully they would have to look somewhere else to solve the crime. If he kept him any longer, he would have to charge him, and he had a sneaking admiration for him. He might look like a runt, but he had not buckled under pressure; he was tougher than Palmer had ever imagined. There was no reason to keep him, they had no evidence, and he clearly wanted to be with his wife at the hospital.

"Right, you can go now. If we need you to help us further with our enquiries we will be in touch."

At last! Eric muttered his thanks. There was only one thought in his mind, to get to the hospital. He could not afford to get a cab from the police station, so he got on the bus to travel home. It was so slow, stopping at every stop, he was willing it through the traffic lights, and when he finally got home to pick his car up, it was already mid afternoon. This must mean they were keeping Evelyn in. If it had just been a checkup, she would be home by now.

He jumped in the car. The journey to the Medway hospital took a while. Once he got off the motorway there were loads of roundabouts, and lorries trundling slowly, every traffic light he came to was red, and he could feel the tension building up in his head. He told himself to keep calm, and when the hospital came into sight he breathed a sigh of relief. Not long now.

He drove round looking for a parking space, and right at the end, under the shade of a tree, there was one, at the furthest end of the car park. He didn't know whether Evelyn would have her mobile on in the hospital, but he was going to take a chance and ring her. He pressed the buttons, and almost immediately it was answered, but not by her, it was Hettie.

"Hi Hettie, it's Eric. I'm here now in the car park. How is Evelyn?"

It seemed strange asking Hettie how his own wife was.

"She's just been delivered, Eric. Congratulations, you have a son!"

Eric felt overwhelmed with emotion at those words. His son was born, they had chosen not to know the sex of their baby, but he had secretly hoped for a boy. It was the best news ever. But it didn't stop the tears of frustration from running down his cheeks. He had so wanted to be at the birth of his son, to see him come into the world and support Evelyn any way he could, but it had been denied to him and he felt he had let her down. Those damn police had a lot to answer for!

Chapter Twenty-five

Sadie was the happiest she had ever been in her life. She was married to the most wonderful man ever, which inspired her to be the loving and caring wife he wanted. She had her beautiful Danielle, and their bond was as close as she could have ever hoped for, and then there were her parents. Oh, how she wished she could have changed all those years when she didn't like her mother. Her mother had suffered during her life and only her strength of character had got her through. Being raped by her own brother, whom she had loved dearly, and then all those years of having to conceal her terrible secret from Daddy, only to find out he had guessed, and still loved them both anyway.

Sadie felt a warm glow in her heart when she thought about Daddy. He would always be her father, he had brought her up, and she was glad her real blood father was not alive as she would not have wanted him in her life. What he had done to her mother would have been very hard to forgive, and Sadie didn't do forgiveness.

She was enjoying her job in the fashion department, and they gave her a discount off clothes, which was a good excuse to change her wardrobe a bit. For the first time in her life it was her own money, and not funded by anyone else. She was quite enjoying the feeling of independence it gave her, and the way Nathan approved. She just had to prove to him that she could hold a job down.

She wasn't sure how long she would be there. She was hoping so much to get pregnant, which she might even be now, and there were opportunities to come back afterwards, although she was not sure about that yet. She could aspire to be manager of the department. They wanted someone, but it would mean longer hours, and would she want to leave her baby with a nanny? She smiled to herself as she realised she was letting her thoughts run away with her, but a wonderful warm glow of contentment swept through her, life just couldn't get any better than this.

She brushed her hair until it shone, then dressed it on top of her head; the more sophisticated she looked in an up-market ladies' gown department the better. Nathan was working from home today, so he would pick up Danielle from school, and they would both be at home waiting for her when she came home from work. Today she decided to wear a smart navy suit with a white blouse. Even though the weather was warm, the air conditioning in the store would keep her cool.

When she was dressed she came downstairs to find Nathan already at work on the laptop. He looked up at her and she savoured the look of pride in his eyes.

"Wow, you look amazing my love, go and knock 'em dead at work. Before you know it you'll get promotion."

She kissed his cheek, but that was not enough for Nathan, he drew her into his arms and kissed her lips. Reluctantly she pulled away.

"Nathan, I have to go, I'll be late!"

He laughed. "I know, but just wait until you get home!" Sadie felt her body tingle at the thought of it, and it took all her self control to leave him right now. But they had their lives ahead of them, and it wouldn't do him any harm to wait.

Their home was within walking distance of the shop, which was another bonus, because trying to get round Canterbury in a car, let alone trying to park anywhere, was as hard as it was in London. This is what she liked about Canterbury, it was a thriving city and community, and they lived in the heart of it, yet their block of town houses were set in a quiet spot by the River Stour.

She pulled the front door closed behind her, after checking she had her key, just in case Nathan and Danielle might be out when she returned later. Her high heels clicked as she walked down the small flight of steps onto the cobbled courtyard which surrounded this block of new houses. She negotiated them carefully, as parts were a bit uneven, and when she reached the pavement she quickened her pace slightly.

She rounded the corner. First thing on a Monday morning the traffic was always at a crawl, so she should be able to make her way across the road by walking past the stationary cars waiting to approach the roundabout.

She found a gap and walked through, and now she was near the roundabout. The shop was about a ten minute walk, and she had twenty minutes to spare.

It wasn't until the door had closed behind Sadie that Nathan realised she had left her mobile behind. Sadie always kept it on silent during the day at work, but that meant he could send her messages and she could reply. He knew she liked having that contact, so he picked it up, then realised he was in his slippers, so went to put his shoes on, intending to run after her. She wouldn't have gone far, she couldn't walk that fast in those heels.

Just as she was approaching the roundabout Sadie heard someone shout her name. It came from the right hand side of the street. A man had just got out of a car and the traffic was all piling up behind him, horns were going, voices shouting, but he didn't seem aware of it.

When Sadie saw him she froze with fear; Ricky had not changed much during the last few years. The voice, that had remained silent inside her for quite a while now, taunted her. Alice's last words came back to haunt her.

"They will catch up with you, and you will rot in jail!"

Ricky had come to get her for selling their baby! He was going to destroy the happiness she had finally found. There could be no other reason for him appearing like that! Panic set in and her body was numb as she tried desperately to think of a way out of this situation. But there was no solution this time, Sadie was like a rat caught in a trap, and she knew it.

The road was filling up with people now. A police car had stopped to see what all the fuss was about, and Ricky was waving his arms and striding towards her. What could she do? Her world was closing in on her, she couldn't lose all she had now, it was all far too precious.

Thoughts tumbled through her brain. Flight was the only answer. She saw that the road was free, and on the other side was a hedge which then led to a small towpath. She had to try anything to get away, even hiding in the bushes.

Sadie ran as fast as her heels would allow her across the road, but in her haste she had not seen the van, which came at such a rate round the roundabout it had no chance of stopping when, too late, the driver saw her. The last conscious thought that Sadie had was a windscreen looming up at her, but she couldn't feel any pain, everything was numb and blackness was descending on her.

"Sadie, my love. Oh Sadie, don't go to sleep. Sadie, I love you, oh my god!"

With a supreme effort she peered through the haze; it was Nathan. She had to fight off that blackness, she couldn't leave Nathan, he was the love of her life.

Ricky was feeling a lot more contented with his life than before. His girls were doing well, he had a happy relationship with Kirsty, and he was rising higher within the FBI and earning more money. All his anxiety over his son had finally been dispelled when he met him, and he was alive and well.

Simon and Jill were so grateful that Ricky was prepared to overlook the way they had got Billy, as he felt they had been punished enough with all the hardship and poverty they had endured for the last eight years.

Meeting Billy had felt strange. When you live with a child every day and watch it grow, it feels like your own, but all of a sudden Ricky had an instant eight year old son. He had noticed the likenesss to himself; he was a bright boy, and in Ricky's opinion, the problems they were having were partly due to the neighbourhood he was growing up in, but he also felt young Billy didn't have enough physical pursuits to keep him out of mischief.

Simon had managed to get a work transfer to a town not far from Greenview, and this meant Ricky would be able to have more input into Billy's life. Together they were going to encourage Billy to do more sport, and one day Ricky hoped he could meet his half sisters, but there was no rush yet, all in good time. He was going to work with Simon and Jill to ensure that young Billy channelled any aggression into his sport, and then he felt sure everything would be OK.

Ricky was not a man who bore grudges, and he had managed

to put behind him the bitterness and hurt he and the family had suffered at the hands of Sadie. They had now rebuilt their lives and moved on. When he went to confession, the priest had encouraged him to pray for Sadie, and since he had found out that Billy was alive and well, he had felt guilty for misjudging Sadie so badly.

Even though Sadie had not wanted her son, and had used him to get herself money, which had obviously hurt him deeply, one simple fact remained. Billy was the end result of their ill-fated marriage, and whether she liked it or not, Sadie and Ricky would always have that connection. The feeling inside Ricky to make peace with her, and tell her that he had been reunited with Billy, was so strong he knew he would have to act on it.

By all accounts Sadie was now married to Nathan and her daughter Danielle was living with them, so she was obviously trying to lead a normal life. Now she had matured there might come a day when she too, wanted to meet her son, and for Billy's sake, Ricky felt that making peace with his mother was the right thing to do.

Dave had agreed to make the visit to England with him. He knew what a big deal it was to Ricky finding his son and, if truth was known, even Dave was interested to see the woman who had created so much havoc in Ricky's life. Even if he didn't get to speak to her, she was still a fascinating creature.

After they had picked up the hire car, they made their way to Canterbury where the hotel was. Dave was looking forward to a hot shower and a beer after travelling all night with very little sleep on the plane. Ricky was armed with information about where Sadie lived now, and the plan was to make contact with her later in the day.

As they were approaching the roundabout, crawling with the rest of the rush hour traffic, Dave stole a glance at a female in a navy suit and high heels, who had just crossed the road towards the roundabout. She had legs to die for, and she looked every inch the sort of woman he dreamed about in his fantasies. He could imagine her, whip in hand, whilst he was tied to the bed post. He chuckled to himself at the thought of it.

"Dave, stop the car. It's Sadie, I've got to get out!"

"Not here, surely?"

Dave's eyes took in the scene of congestion, such narrow roads in England, no wonder they had all this nonsense.

"Yes here!"

206

Ricky's tone was so urgent, reluctantly Dave pulled over, and Ricky sprang out. He hoped he would be quick, as already he was holding up the traffic even more, and he could see a cop's car approaching them.

But Ricky was oblivious to it all. He shouted to Sadie and waved his arms in the air, and Dave watched fascinated, as he attempted to run towards her. Somebody honked behind him, but he had nowhere to go, so he tried to pull the car in more towards the kerb.

Sadie had spotted Ricky now, and he watched with interest her reaction. She didn't wave back, and appeared to be glancing around her for an escape route. A cop was coming towards the car, so Dave jumped out and produced his ID card. It might get them off the hook if the cop knew they were from the FBI.

Dave was not prepared for her next move. She dashed straight across the roundabout. He saw the van coming and he tried to shout and warn her, but it was too late. Even the cop had stopped in his tracks, as they waited for the inevitable. Sadie was flung against the windscreen. The impact was loud, and her body was tossed into the air, coming to rest on the road. She had landed on her back, with her arms and legs splayed out like a rag doll, and with horror, Dave noticed the blood seeping out from the back of her head.

The moment passed, then everyone sprang into action. A man he guessed must be Nathan was kneeling beside her, imploring her to wake up. Ricky was telling him not to move her, but Nathan was so distraught, he cradled her head on his lap, and Dave could see tears running down his face.

For Ricky it was all a blur. The people, the noise of the traffic, the cop who was attempting to direct the traffic around all the chaos. He watched, with horror, Nathan trying to will her limp body to respond; there was blood coming from her mouth when she tried to speak. It didn't look like Sadie was going to make it, and it was his fault for frightening her.

Nathan was not going to leave her, he didn't care that the blood was all over him too. He willed Sadie to speak, and with a supreme effort her eyes flickered open, but they no longer gleamed with passion, they were dull.

Sadie knew she was dying. She could feel a huge curtain closing her off from Nathan and she didn't have the strength to open it. Her life was flashing before her; she saw her parents, Jeremy and Matt, and tears pricked at her eyelids. She saw Sunita, her one true friend; Danny, and their beautiful daughter Danielle. She had so wanted to live to see her grow up. Her perfect life with Nathan, her one true love, and Danielle was not meant to be, and in her dying moments she asked God to forgive her for obeying that voice in her head. If only she could have resisted it. With a last supreme effort her words came out as a feeble whisper that only Nathan could hear.

"Please forgive me, Nathan. I will always love you, it's all there in the box."

And then with a sigh her body relaxed, her eyes became lifeless, and Sadie passed away.

Chapter Twenty-six

One year on. . .
Nathan was so glad that the last year was behind him. His devastation after losing Sadie had affected him so greatly he had been tempted to drink himself into oblivion to try and cope. But he knew it wasn't just about himself; Danielle had taken it really badly, as had Sadie's parents, so he summoned all his strength of character to try and give them the support they needed, and in return, they also helped him.

He left his house in Canterbury because it had too many memories of Sadie. He couldn't even sort through her personal belongings, they were just all hurriedly moved into the loft. Isabel, Philip and Danielle welcomed him back at Herne Bay, and because it was so hard for him to make any decisions at this time, he rented his house out for a year to a businessman and his family from Japan.

There had been an inquest into Sadie's death, and a verdict of accidental death was recorded. Nathan began to understand more on that day. Finding out that Sadie had married whilst in the USA, and even had a son by Ricky, had been a huge shock. Ricky had explained that their marriage had not lasted long and he had not been around when their son was born. He had reunited with him after Sadie had him adopted, but the need to let Sadie know he bore no grudges, and if at any time she wanted to see her son she could, was so strong, it had caused him to come to England.

Nathan assumed Sadie's reaction when she saw Ricky, wanting to flee, was because there had been so much bitterness before. He had told Ricky it was not his fault, what else could he say? The man had no evil intent, but Sadie's reaction had been remarkable, and the pain he felt that she had concealed her marriage and her son from him had only added to his grief. He assumed this was what she had tried to tell him as she lay dying.

In the beginning Danielle had terrible nightmares, frequently waking up screaming; she felt the loss of her mother greatly. So Isabel found a new person to help them, not exactly a nanny, more like a companion, someone to help with the ironing, and take Danielle to all her after school activities. During the school summer holidays, Lydia had organised various outings for Danielle, taking the weight off Isabel's shoulders at a time when the grieving process was still very ongoing.

Nathan had vowed that he would never remarry, he just wanted to be faithful to Sadie's memory, and somehow he didn't think that any woman could live up to her because, in his mind, Sadie had come so far, and changed so much. Her looks, her spirit, the fun they had, the love they had shared, it had been so special, and he believed that you only meet your soul mate once in a lifetime.

Lydia had suffered her own heartbreak, although she seemed to have coped. She had been married to a violent man and suffered several years of being physically abused. She had explained she only stayed that long because he had two sides to him, and when he was being nice, she truly loved him. When she found herself pregnant, she had hoped the responsibility might change him. But during an argument one day, when he had forbidden her to leave the house, he pushed her down the stairs, and at seven months she had given birth to their stillborn son. He was now in prison for his offences, and there was a court order against him coming anywhere near to Lydia when he came out.

Hearing about this made Nathan realise they weren't the only family with troubles, and he warmed to Lydia. She was a decent young woman, who had not deserved to be treated in such a way. He was glad that Lydia was so different to Sadie. She had blonde hair, which she wore short in a bob, very blue eyes, and she was a good listener. He had unburdened himself to her often about Sadie. They had actually helped each other, and he now thought of her as a great friend.

For Philip and Isabel, it was the heartbreak of losing yet another of their children. The only thing that comforted them was the knowledge that all old wounds had been healed, and they believed there were no more skeletons left in the closet. They too tried to stay brave and stable for Danielle, and with a little bit of counselling for the whole family, after a year, they were beginning to get their lives back on track.

For Danielle, the tragedy of losing the mother she had been given back was devastating, but with the kindness and help of Lydia, her bad dreams were subsiding now, and she was starting to form an attachment to her.

After a year, Nathan realised he needed to be back in his own home. He would either have to bear the memories of Sadie, or sell it and move somewhere else. He spoke about it to Lydia, who agreed, and she offered her support on her day off to go and help him to clear it out. When they arrived the cleaners had been, following the departure of the Japanese family, and everywhere was gleaming and ready for whoever might choose to live there.

But today was the day that Nathan had vowed he would sort through Sadie's possessions. It was a job that had to be done no matter how painful it was. He went up to the loft and found the black plastic bags and the boxes that contained much of Sadie's past life, and braced himself to deal with it.

Lydia was there to give him support. He didn't know it, because he was still wrapped up in his grief, but during the past year she had grown to love Nathan. He was the complete opposite of her violent ex-husband, and knowing him had restored her faith in men. Whether he would return her love one day was another thing, but she still couldn't help how she felt, and the way he made her feel safe was something she wanted to enjoy.

Nathan sorted through Sadie's clothes. Lydia noted they were all good quality and expensive.

"Would you like any of these, you are about the same size as Sadie was?"

"Well, not if it upsets you to see them on another person."

"To be honest, Lydia, she had so many, she used to buy them and not always wear them."

Lydia relaxed a bit more. She didn't want to be a carbon copy of Sadie, but they were far grander than anything she had, so why not? She murmured her thanks, and then her attention shifted to a big iron box, which Nathan had brought out from the loft and was now trying to open.

"I can't find a key for this, I wonder what is in here?" Then he remembered Sadie had mentioned a box as she lay dying. This must be it.

His desire to find one little piece of Sadie's life to keep with him and cherish was so strong, that after a lot of fruitless searching for a key, he took a quicker route, and found a hammer to smash the lock in. As he opened the lid, he was not prepared for what he found; bottles of pills, unopened, and a thick red book, which smelt a bit musty, but appeared to be some sort of diary.

He picked up the bottles to examine them. The pills were dated just after Sadie had returned home from rehabilitation, and next to them was a repeat prescription which had never been taken to a chemist.

"Whatever were these pills for?" he asked wonderingly.

Lydia had trained as a nurse, and one look at them confirmed her suspicions.

"They are to treat chemical imbalances in the brain, without them Sadie would have been very much at risk," she said gravely.

Nathan suddenly realised this was a side of Sadie he had not known about. He had not realised she was still on medication, but why on earth had she neglected to take them? He would have been supportive if she needed them. He opened the musty pages of the red book, and read from a page where Sadie had made an entry.

Today I feel great. I am home with my family, and I want to put it all behind me. I need to get on with Mummy and make Danielle proud of me. I don't need medication any more, I am cured, that voice inside me is gone.

Then he found her last entry, and as he read it he felt sick, and the horror of realising just how mad Sadie was hit him.

Nathan and I are now married, he's the love of my life, and now I need to say a prayer to the lord for all my past crimes. I want Nathan and Danielle to love and respect me forever.

I killed my brother Jeremy, to pay Mummy back for making me destroy my own baby.

Petra the maid, who may have been more than that to Danny.

Melissa, for so clearly trying to steal Nathan from me.

Mia, for suggesting Nathan would leave me.

I have found love, true love with a good man, and I am telling that voice to stop plaguing me, it has no place in my life.

He looked up, and the agony in his eyes moved Lydia, and she went over and put her arms around him. "She did all that because she was ill Nathan, and it got worse when she stopped taking her medication."

"But how can I tell her parents and her daughter just how ill she was. Haven't they suffered enough pain?" he said angrily, remembering that Philip had said that Isabel's spirit had become fragile since Sadie died, and there was always the worry of the cancer returning.

"You don't have to tell anyone," said Lydia calmly. "No good will come of it now. Let them go on believing Sadie had reformed. Part of her had, it seems, but without her medication, she would always revert."

"Would you really do this for me?"

Nathan looked into her eyes and saw sincerity, and the feel of her arms around him felt right. It was a shock to find Sadie was not the woman he had thought she was, and he realised he had built up a picture that did not exist.

"Yes Nathan, I would."

He felt overwhelmed with sadness for the woman she had tried so hard to be. He remembered how she had loved and cared for her daughter, and then nursed her mother back to health. Inside bad Sadie there had been a good Sadie struggling to get out, and he had loved that Sadie with all his heart. Perhaps it did all stem back to what her blood father had done; he was clearly not in his right mind, and maybe Sadie had inherited his unbalanced nature.

Now he turned his attention to Lydia. What a rock she had been; and suddenly he knew what he wanted in his life, not someone unpredictable, but someone who was stable and calm, and who also loved Danielle. Did he mistake that look in her eyes as love? He gently took her hand.

"I don't deserve someone like you."

"Oh, you do," she said, and then it slipped out before she could stop it. "Because I love you."

So he had not misread the situation. Lydia did care, she wasn't just a mate.

There was one more thing he had to know before he allowed himself to love again.

"One day Isabel and Philip will be gone, and whoever I marry will have to be prepared to take Danielle on as their daughter until she is old enough to leave home."

For Lydia the word 'marry' was a bit of a shock, but she loved the thought of being his wife.

"Oh, I am sure that can be arranged. I love that little girl!" she murmured as their lips met, and Nathan suddenly felt free, and able to move on. The spell Sadie had cast on him was now broken.